A
New
Dawn

Printed in the United States of America

Published by Author Academy Elite
PO Box 43, Powell, OH 43065
www.AuthorAcademyElite.com

Identifiers:

LCCN: 2021915994

ISBN: 978-1-64746-876-7 (paperback)
ISBN: 978-1-64746-877-4 (hardback)
ISBN: 978-1-64746-878-1 (ebook)

Available in paperback, hardback, e-book, and audiobook

Book design by Dragonpen Designs.
Cover design by: Kimmo Hellström.
Illustrations by: Steven Bell

Book 3

A
New
Dawn

Kingdoms of Islandia Trilogy

J.J. Johnson

This book is dedicated in loving memory to Danette Tropansky.

Without your love and support Danette, this book would not be possible. I cherish the day we can see each other face to face once again.

TABLE OF CONTENTS

Acknowledgments

Thank you to my loving wife and daughter for allowing me the countless hours to make this dream become reality. I also want to bring special attention to every person who helped give feedback and critique. Sheena Monnin, thank you for putting in the effort to help craft this book into what it is today. Your editing services were a huge help in making this story great! Thank you to my friends and family for your amazing support. Without your belief in me and this story no one would be reading it today. Last, but certainly not least I want to give glory to the Name above all names. He is the true morning star and the dawn bringer of our story. His name is King Jesus. He deserves all the honor, glory, and praise.

PRELUDE

THE SOUND OF bell towers filled the air. The smells of the coming autumn brought with them a familiarity that countered the tragedy that had befallen the once proud city of Kingshelm. Too many tears had been shed in the ancient city. Today, however... today was a wondrous day. The woman embraced the refreshing breeze, face upturned toward the sun. Just above her stood the pristine white towers of Kingshelm's palace. They stood proudly, slowly being restored to their former glory.

"Are you ready?" Geralt asked her. The grizzled warrior stood freshly shaved with his hair pulled back from his face. His usual leather-laced armor was replaced by formal attire. Despite the soft fabric, there was no denying his strength or readiness to fight. The man's gloomy demeanor of late softened into satisfaction as he looked at her. She was radiant.

"I am," Lydia said with barely restrained glee.

Without a word, Geralt moved to open the wooden door before them. Light beamed in, washing away all thoughts of war and conflict. As she blinked to adjust her eyes to the light, a host of guests stood to welcome her arrival. Each wore a grin that stretched from ear to ear as they marveled at her. Lydia's auburn curls had been made into a beautiful plait of braids and loose strands that flowed gently onto her shoulders. The elegant dress she wore was a masterpiece of embroidery. Small flowers weaved into the smooth cream colored fabric. The guests waited in a beautiful palace garden filled with a kaleidoscope of color. Any visitor to this place would have been lost in awe of its magnificence. Each color and scent was intoxicating to the senses, leaving most visitors uncertain where to look. But Lydia's eyes were fixed on one—*her* one.

He stood tall, waiting on a platform just ahead. His face morphed into overwhelming emotion upon seeing her. Joy radiated from him as he awaited his bride. Slowly, she stepped forward down the path marked by white cloth. Onlookers whispered their congratulations with exuberant smiles and tender nods. She drank in the scene and saw it all in slow motion, tucking it deep into her memory.

The faces of the people she had known throughout her life, both old and new, had come to bear witness on this special day. Imari, the mighty Khosi of Khala, paid his respects with a bow. The white dashiki he wore for such an occasion was intricately embroidered with shimmering gold thread. Lancelin cheered beside him. His face was creased with a broad smile. His sandy blonde hair was pushed back and he wore a formal tunic in the colors of his home. Even her reluctant brother stood near the back. Likely the only gloomy face present. She forced herself not to think of all the empty spaces she had wished to be occupied.

Her parents' absence stood as an unmistakable void beside her. She knew the one who would take as much joy in this moment as they would have was missing as well. Eloy, the High King who had given his life so that this moment could be possible. Not just this moment, but all future moments of peace, prosperity, and hope still to come. Stepping closer and closer as the crowd watched, her eyes drew upward to her waiting groom.

Titus reached his strong hand out to help her onto the platform. His face held a tearful smile. She couldn't help but feel hot streams of her own tears run down her slender face, an embarrassing moment for a shield-maiden. They stood hand in hand before the people. The royal councilor of the court who was residing over the wedding cleared his throat.

"We have gathered on this joyous day to witness the union of High King Titus and High Queen Lydia."

She exchanged a happy smile with Titus at those words.

"We gather as a witness to this union but, as the high courts require, are there any from these parties who wish to speak against such a royal union?"

It took all Lydia's strength not to glance at her brother. As the moment of silence carried, she sighed a breath of relief.

He has not come to ruin this day after all, she thought.

"As a member of the royal court, I stand as official witness to the uniting of these two. May they reign over us with all knowledge, wisdom, and strength."

"And may their reign be long lived," answered the crowd in unison.

"What vows do you give?" asked the councilor.

Titus took a step forward. "I, Titus, vow that so long as I draw breath, I will love, serve, and protect you. I will stand by your side until my last day. No matter how dark the night, no matter how difficult the day, I will be yours to the end of this road."

She wiped away a tear from her eye as a warm smile filled her face. "I, Lydia, vow to stand with you, my King, all your days. To love, cherish, and defend you. You have stood beside me in my darkest days. You have loved me even when all would declare us enemies. I will stand with you until my last breath. The road behind has not been easy, but, with you by my side, I will gladly walk the road ahead."

"We who are witnesses shall hold these words as bond. With that, I declare you High King and High Queen of Islandia. You may kiss your bride."

Titus moved to embrace her. With tenderness and passion they kissed. Their bond was sealed before their people. The crowd erupted into cheers. Thunderous applause filled the air as those gathered embraced their new High King and Queen. Parting from their embrace, the young couple turned to join the crowd's celebration. With lifted arms they rushed forward ready for the evening's festivities to begin.

The night was filled with laughter. Lydia hadn't felt happiness in so long, and now, she was married to the man she loved. Her heart could barely contain her bliss. She couldn't believe the joyful sights and sounds within the palace halls. Even Geralt joined in the celebration by dancing, something she had never seen in her whole life. He traded his downcast demeanor for a small twinkle in his otherwise serious eyes. He wasn't half bad either. He swung from partner to partner with ease.

"Kind of like a fight," he joked to those who watched him in surprise. "Just without swords."

Imari and his companions stole the show as they displayed the traditional dances of the Khalans, typically reserved for their own celebrations. She and Titus enjoyed a laugh as Lancelin moved to give the dance a try. His fumbling attempt made the typically smooth man look like a newborn fawn.

Most of all, Lydia loved being with her king. Titus gave her a knowing smile as they both relaxed in the first real moment of peace they had ever known. They had never had this type of freedom before, to laugh, love, and be with one another without darkness or impending doom. They drank in the scene of the torchlit hall from their seats at the royal table.

"Shall we dance, my Queen?" Titus asked, extending a hand.

"We shall," she said with a delighted grin.

The rhythm carried them away into the night. She twirled, dipped and laughed until she could laugh no more. On this special night all the pain, all the hurt, and every difficult thing that they had endured was washed away. Hours passed in this happy reverie. As the crowds began to disperse and the halls quieted down, Titus took her hand.

"Shall we retire, my Queen?" he asked lovingly.

4

She laid her head on his chest. "Yes, I think we shall."

She let out a surprised yelp as he lifted her in his arms. A playful look crossed his face. They laughed and kissed as they made their way through the halls to the royal chambers. As they entered, he placed her on her feet once more. His hands clasped her shoulders gently.

"Lydia, I want you to know something."

She looked him in his eyes. Behind the dark green depths, a look of tender love resided.

"I cannot express how much you mean to me, without you... I..."

She lifted a hand to his cheek. "I know."

She pulled him close with a passionate kiss. She had found the one her heart had longed for, and now until the end she would hold him near.

1

TITUS

One Year Later

ITUS STARED DOWN at the parchment in his hands. He
found himself subconsciously rubbing his thumb and forefinger
over the coarse texture of the document as he read its contents.
He held a message sent from Samudara Port. Its contents spoke of
strangers arriving from faraway lands. Strangers landing on those shores
was not unheard of since Samudara was the only city that traded
with outsiders, but this... this was different. Hundreds of ships finely
decorated had arrived at the docks. The crew arrived with barely any
supplies remaining, but all of them stood armed as fighting men. The
letter was more vague on details than he would have liked.

His frown deepened. This was disturbing news indeed. This potential
threat was not helped by the absence of almost the entirety of Kingshelm's
and Leviatanas' forces. The armies were away near the Forest's Edge

to resolve the conflict between New Valkara and Aiden's rebel forces. Titus let out a sigh as he put the parchment down.

"And here I thought the days would be easier now that the Felled Ones were gone," he mumbled to himself.

"No days are easy, sire. Even the easy ones," said the voice of his royal advisor, Markus. He was a thin man, beginning to bald, and usually had a bad sense of timing, but he was an honest man. Titus needed more of those.

"True," Titus said curtly.

"Shall I request a convening of the council, my lord?" asked Markus.

"Yes, they should hear of this news."

Markus turned to leave. Before he vanished, Titus spoke again.

"And make sure Lancelin and Lydia are sent word of this." His voice carried the authority of his position.

Markus gave a bow of acknowledgement and scurried down the hall.

"I should be with them," Titus sighed to himself. Lancelin had been given charge of the army to make sure the Riverlands were safe from the conflict brewing at their borders. In the last few weeks, movement had been seen around the forest that divided Valkara and the Riverlands. The reason soon became clear. Jorn had ordered a path cleared through the dense woods in order to circumvent the long journey south. Titus knew the man's target immediately: the true Valkaran king, Aiden.

He and the collection of men he had gathered from all of Islandia had retreated to the far north near the town known at the Forest's Edge. There they had set up a base of operations into which they would recruit others to their cause. They sought to win back a kingdom of their own. Titus didn't necessarily love the idea of a freely roaming army in his lands, but as long as they kept away from those in his charge, he saw no need for aggression. All that had changed now.

Jorn's legitimacy was at stake as long as the true Valkaran royalty lived, so now he planned to end any threat to his claim. Of course, when Lydia heard all this she had demanded to go. Titus knew better than to stand in her way. Besides, family was family no matter how frustrating.

"If only I could stand at your side, my love…" Titus thought ruefully.

He would have overseen the march himself, but strange rumors had reached Kingshelm of a force on the horizon. His kingly duties clashed with his heart. He felt he had to stay if the rumors happened to be real. When the whispers turned out to be true, he felt better for remaining behind.He still regretted not being with Lydia as she faced her past. She had understood. She always did. Her clarity of purpose was one of many reasons she made not only a great High Queen, but a wonderful wife.

He gently placed the parchment down onto the table before him. Slowly he moved to a basin of water in the corner of his chambers. Dipping his hands into the bowl, he brought a refreshing splash of the cool liquid onto his face. His gaze lifted to a tiny mirror placed over the basin. In its reflection he saw a familiar face with a subtle change in his expression. Where once he had stood as an untested youth, a more regal and wise man now stood before the mirror and stared back at him resolutely. His physical form had broadened with muscle from the past year of conflict and hardship. He still kept his brunette hair closely trimmed on the sides while keeping its length on the top.

The biggest difference he noticed was in the eyes looking back at him. The hazel pools carried a burden, one that felt the weight of a kingdom resting on his shoulders. How he wished his father or Eloy, or both, were there with him. How inadequate he felt for the tasks ahead. He knew Lydia would scold him for such talk. Somehow she would find the words to make him feel that even without decades of experience, they could stumble upon a solution to any difficulty. But, all alone in the palace he felt less sure.

Stretching to shake off the midday weariness, he moved out into the palace halls, stopping only to grab his trusted blade, Dawn Bringer. The halls were filled with activity. Servants busied themselves with the day's tasks. They all seemed thankful for a life of normalcy again. He wasn't as sure. Had life returned to normal? Something deep inside him felt that the world had forever changed, and would continue to change, no matter what he did to rule and protect his people. He didn't understand his feeling. He wished Lydia were there to help him make sense of it.

As he glanced around the halls he couldn't help but question his feeling. He smiled as he beheld the beginnings of restoration. The work would take years, maybe even decades, before Kingshelm could be fully restored to shine in its former glory.But the work being done had brought back some utility to the place. He caught sight of Markus' waving hand, breaking him from his trance.

"The Royal Council is awaiting you, my King," Markus said with a respectful bow.

Time to break the news to them, Titus thought.

Markus led the way with a quick pace down the hall until they reached a broad wooden door resting beneath the throne room's double stairway. He extended his hand to open the door to the council chamber and usher Titus in. Several members of the royal court sat in the room, waiting expectantly.

"Greetings, council members," Titus said with a nod as he took a seat.

The members stood in honor of his arrival and each returned a greeting of their own. They had all been newly appointed to their positions. Titus could sense that each of them stumbled about with their words and actions, as if they had entered into completely uncharted territory.

"Word has reached me that no small force has landed on our shores at Samudara Port," Titus began.

"No small force? What exactly does that mean?" asked councilor Ambrose, a young, regal man with jet black hair.

"At least a hundred ships full of armed fighting men," Titus announced, assessing his councilmen.

"This could be nothing less than an act of war!" cried Adrian, an older man with graying hair.

Titus lifted a hand to calm him. "They arrived without supplies or cargo. This could mean that they have fled to our lands."

"If so, from whom, and where?" asked Ambrose ominously.

"They might have failed to plan for such a journey and now they want to take what we possess. The people are weary of war. We cannot let them know an army is on our shores," Adrian's face drew downward in concern.

"We are all weary of war, Adrian. Soon enough this rumor will reach even the most remote areas of Islandia. We must act cautiously. We do not know if this is friend or foe," said Titus.

"So what do you suggest, High King?" asked Cornelius, making his voice known. His face was creased from age, but Titus knew that those creases had years of wisdom behind them.

"I will travel to Samudara Port to greet our new arrivals personally. This is the only way I can be certain of their intentions."

"My lord, there is no reason to put your life into unnecessary risk," said Adrian.

"I will take a small guard with me. Enough to prevent any attempts on my life but not enough to threaten them."

"There is no convincing you?" Ambrose asked.

"There is not. I held this council so you would know why I am departing. If all goes well, I should return within a few days."

The council stood as Titus rose to his feet. Each member stepped from the room with a respectful nod to the king. Titus watched each man as he left. Markus came shuffling up to him.

"You are brave, my King, going by yourself."

"We will find out soon enough if it's bravery or stupidity," Titus said. He turned to leave.

As he stepped out of the room an arm reached out and a hand caught hold of him. Titus looked to see the cheerful face of Imari. The

Khosi's hair had grown and was woven into an elaborate set of braids. His attire was a formal dashiki of brown and gold. The sharp features of his face smoothed into a smile.

"High King, I apologize for taking you by surprise."

Titus embraced him. "None needed. I thought you had departed after your meetings with the tradesmen's guild."

"I planned to leave immediately but I thought I should see an old friend before I left."

"I'm flattered, but you didn't need to delay your trip when you had seen me just before your meetings, friend."

"I'm sorry High King, I didn't mean you. I went to visit Geralt," Imari said in a somber voice.

Geralt. He had taken the death of Eloy harder than expected. Geralt's sorrow was strange. At times he had been Eloy's biggest critic but after his death... well, Titus couldn't blame him. Geralt had lost more than most.

"How is he?" Titus asked.

"The usual, in many ways, but something isn't right with him. He is claiming what cannot be. He claims to have seen... Eloy," Imari whispered the words, not wanting any listening ears to hear.

Titus shook his head. "Another drunken hallucination. Listen, we all wish Eloy was alive, but I can't afford to wallow in all I've lost. Too many are counting on us."

"I didn't believe him either. I told him to sober up and get some rest, but he wouldn't stop. He begged me to listen and, when I turned to leave, he showed me this." Imari carefully withdrew something wrapped in cloth from his belt. With delicate hands he unfolded it, revealing a pristine white dagger with a golden hilt.

"A dagger? What does that have to do with Eloy?" Titus asked.

"This dagger is the gift Eloy gave me on my way back to Khala over a year ago. This saved my life. That night before 'they' came... I returned it to Eloy. I made sure it was on his person when we sealed the tomb. A memento of remembrance, I suppose."

Titus stiffened. "What are you saying, Imari?"

"I am saying unless someone broke into the tomb to take this, the last person to possess the dagger was Eloy."

Titus' heart stopped. What Imari was suggesting couldn't be true. After all this time? No, someone must have raided the tomb and was playing a sinister trick on them. His face flushed with anger. "Come, we will find out soon enough."

Without waiting, he strode with firm steps to the royal tombs. Why now, of all times, would someone choose to do this? Why show the dagger to Geralt, and how would the person know that Imari would visit Geralt and come across the dagger? The questions made him quicken his pace, not waiting for the men already following behind Imari. Titus rushed forward, barking at the posted guard.

"Open the catacombs!"

The apathetic guard shot to attention, his eyes wide in surprise. Nervously he fumbled with the handle. "Of course, High King! What is it? What has happened?"

"I gave a command. Open it." He knew he shouldn't speak to the man in such a tone but his panic, fear, rage, and pain were all rising to the surface. Without another word the guard opened the wooden door. Down the damp and cobwebbed steps Titus went. The cool blast of air brought a shiver across his skin. Grabbing a nearby torch from the wall, he descended into the depths below ground. Gray, lifeless stone lined the walls. Each carved stone was decorated with the various symbols and monuments of long dead kings.

Forgetting any respects that ought to be paid as he passed the tombs, Titus pushed on until he found a small, circular room. All along the walls were shelves occupied with mummified residents. In the center was a circular stone slab. Adorning its top rested a sepulcher. Titus stood still, observing the place. Imari arrived behind him, panting.

"High King, what are you…"

"We must open it to find out the truth," Titus said coolly.

Imari's worried expression turned to horror at the king's words. "Titus, that is…"

"I know what it is, Imari, but I can't have baseless rumors filling the streets," Titus said. His eyes held a determined look that would tolerate no disobedience.

Imari stepped forward with a gulp and touched the cool, dark stone. Titus flexed his hands and placed them on the stone lid. With a push he felt the top begin to give. He looked at Imari and with another expenditure of strength the lid fell heavily to the ground with a dull thud. Dust wafted into the air and temporarily blinded them. Swatting away the particles, Titus moved to the small steps to peer into the grave.

He could feel Imari's anxious energy approach behind him. With a final step, Titus steeled his nerves and looked down into Eloy's resting place. To his utter shock, the tomb was empty.

2

GERALT

THE TAVERN WAS a dingy place. The odor of stale beer and moldy bread clung to every surface. Or, was that him that he smelled? Barely a soul filled the poorly lit establishment. Not surprising, as it was only a few hours past noon. At night the place was full of merriment, dancing, and the occasional angry drunk.

"Another," he grumbled to the barkeeper.

"I think you've had enough. Take a few hours, sober up, and you can get your fill tonight."

"I'm fine, old man," he snarled. He knew that was far from the truth. He wasn't fine. That's why he was here. A look of restrained fear filled the barkeeper's face, as he decided how he should handle this well-armed agitator.

"Fine. I'll leave, old man, but you owe me a drink when I come back tonight."

Geralt slammed a sack of coins onto the bar and stomped off. Stumbling into the streets, he was greeted by the blinding light of the sun. Around him, people scurried about, busy rebuilding their lives in the city that was being restored day by day. He could see another large building being erected not a stone's throw away, a public bathhouse by the look of it. At least Titus was rebuilding the essentials. He glanced up at the sign swinging freely in the breeze above him. The Drunken Raven.

"Soon enough you'll get some competition around here. Then we'll see if you kick out your paying customers," he said grumpily as he spat on the ground. He stumbled his way down the street, paying no attention to the townspeople around him. He saw a group of small boys kicking a ball in the street, their smiling faces affecting his own. That's when the vision came: the cold corpse of a child crushed into oozing mud, eyes lifelessly staring up into the overcast sky.

As quickly as the vision came, the face of the young boy playing in the street reappeared. The child stood cautiously staring at the grizzled old man. Geralt let out a grunt and turned away. He headed down the street, the thought of more ale weighing on his mind. He reached a humble wooden abode. A single, small window was all that adorned the exterior.

He moved his hand unsteadily to open the door. With a burst of strength it flew open, smacking into the wall and sending the contents from the shelf clanging to the floor. With an annoyed grunt he bent down to pick them up. As he reached for the small dagger the flash of his brother's dead face appeared before him. Valkin's cold, unyielding eyes pierced into his own. A stream of blood flowed from the dying man's mouth.

"Was it worth it?" the man in his vision moaned.

The nightmare vanished with those haunting words, leaving Geralt alone and trembling as he collapsed to the ground. In fury he tossed the dagger across the room and curled into a ball on the floor. Tears and snot began to drench his face. His mind raced for an answer but found none. Soon his unyielding grief succumbed to sleep. He didn't know how long he stayed on the cold and dirty floor. Only when he was greeted with a pounding headache did he awake once more. The darkness of night filled his room. Just outside the window he could hear voices full of laughter. With a grunt he lifted himself from the ground. Rubbing his face he moved toward a container sitting on a simple wooden table. Lifting it to his mouth for a drink, he waited for the sweet embrace, but nothing came.

"Empty. Always empty!" he roared and threw it against the wall, shattering the vessel into a hundred pieces.

He massaged his shoulder and with resentment on his face he moved to the door. He failed to notice the wondrous majesty that filled the sky as he stepped onto the street. Pockets of shining orbs spread across the dark sky. A spattering of small campfires burned on the ground, keeping the coolness of spring at bay. While such fires had been outlawed, the poorest communities in Kingshelm seemed to get away with these small indulgences. Geralt wondered how the small fires didn't create dread in the returned inhabitants. He fought back the visions of skulking figures revealed only by the light of fire. Their menacing fangs and murderous eyes peering from the darkness. With a shake of his aching head he banished the memories from his mind.

He glanced at the families sitting by their fires. The faces revealed by the flickering lights showed expressions of joy and contentment. Something he deeply yearned for himself. He wandered through the night until he reached his home away from home, The Drunken Raven. As he entered, he took note of the plethora of people now gathered inside. The smells were the same, only intensified by the number of warm bodies in the place. The sound of stringed instruments traveled into the night air, the silky voice of a woman singing in unison to the tune. She sat in a revealing red gown, her blonde hair casually draped on one shoulder as she sang a smooth melody. Her eyes stared seductively out into the onlooking crowd. Cheers rang from the opposite side of the room followed by disgruntled complaints at a card table. Geralt brushed past the music and the crowd and made a beeline for the bar.

He moved to his usual spot where a youthful, skinny man sat. The man took note of Geralt's hovering presence.

He raised protest in a nasally voice, "You got a problem? By the smell of it you could use a change of clothes. Heard they got a wash basin for the pigs out back. Maybe you should find yourself there." The young man jabbed a finger into Geralt's torso as he said the words.

Without moving a muscle Geralt glared down at the drunken fool. The young man squirmed uncomfortably in his seat.

"Alright, what you want brute?" he asked after Geralt remained silent.

"You're in my seat, lad," he grumbled.

The youth's eyes darted to and fro, but he took the prudent path and rose to his feet. Swallowing his pride he scurried into the crowd. With a tired sigh Geralt collapsed onto the stool. The bartender caught his eye and gave a weary sigh of his own. Slowly the barkeep moved his way, cleaning a mug as he went.

"Didn't think I'd be dealing with you again," the bartender said curtly.

"After every other night you thought I wouldn't show? Just give me the usual and shut it."

The bartender rolled his eyes as he turned to take another's order.

"And don't forget it's on the house for earlier!" Geralt barked.

In return he was given an unsavory gesture. He found himself nursing his fifth drink as he stared out at the blur of faces in the crowd. He wondered where they all had come from? What stories they carried? What pain? He was taken aback suddenly by a face standing out from all the others. The dark olive skin stood out in stark contrast to the pale faces of the River Folk. His deep brown eyes carried a penetrating stare and they were looking directly at him.

"Eloy...?" mumbled Geralt. A hulking figure came bursting in front of him, blocking the room from his sight. He looked up to see a round-faced man. His body was two sizes too large and his breath sent vomit rising in Geralt's throat. He heard a nasally voice just behind the hulking man.

"Yeah… that's the one, brother! He told me off, treated me like some gutter rat!"

"That so?" the hulking man asked. "You treat my brother poorly?"

"Move out of my way you mass of filth," Geralt snarled as he rose to his feet. He felt the room spin and caught himself on his stool.

"Seems this one's had a bit too much to drink," chuckled the fat man.

"Easy prey, brother!" cried the scrawny youth.

"Still sober enough to take you, fat lacka." He moved to strike the man, but felt his balance betray him.

The hulking form gripped Geralt by the shoulders and sent him flying across the room. Cries of panic filled the air as he came crashing to the ground. The music screeched to a halt and all eyes darted to the scene. Geralt moaned as he got to his knees.

"Good first hit," he muttered.

"ENOUGH!" yelled the bartender. "Get him out. He's been enough trouble."

He turned his gaze to Geralt. "I don't want to see you here again, understand?"

The bruiser came crashing forward, his stumpy fingers locked around Geralt once more and hoisted him on to his broad shoulders. Geralt found himself being carried outside into the dark of night. With a sudden loss of gravity, the world around him began to spin. It only stopped as he was greeted with the vision of brown muck oozing as if on its own. Before his world went dark he vaguely heard the snorting of pigs.

"Geralt."

"Geralt."

There it was again. That familiar voice. His eyes blinked open. Between the clumps of mud distorting his vision he could just make out the form of pigs and a pair of feet.

"Geralt, I need you to wake up. I have an urgent task for you."

He groaned as he rose to his knees. He looked up and his heart stopped. He felt his jaw drop as he stared into the eyes of Eloy. His strong, regal face cracked into a smile from the acknowledgment of his friend. Fear pierced Geralt's heart and he scrambled backward.

"Don't be afraid, friend. I am not a ghost," Eloy said kindly.

"You... how drunk am I?" Geralt mumbled in confusion, grabbing his head.

"Very drunk. I promise this is no hallucination."

"Why? How?" Were the only words Geralt could muster.

Eloy let out a soft chuckle. "Important questions, but not answers I can provide now. I need you to deliver a warning and also spread good news. A grave danger is on the horizon, Geralt." Eloy paused to let the drunken man absorb the warning. "You must tell the others that I am alive."

Geralt found himself fumbling for words again. "Do the others know?"

"Not yet. You haven't told them," Eloy said with a wry smile.

"Me? What do you mean? Are you not going to tell them?" Geralt's head was swimming and his thoughts were confused.

"I will, at the proper time, but the task of sharing this news I give to you."

"You don't understand, I haven't seen them... well it's been awhile."

"That's exactly why you should tell them," Eloy said not unkindly.

"They won't believe me if I do! They'll say I was drunk, and making it up or seeing things."

"What you say is only partly true," Eloy said with a chuckle.

"This isn't a joke! You have the wrong man," he protested.

A flicker of sternness flashed across Eloy's face. "Are you questioning my ability to declare you to be fit for a task?"

Humility suddenly struck Geralt and he dropped to a knee. "Of course not, my King."

"I didn't think so. Now get yourself cleaned up. You have a message to deliver."

Geralt found himself nodding with affirmation, and as he looked up Eloy extended a white bladed dagger toward him. The blade hummed with a faint energy similar to a Dawn Blade.

"What's this?" he asked.

"You may need help convincing our friends when the time comes. This is to help your case."

Geralt took the dagger in hand and looked it over. "I don't understand."

"You will. We have a mutual friend who will know what it means."

Eloy now extended a hand and lifted Geralt to his feet. His mind whirled at the feeling of Eloy once again in the flesh. The strength of Eloy's firm grip caused his brain to spin. He mulled over the person before him. The man before him looked like a deeper reality than he had ever experienced standing in the presence of any other person. In a blink, that reality was gone and Geralt was standing alone in the mud.

He had laid awake all night staring up at the ceiling, mind racing. Could it be true? Had Eloy really returned? He knew the answer, yet he fought to believe it himself. How could he deliver the message to the others? With a groan, he rose from the cold ground. An outline of mud had stuck to the ground where he had laid. He felt a soberness that had been long in visiting him. He drew up water and filled a basin to wash away the filth from the evening before. The long night had ended, and it was time to start living in the day again.

He let the refreshing chill of water bring new energy to his soul. Releasing a deep breath he hoisted himself up. A small wooden chest rested in the corner of the room. He moved to it, pausing just before opening it. A tinge of doubt rushed to his mind. Would they really accept him back at the royal court? The last time he had visited, it ended on poor terms. He had arrived intoxicated and made a mockery of all in attendance.

He could still visualize the sour faces of Lydia and Titus as he accused them of moving on with such ease. A blossom of shame filled his cheeks. That was in the past. Now, he had a fresh chance. He flicked the chest open. Inside rested the black and white tunic embroidered with three wolves' heads. Underneath lay a Light Bringer and wrapped around it was a beaded necklace made from his long passed mother.

With delicate care he raised the necklace over his head. Its simple patterns made of alternating blue, white, and silver reminded him of home among the hills. He donned the royal tunic and fastened the Light Bringer around his waist. If he was to attend the royal court he best look the part. He was taken by surprise by the knock that sounded at the door behind him. No one ever visited him here. Could it be the lackas from the night before?

"Geralt?" asked an accented voice of the south.

"Imari, is that you?"

"It is. May I come in?"

Geralt scrambled to the door, fiddling with the lock. The door swung open to reveal the blinding light of day. As his vision returned, he saw the slender form of Imari standing in the doorframe. The Khosi was dressed in a formal brown and gold dashiki. His face's sharp features were warmed by the sight of his old friend.

"I like the hair. Growing it out, huh?" Geralt asked casually.

"It's been nearly six months and that is your greeting for me?" Imari said, laughing.

They embraced and Geralt motioned for the man to enter. He could see Imari trying his best not to look too closely at his current residence. Geralt knew his place had its own unique smell he had grown accustomed to. He pulled up the single chair in the room and offered it to his friend. Imari sat and glanced around.

"So, you have been staying here?" he asked.

"Yea, closest place to the tavern and, well…" he didn't finish. "What brings you down to this part of Kingshelm?"

"You, my friend. It has been awhile since any have heard from you."

Geralt nodded his head and mulled over how to start what he wanted to say. "Something strange happened at the tavern last night."

Imari shifted uncomfortably in his seat, not sure if he cared to know the tale.

"It wasn't another drinking binge. I mean it was, but that's not the point."

Great start, Geralt. he thought to himself.

"I was thrown out into the pig pen last night by these fellows. After I shook off the beating, something amazing happened." Geralt's stomach lurched as he revealed his secret. "I saw Eloy."

Imari's eyes narrowed. "What do you mean you saw him? Like, a vision?"

"Yes. But more so! I could touch him. He was real, tangible, like you or me but in a strange way even more so."

Now Imari's face shifted to disbelief. "Geralt, you were drinking. This was likely a hallucination from the amount of alcohol you've been consuming." His eyes flickered over to the shattered bottle on the floor.

"I swear! It was him. I know it was him. He told me to warn of a coming threat and to tell you and the others he is alive!"

Imari rose to his feet. "Get some rest, Geralt. Sober up and you'll see it was all just a dream. I can see myself out."

The Khosi turned to the door and panic filled Geralt. He knew they wouldn't believe. How could he ever be so foolish… then he remembered the dagger.

"Wait! He gave me this as proof!" He quickly fumbled under his tunic and pulled out the shimmering white-bladed weapon. Imari stared at it in disbelief.

"Where… where did you get that?" he asked.

"He gave it to me! He said we had a mutual friend who would understand what this dagger meant." He motioned eagerly for Imari to take it.

Imari stretched out a cautious hand. He rolled the blade over, inspecting every inch. The Khosi stood frozen in disbelief, his eyes glued to the glowing blade.

"This can't be," he muttered. He lifted his gaze to Geralt. "Why would he choose you to give us this message? Did he not know we would doubt you in your... state?"

A wrinkled grin crept onto the leathered face of Geralt. "It's Eloy, Imari. Does he ever do anything simple?"

Imari choked out a laugh. "I guess not." He tucked the blade into his belt and turned to leave again.

"Where are you going?" Geralt asked, confused.

"Titus must know of this."

"I'll come with you."

Imari gave him a careful look. "I think it is best that I approach Titus alone. I'll bring word if anything changes."

Geralt felt his shoulders sag at the words. "Fine, but you better return to me."

Hours had passed and yet no word had come. Geralt felt frustration welling up in him. Wasn't he the one who was to give the message? Pacing the room he crossed the small mirror that hung on the wall. In it he saw the reflection of a scraggly, bearded man. His graying black hair was disheveled, but there was something different about his eyes. Behind the dark jade pools a light had returned, one he had not seen since his childhood. With swift action he grabbed a razor and watched as clumps of hair plummeted to the ground. After fighting against the tangles of long neglected hair, he stepped back to observe his work.

His face, now freshly shaved, showed the accumulation of wrinkles and scars he'd gained over the years. His hair, which he had always kept long, was now cropped short. A smile crossed his face at his handiwork. Maybe this could be the start of a new beginning. A sudden knock came from his door. Without waiting for an answer, Titus burst through the frame.

"Impatient are we, my King?" Geralt asked, only a little annoyed.

The young ruler stood keeled over and out of breath. He extended a hand, gesturing for Geralt to give him a moment.

"It's empty," he said between breaths.

"What are you talking about?" Geralt asked.

Suddenly Imari came bursting through the door just behind Titus. Both men looked as though they had run all the way from the palace. Titus stood straight, able to control his breathing again.

The High King's voice held a mix of confusion and barely restrained hope as said the words that lifted Geralt's spirit. "Geralt, the tomb is empty. Eloy isn't there."

3

LANCELIN

A WEEK PASSED SINCE their arrival. Even before the combined forces of Kingshelm and Leviatanas had reached the Forest's Edge, battle lines had been drawn. Tucked within the tree line of the northern woods, using the Atlas River as a natural defense, stood Aiden's forces. His army was a motley crew of disgruntled Riverland folk and old Valkarans. Their weathered faces told of what they had endured to survive the past year. Each stood behind chest high wooden spikes, some brandished the various banners and markings of their home. Their weapons were an assortment of old farming tools, simple spears, a few axes, and swords. The latter had been reserved for the veteran fighters among them, but their numbers were far fewer than the foe they faced.

In the open field just outside the town loomed the forces of New Valkara. The name had been given to the kingdom now possessed by Jorn and his followers. Each man stood equipped with chainmail and leather plating. A silver fox was stitched onto each man's chest. This was the symbol Jorn had claimed for himself. The mens' heads were crowned with the traditional helmet of Valkara, only the face of Odain had been replaced by a snarling fox for the mask. They were an imposing force to the ragtag assembly huddling in the woods. The uniformity of a trained army opposing the uninitiated could not have been more pronounced.

He must make the difference. He glanced over at the two commanders standing around the table. His tent looked out onto the battlefield. A light breeze passed through the large open space of the tent. His eyes caught Lydia's in the midst of the heated discussion.

"If we openly side with the rebels, what precedence does that set? High King Titus offered them amnesty if they would lay down their arms. They refused," complained the commander of Kingshelm.

"So we fight both armies at once? We may have either side outnumbered but not both. Besides, most of the lads in the army are fresh recruits. We lost a majority of our veterans at The Stand," countered Leviatanas' commander.

The Stand. This was the name given to that wretched night. How he wished he could blot it from his memory.

"What do you say, Queen Lydia?" asked Lancelin.

Both commanders grew silent realizing that they discussed the fate of the queen's brother in such a casual tone.

"Jorn is the last great enemy of Islandia. What is there to discuss?" she asked disgustedly.

"My Queen, with all due respect…"

"Don't pity me, commander. You may preside over Kingshelm's army, but you do not rule a kingdom. Besides, I believe Lancelin and I have the final say."

Kingshelm's commander retreated into embarrassed silence. Lancelin found himself stroking his chin as he mulled over the dilemma. While it was true that Jorn was the true enemy, a band of rebels running their own kingdom in the north not only set a bad precedent, it could eventually become a rival faction. Many had become dissatisfied with the unending year of violence. Few wanted it to continue, which played into Aiden's hands. If they acted against him even more could flock to his cause. If they were to depose of Jorn? Would Aiden take hold of Valkara and use it against Kingshelm in retaliation? He rubbed his tired eyes.

"What if we asked for terms? Maybe we could convince Jorn to retreat back to Valkara now that he is outnumbered. After, we could offer Valkara to Aiden on the terms of a coalition against Jorn and the return of peace when all is settled."

"You do not have that kind of authority to offer such terms!" exclaimed Kingshelm's commander.

"No, but she does," Lancelin said looking to the High Queen. Lydia's eyes probed his, ascertaining what his aims might be. He had been hesitant to let Aiden walk free in the King's council some weeks before, but now he could see no other way.

"So, we let Aiden not only walk but receive a kingdom?" Leviatanas' commander asked.

"One that rightfully belongs to him," Lydia chimed in.

"He is the true heir of Valkara," Lancelin conceded. "I see no other way. Besides, do we not strive to be a kingdom of mercy?"

Kingshelm's commander let out a disgruntled noise. "So we set the precedent of pardoning any member of the royal family no matter if they commit treason? This is a dangerous slope you two are heading down."

"I have heard enough. My brother has endured much in the way of treasonous behavior from the likes of Kingshelm. If we all want to hold to account every poor action a royal member makes, we will have nothing but enemies remaining," Lydia spoke confidently.

"It's settled then? Shall I send word for a parley with New Valkara and Aiden?" asked Leviatanas' commander.

"Send it," Lancelin ordered.

The two commanders bowed rigidly and exited the tent. Lancelin felt himself exhaling a deep sigh.

"That went well," Lydia said with sarcasm.

"You achieved what you wanted, did you not?" Lancelin asked tiredly.

"It's not about what I want, Lancelin. This is about what's right. You know as well as I who the true monster is on that battlefield," she said pointing to the tent opening to the waiting army beyond.

"When did what was simple become so complicated?" he muttered.

"It was never simple. We just wanted to look at the world in simple terms. It's easier that way," Lydia replied.

"At least we will rid the world of a monster today."

"This day has been a long time in coming," she said in agreement.

A bright blue sky hung above the lush green plain. Before them was a small, white canopy that had been propped up near the three forces. Each army stood ready for battle. An entourage of soldiers from each side slowly approached the meeting place. Each group presented themselves in a straight line across from one another. Aiden took the initiative by stepping forward from his men. The young Valkaran had the signature auburn hair and green eyes of his family. His oval face was common looking and peppered with freckles. His frame had filled over the year of hardship. Despite that, Lancelin could still see the scars creeping up his neck. Forever a reminder of the torture he had endured at the hands of Eli. The Valkaran prince wore chainmail covered by plated armor. A small ram's head was stitched near his heart on the tunic he had draped over the shining steel.

Opposite him stood Jorn. The man who had taken so much from Aiden and Lydia. He adorned himself with armor of ebony.

Lancelin had never seen such armor. Embedded into the plating were swirls of gray. The swirls gave the appearance of smoke rising from a fire. Jorn's face held a sneering smile, his countenance accentuated by silver eyes that glowed with malice. An air of confidence exuded from him.

Lancelin shifted his eyes to Lydia to catch her reaction upon seeing the man. Her emerald eyes stared coolly at her foe and the demeanor of her round face showed only calm. Her hair was pulled back and braided for battle. He checked his own armor. Each piece had been reforged and repaired. The familiar jade color was now set in a pattern of scales stretching up his arms and legs, coming to rest on newly polished steel. His armor had been reborn, much like himself: stronger. He was thankful for the newly crafted suit now more than ever. Looking across from him, he knew he could not trust either of these men. Clearing his throat, he moved to the center with Lydia by his side. Jorn and Aiden quickly followed suit.

"Was the message sent?" Lancelin asked Lydia under his breath.

"Yes. Aiden will know the plan."

An awkward silence filled the air as the three opposing sides approached one another. A spring breeze floated through the air, stirring the cloth of the canvas above. Its gentle movement was the only noise among them.

"I suppose I'll start," Lancelin said.

"Save it," snarled Jorn. "You think I have come this far to back down to the likes of you? Here you've brought me both my prizes. I might not get a chance like this again."

Lancelin was taken aback at the words, but knew he couldn't back down now. "You really think you can attempt an assault on us? We outnumber you at least three to one with Aiden's men."

"Ahh, but without his men?" Jorn asked threateningly.

"What did he mean…" Lancelin began, but was cut off by the angry man in front of him.

Suddenly Jorn began to speak at the top of his voice so that even those hidden in the woods might hear. "Men of both Valkara and Riverlands, you have rebelled because you seek a kingdom of your own away from the tyranny of kings, do you not? I am of the same mind! I am not here to kill you, only this man." His gaze fell to Aiden.

"If you will side with me I will make sure that Kingshelm can never march against you again. You can rule yourselves however you wish. Join me in this battle and we will return to Valkara and allow you to build a kingdom of your own making. If you so wish, call upon us and we will march with you to the very gates of Kingshelm!"

"You lacka!" hissed Aiden. "My men are loyal to me!"

A sudden murmur filled the forest. Lancelin could see a slight panic begin to fill Lydia's eyes.

"Lancelin, this may be a greater conflict than we imagined," she said breathlessly.

A loud clang of steel rang out in the woods followed by shouts.

"What have you done?" Aiden growled.

"Sabotage, my young prince. Do you remember the influx of Valkarans you received some months back?"

Aiden's eyes narrowed at Jorn's words.

"Well, you see, rumors are like a seed. Truth or falsehood, it doesn't matter. Once the words are spoken they grow in the mind. As time goes on people make them their reality."

Lancelin found his hand moving to his sword. "Speak plainly, Jorn, before I end you here."

"Bold words, but I suppose you alone possess a weapon that could defeat me," Jorn said patting the Dawn Blade at his hip. The dark metal glistened in the midday sun. His gaze shifted back to Aiden.

"You see your men, well, really, my men, began to spread the word how New Valkara was all about freeing the kingdom from the rule of Kingshelm. The truth, might I add, and that truth has been growing

in your ranks. This idea that maybe *we* are the ones who can liberate you after all."

"My men would never believe you! They have seen firsthand what you've done to Valkara. They followed me because of you," Aiden protested.

"But not all in your ranks are Valkaran, now are they? Did you not profit off the disenfranchised of Kingshelm?"

Realization dawned on Aiden. His face turned downcast at the revelation of what Jorn had done. Jorn's eyes flickered to a captain among Aiden's men.

"Captain Antony, who is your enemy?" he asked.

"Kingshelm, sir!" was the man's reply.

"So will you aid Kingshelm this day?"

His answer was a drawn sword. "I will not."

In that moment, a clamoring of swords being drawn echoed out over the peaceful plain. Lancelin withdrew his own blade and charged at Jorn. The man's eyes flickered with recognition as he moved his arm to his sword. The ringing of steel sounded as the Dawn Blades collided. Lancelin knew Jorn was no proper swordsmen and had relied on the superiority of his weapon to bring down those who opposed him. He pressed his attack pushing the man backward with each swing. He could see panic begin to grip the vile man.

"Let him fear me," he thought.

Behind him he heard Lydia cry out, "Lancelin wait!"

He stopped his press and observed his surroundings. Suddenly he realized Jorn had feigned his fear. Closing in on him was the host of New Valkara and, far off in the distance, stood his own forces. Jorn had lured him away from all his help.

"You really are a snake!" Lancelin cursed.

"Ah, here is a serpent calling out another," Jorn said with sickening glee.

Lancelin braced for the coming tide. A host of faceless warriors moved to engulf him. He bolstered his hope when the sound of thundering hooves drew near. On the mount was Aiden, his face a mix of fury and pain. He came to a halt beside Lancelin.

"Get on!" he shouted.

Lancelin took the extended hand and mounted the horse. Jorn's face morphed into rage and he cried out for his army to make chase. With blinding speed Aiden darted to Kingshelm and Leviatanas' battle lines. Lancelin could see that Lydia and the other commanders had already fallen back with the rest of the men who stood in formation.

"Thank you," he shouted over the galloping steed.

"Thank my sister. Besides, you're not a son of Kingshelm."

As they reached the frontlines of the army, Lancelin could see the commanders already giving orders to the men. The host of New Valkara steadily drew near behind them. Aiden motioned for Lancelin to dismount as he steered them beside Lydia.

"Are you not staying with us?" Lancelin asked as Aiden turned to leave.

"I must rally my men or, what remains of them."

"Aiden, you can't! Jorn will sweep over your men now that they are fighting amongst each other," Lydia said pleading.

"I must, sister." With that, Aiden spurred his horse to the tree line.

Lancelin turned his gaze to the encroaching army. He placed Dawn's Deliverer back into its sheath. He had taken the same lesson that Titus had learned the hard way, no blood of man would be spilled by the blade. Turning, he scanned the army at his back. The men of Kingshelm stood ready in their silver and gold armor. Beside them the polished silver and jade of Leviatanas held spears at the ready. Lancelin motioned for a nearby soldier to hand him an extra sword to wield. Weapon in hand, he took his place next to Lydia, ready to embrace the coming tide.

"Well, it should be more interesting now," he said.

She gave him a disapproving grunt but shot him a grim smile, "I've got claim on Jorn."

They both braced themselves as the New Valkaran forces charged. Lancelin could just make out a segment of their army breaking off from the rest, now headed to the woods. Divide and conquer, the age old strategy. A horn rang out giving the order for their own forces to begin their charge. With a cry, he rushed forward with the collective army. A flash of sounds and visions greeted him as the two lines collided. Steel and flesh met for yet another deadly dance.

Cries of agony filled his ears as he fought through the line of foes. With a sweep of his sword he severed a spear and followed with a deadly thrust. He felt the swoosh of Lydia's sword beside him as she cut down her foe. Side by side they pushed forward through the crowd of enemies. Men had come to know of the fighting prowess of both the jade armored prince and the red-haired queen.

A host of arrows took them by surprise as they rained down from the edge of the forest. Aiden and his men had been able to rally, sending some relief to their allies in the field. Lancelin could just make out the New Valkarans swiftly moving to Aiden's position. His mind returned to the battle at hand when he was forced to deflect an incoming blow. He held his opponent's sword high in the air as Lydia went low, sending a thrust into the man's abdomen.

"Your brother's in trouble. We need to help him now," cried Lancelin over the sounds of battle.

"How?" Lydia asked as she cut down another of Jorn's men.

How indeed? he thought.

Then, an idea sprung on him: a false retreat.

"We can feign a retreat to the tree line. From there we can hold the New Valkara forces at bay while the back lines can defend your brother."

Lydia grunted as she kicked her opponent to the ground and finished him with a downward heave of her sword.

"Sounds like a good way to die. Let's do it," she huffed, standing ready for the next opponent.

He gave her a nod and moved to find the nearest signal horn. He spotted the man near the back of the formation. He began to push his way through the men who were still eagerly awaiting their turn for battle. Panting, he reached the signal caller and gave him the order. The strange order made the man's face drop into a distrusting look.

"I said do it!" Lancelin barked.

Shaking his head, the signal caller sucked in a breath of air and bellowed out the order. Soon Lancelin could feel the formation shift to the tree line. The mass of humanity stumbled to keep their formation in tact as they moved. He rushed to the back and directed his forces to their new target. Those in the back now saw their opportunity to fight and rushed forward to greet those attacking Aiden and his men. The maneuver worked. The New Valkaran forces turned in horror at the army rushing their flank. Many scrambled to pull together a defensive position, but they were smashed between the hammer and anvil.

Lancelin and the others cut them down with ease as Jorn's forces fought from both sides. Soon Lancelin and his men would experience the same, but he was confident they would break their foe before it would come to that. He watched as that belief came to fruition before his eyes. Slowly, panic began to settle over the New Valkarans. Row after row fell to the sword and a small number threw down their arms and fled. That small number grew until the whole regiment burst into unorganized panic. Warriors abandoned their lines, leaving their comrade's flank exposed.

As the New Valkarans fled, Lancelin could see into the tree line. A small skirmish had broken out between Aiden's men and those who had switched sides. He looked over his shoulder and saw that Lydia and the others were holding their own against Jorn's remaining forces. With a motion of his hand he called for a unit of men to follow him into the woods to aid Aiden in his desperate fight.

The scene was chaos as none of the men bore the mark of the enemy. Each man fended for himself as he fought amongst the trees.

Arrows zipped past, sinking into birch trunks and flesh alike. His concern was to find the young Valkaran prince in the midst of the chaos. He and his men fought their way into the woods and cut down any who approached. Finally, after some time, he could see a cluster of captains holding a defensive position among a small outcropping of rocks. As Lancelin and his men approached, a hail of arrows rained down on them.

"We are on your side!" Lancelin barked.

The men paid no mind and sent another set of darts raining down on them. Behind, a new group of soldiers were rallying together to take their shot at the foolish Leviatanas unit that had wandered into the woods. A soldier beside Lancelin gave him gave a chilling look.

"I know, not good," Lancelin said despairingly.

That's when the horn to retreat rang out. Each man turned to see Jorn and his army melting away in the distance. Somehow, despite the treachery, they'd won. He glanced around and saw the faction who had placed their hopes in New Valkara flee into the open field, chasing after their new master. The rest hurriedly vanished deeper into the woods. Even the small battalion guarding the rocks behind them had disappeared. Each man with him breathed a sigh of relief.

It wasn't long before Lydia came searching for them in the woods. He cracked a smile at her approach but was greeted with a frown.

"What's the matter? You look as though we didn't just survive a treacherous battle."

"He got away, Lancelin," she said, fury causing her voice to shake.

"Who..." he started to say, then stopped. *Ah...who else could it be?* he thought. "There will be a day when he pays for what he has done."

"We keep saying that, but that day still has not come," she said crossing her arms.

He let out a breath, knowing now was not the time to argue about such matters.

"We should find your brother."

"He's not here?"

"He and his men have retreated into the woods," Lancelin said, motioning with his head.

She shook her head. "What have we really accomplished then?"

"Sometimes, it's just survival," he answered.

Lydia fixed her gaze on the woods. "I'll go speak with him."

"What will you say?"

Her emerald eyes hardened. "It's time to end this."

4

IMARI

MARI WATCHED AS Geralt stooped down to stare into the empty tomb. His wrinkled face bore an expression of joy at the sight. With giddiness he turned to face Titus and Imari. "I told you! He is alive. This confirms it."

Titus held his chin, unsure of what to make of all this. Geralt sighed at the skepticism painted on the High King's face.

"You believe me, don't you, Imari?" he pleaded.

"I... I cannot doubt what I see. The tomb is empty. It's just..."

"Why would Eloy appear to the drunkard out of all of us? Is that what you want to say?" frowned Geralt.

Imari could feel the heat of embarrassment creep up his neck. "Why would he not appear before us as well? Why leave you with the message?"

Geralt threw up his hands. "How should I know? Has Eloy ever done anything that didn't have a shroud of mystery around it?"

Titus spoke abruptly, "We need to keep this to ourselves."

Imari and Geralt turned to to the king, his face still frozen in thought.

"And why is that? This is good news!" Geralt protested.

A flash of annoyance filled Titus' face. "We still do not know what has happened. Imagine if word gets out that Eloy is missing. Every beggar who knows a corpse will come out of the woodwork proclaiming it's him, and we will never discover the truth."

"So what?" asked Geralt.

"We do what we can to discover the truth."

"What if the truth is already in front of you?" countered Geralt.

"Then it will be made plain soon enough," Titus said in a tone to end his protests.

"Friends, we will find the root of this mystery. No need to hold hostilities toward one another." Imari said.

They both gave a faint smile as they looked to the Khosi. Imari only hoped he was right. This was a mystery that could quickly become clouded in myth and falsehood.

"We should go back up top. I am sure there are already rumors I will need to squelch with the guard."

"What would you have me do?" asked Geralt.

"There is another mystery that needs to be tended to that I would like your assistance with," Titus said.

Geralt gave him a nod. "Anything is better than waiting in the slums for you two to try and solve this."

Titus turned to Imari. "What about you, Khosi? What will you do now?"

"There are still a number of things that I need to handle back in Khala. After they are taken care of I will return to help you in anyway I can."

The two men embraced. "You have been a faithful friend, Imari. Know that you and your kingdom are always welcome."

Geralt gave Imari a pat on the shoulder. "Good to see you again, Khosi. Thanks for delivering the message." His eyes flickered over to Titus.

"It is my pleasure. I see you took a cue from me about the hair," he said, chuckling at Geralt's handiwork.

"Ehhh, you have a good idea here and there," Geralt said with a smirk.

With that, Imari bowed and took his leave. Ascending the stairs he was greeted by a squad of guards whispering as they peered down into the catacombs.

"Titus will have his hands full indeed," he mused.

He wasted no time in finding the Khalan envoy that had accompanied him. They had followed his orders and had prepared for their return journey. He had left later than he had wished, but the sweeping plains on the way to Khala were a familiar road to travel, even in the dark.

Finally, the day arrived when the royal envoy reached the towering walls of Khala. The palace was shaped in a ziggurat and could be seen over the walls as they approached, as if to greet them. The four pillared towers stood sentinel over the city. Their watching eyes awake for any who would dare strike again. Khala's sufferings, however, had not come at the hands of the obvious invader but through treachery and deceit. This type of infiltration had hounded both his father and himself. The violence done a little over a year ago had created doubt in many of Khala's clansmen. Not to mention, he had marched their able-bodied warriors north not two days after the assault and only returned with a meager force.

He did not question his decision. He knew he had chosen what was right. The consequences were what he dreaded. The bronze gates of the city creaked open as they received their Khosi. No grand celebration awaited him like his first return, only cautious glances and doubting eyes came from the people in the streets. Most of the city had been repaired. The markets flourished once more and the people crowded the streets in their usual trade. The wealth and resources of their home remained secure. The trust and allegiance of his people had been fractured.

As they approached the palace, the muscular form of Khaleena and her trusted Masisi warrior Lombaku stood ready to greet him, a gesture Imari did not appreciate. The city was on the edge of fracturing and Khaleena had finally taken his old offer of inviting the Masisi into the city. She claimed it was to defend their people since Khala had so few warriors remaining after The Stand. Imari couldn't fight the creeping suspicion that his sister doubted his leadership.

Surely, she isn't making a play for power? he thought.

She moved forward to greet him, her vibrant red and black dashiki that could not conceal her scars swished in the breeze. Tight braids of hair were pulled back, revealing the deep wound that ran down the side of her cheek.

A formal smile crossed her face as he approached. "Welcome home, brother. I trust your journey to Kingshelm was fruitful?"

He shot a questioning glance at Lombaku before fixing his gaze on Khaleena. "It was. The tradesmen have promised us another year's worth of stone to help build irrigation systems outside the city in exchange for precious jewels."

I found out Eloy may be alive in a miraculous rising from the grave, was also what he wanted to say, but he kept that thought to himself.

"Very good. I am sure the prospect of a more secure crop output will make many of our people happy," she said coolly.

What are you hiding Khaleena? Do you plan to supplant me? Do you think I have failed our people so badly? he wondered.

He shifted his eyes to Lombaku. The man towered over most who encountered him. His arms were as thick as tree trunks and his face, covered in traditional piercings, was perpetual stone. Like most of the Masisi, he was not known for his social etiquette.

"Good to see you as well, Lombaku."

The Masisi warrior let out a disinterested grunt in reply. Unfazed, Imari turned back to his sister.

"How have things been in Khala in my absence?"

"An interesting development has occurred, brother. One that will demand your attention."

"What matter is this?"

"Visitors from a most intriguing place. They await your arrival in the throne room."

With a cautious look, he stretched out his hand. "Lead the way then, sister."

She gave him a slight smile and turned to order the palace doors to open. Inside, the refreshing sound of water trickling reverberated off the walls. Imari took in the familiar sight of lush vegetation lit by the hollow ceiling. Their green display surrounded a fountain at the center of the room. The ancient fountain decorated with tales of Khala's history now carried a plastered line across its face. A scar to remind them of the danger of Sahra. At least that was the rallying cry many clung to these days.

The small party ascended the stairs to the right and moved up the layers of the palace until they reached the throne room doors. Two Bomani stood sentinel. A feeling of sorrow passed over him as he inspected them. The Bomani had been whittled down to dust in the conflicts that had happened a little over a year ago. Even the famed leader and drillmaster Imamu had paid with his life. Only now had the Khosi's ancient guardians begun to regain their strength under a new leader.

The throne room's doors swung open and out of them came just that man. Impatu stood tall. The year of trials and battle had crafted the young Khalan into a seasoned warrior. His once thin and youthful appearance had filled in its form. His hair was shaved to the skin on the sides and pulled back tightly on the top, in the traditional way of the Bomani. His face cracked into his familiar smile at the sight of Imari.

"Khosi! You've returned. Incredible timing at that." He moved to embrace Imari in a manner that few dared. Imari opened his arms to greet his friend. Pushing him away, he examined the young warrior.

"I noticed a few more dressed in the Bomani fashion around the city on my arrival. This is good news, so long as you aren't going easy on them, friend," he said chuckling.

"I would never, Khosi. It is true our numbers are finally beginning to rise. The first class of Bomani have passed their trial not two weeks ago."

Imari's eyes shifted to peer inside the throne room. He could just make out a cluster of men in varying colored robes. Impatu took note of his gaze.

"Our new arrivals," he said.

"And what does my captain of the Bomani make of them?" Imari probed.

"It is yet to be seen, but they have not shown any signs of hostility."

"The most dangerous enemies don't," said Imari. He stepped forward into the chamber to greet his distinguished guests. Sunlight bathed the tiled floor. The speckles of gold glimmered between its blue and white companions. The large overhanging gardens gave the room a sweet fragrance. Massive tapestries hung on either side displayed a pouncing leopard. All these things drew the eye to the throne upon its pedestal. Standing before that throne the group of men turned as he entered. Imari spread out his arms in a welcoming gesture.

"Welcome to the kingdom of Khala. I apologize I was not here to greet you sooner."

A man stepped forward from the group. His neck and torso were wrapped with a smoky colored cloth. Underneath his scrappy form Imari could see a sliver of dark plated armor. Gray eyes sat fixed in a face worn with signs of long exposure to the sun. His faded brown hair fell loosely above his shoulders. The others in his party had various appearances. Some were dark skinned like the Khalans, others a pale complexion with narrow eyes and sharp features unlike any who dwelled in Islandia. The rest had an appearance similar to those of the Founders' descendants. This was a strange visitation indeed.

"We thank you for your hospitality, Khosi. I was told that is your title. Please correct me if I have misspoken. My name is Cedric and my men and I hail from, well… the rest of the world," Cedric said with a musing smile.

Imari was taken aback by the man's words but quickly regained his composure. "You have not misspoken, Cedric from the world. My title is Khosi. Sadly, I must say if you wish to speak to the highest ruler of the land I am not he, but I can speak for my people here in Khala."

Cedric gave a reassuring smile. "Rest assured we have come to speak with you, Khosi. Our leader, Ulric, insisted that a representative of our people go out to each of the kingdoms of your land. I hope this does not intrude on this… ruler of yours."

Imari felt a tinge of unease at Cedric's words. They were a slight at the High King's claim, hidden in the drape of formality.

"So what is it you and your leader Ulric want, Cedric?"

Cedric turned to the others and cleared his throat. A large chest was brought forth and placed on the floor before Imari. One of the men clicked open the lock and carefully lifted the lid. Inside rested a dazzlingly array of gold, gems, and an assortment of riches.

"We are refugees in search of a new home. Our lands have been decimated by a dark force. We call them servants of the moon. Vile creatures that once were men but have been taken over by a Dark Master, as many of our people call him."

"I am familiar with these beings," Imari responded.

"Then, I will move on to why we are here. A little over a year ago something changed. All of our homes had been subjected by this fell being, but he had allowed us to live in relative peace as long as we answered his call. That is until The Reckoning."

"What is this 'Reckoning'?" Imari asked, playing along.

"Something strange happened. Something that made the Dark Master very upset. Many of our homes were ordered to be destroyed and our people were slain, or worse. We didn't understand why this was happening. The Dark Master profited from many of our civilizations but something had caused him to be so enraged that he no longer cared."

"Do you know what that might be?" asked Imari.

Cedric shot him a sideways glance. "We heard rumor of a land far off from the rest of the continents, one that had not yet come under the Dark Master's rule. Word was this small kingdom had thrown back his army and stood against the Dark Master himself. We traveled far and wide looking for this rumored haven, and at last it seems we have found it."

Imari examined them with a careful eye. He looked at the chest lavishly displayed in his hall and the men surrounding it. Something wasn't right.

"You say you are refugees, do you not? How would refugees come to have such treasure? Did you have time to empty your treasuries before you fled? You also say you heard rumor of our lands and it took you some months to arrive on our shores. I knew a man once who had departed from here and it took him years to find his destination."

Cedric swallowed, weighing his next words very carefully. Imari could feel Impatu and the other Bomani scattered around the throne room tense at his words.

"My Khosi, these things are all that we have left of our most precious belongings. We were not beggars where we lived. The Dark Master has turned us into such. As for the journey, word has spread of your High King's escapades across the seas. It was not hard to trace them to the source, especially when those who knew the rumors joined us."

"So, what is it you seek?"

"A home. A place where we can live without fear of evil. A land to share," Cedric said.

"A home..." mused Imari. "So you intend to stay in Islandia?"

"If you will allow it, yes."

"Do you hope to buy yourselves a home?" Imari asked pointing at the treasure. "Or do you intend to take it?"

Cedric looked uncomfortably at the piece of armor peeking out of Imari's robes. "We come in peace, as weary travelers seeking a place away from the rule of darkness. We believed that Islandia was such a place."

Impatu leaned in to Imari's ear. "I do not like the look of this. These men do not appear to be starving survivors to me."

Imari was glad to have another who felt the same. He turned to look at his sister who gave no inclination either way on how she felt, but he doubted she was feeling trustworthy toward any outsiders. He turned to Cedric once more.

"I am afraid your timing is poor, Cedric. Our people have endured much at the hands of outsiders."

"So will you turn us away to wander the seas?" Cedric asked.

"No, but this is not a decision for Khala to make alone. You will return to your leader Ulric and tell him that this is a matter for all of Islandia's rulers to decide. Tell him we will gather a council at a city called Kingshelm. You are welcome to stay the evening, then I think it best you deliver this message."

Imari could see the frustration on Cedric's face, but the man pushed his emotion aside. "We will abide by your council, Khosi."

Imari gave him a bow and turned to leave. Impatu was quick to his side.

"Make sure the Bomani keep a close eye on them. I want them gone from the city by tomorrow morning, and make sure they do not get a chance to see our defenses," he ordered.

Impatu gave him a bow as he stepped aside to convey the order. Khaleena came rushing to his side.

"Where are you going now, brother?" she asked.

"I need to pay a visit to Sahra."

"Sahra?" she said taken aback. "Why would you go to our enemies now?"

He gave her a disapproving look. "I need to know if these same outsiders have sent messengers to Nabila. If so, I need to know what Sahra intends to do, and if they haven't... Nabila deserves a seat at the council regardless of the past."

Khaleena shook her head and stomped down the hall, muttering under her breath.

Imari let out a sigh. He hoped of all the new threats rising that the most dangerous one didn't share his blood.

5

LYDIA

S HE PUSHED DEEPER into the woods, following the trail of trampled flora and broken branches. It took her back to simpler days. She envisioned her sister running ahead of her, excited to keep pace with the deer they stalked. An exasperated Geralt kept reminding them they would find no deer if they couldn't keep quiet. Even her brothers had joined in on the hunt. Brayan held his typical shy demeanor but Aiden was eager to prove himself.

As they approached a sharp ledge within Valkara's woods they had spotted their prey. Aiden, without advising the others, rushed ahead, unaware of the cliff. His recklessness sent him crashing to the ground with more than his pride injured. Needless to say, the buck had escaped and it was a long, disheartening trudge back home.

"Oh Aiden, I hope you don't repeat your mistake," she sighed to herself. She had made the decision to seek out his surrender. He must lay down his arms and in exchange they would finish Jorn off once and for all, together. And after? After there could finally be peace. At least, she hoped there would be. Something told her it would be much more complicated.

Just ahead, she spotted a wooden palisade with patrols of archers at its base. The last remnants from the fight were trickling in behind the defense. She mustered up her courage. These men may be led by her brother, but they all had experienced treachery by those they trusted. She was thankful Lancelin was willing to hold back the army and give her the chance to speak with Aiden alone.

She moved toward the encampment with her hands raised in the air. Her sword hung sheathed at her side while her shield draped loosely against her back. At the sight of her arrival the patrol of archers bolted into action. Each tightened their bowstrings with arrows notched. One shouted out to her, "Stop now if you value your life!"

"Kill her. She's seen our camp already!" cried another.

"My name is Lydia, sister of Aiden. I come in peace," she shouted back.

Hesitation crossed the face of the first guard as he lowered his bow.

"Are you mad? She is the enemy! Was she not part of the army that marched up here to wipe us out?" protested the anxious comrade.

Lydia looked each of the men in the eyes, searching for pity. They were a mixed company, with some still desiring a home of safety and freedom. Others were eager to be done with the wretched day.

"Men of my brother, I wish you no harm. I only desire peace."

"Peace," scoffed one of the men. "Yeah, we've seen enough of the type of peace your kind brings."

"Please, I do not want more violence on this day." Slowly she reached for her sword, slid it from its sheath and threw it onto the ground.

"You may spill my blood if you like, but it will be the blood of an unarmed ally."

The leader of the pack let out a disgusted noise. "Come lads, drop your bows. If it's Aiden she wants let him decide for himself what to do with her."

"But sir, the commander is in no shape to..."

"Silence lad!" the captain's face flared with annoyance at the loose lipped underling.

No shape for what? Lydia wondered. Had her brother been injured in the fighting?

"Come, lass," waved the captain, ushering her forward. With quickened pace she moved to the opening in the camp's wall. Inside, a host of wounded men rested, tending their injuries. Those who were healthy enough to stand rushed to and fro doing whatever was necessary. She was led to a small longhouse that stood in the center. Its timber walls were decorated with the symbol she knew well, the blue field and black ram. Alongside it many different symbols hung on display. Each represented the collaboration of the movement. A cause that now had reached its death throes.

She was escorted inside a dimly lit room. A group of armed men stood huddled over a cot. Their heads turned as the unexpected visitor entered.

"I thought we said no visitors!" One of the captains barked.

"This is no simple visitor, captain..."

All eyes fell on her. Each of their faces softened with realization. They parted from their circle to reveal Aiden reclining, his breathing labored. From his right shoulder protruded the shaft of an arrow.

"Brother!" Lydia said with concern as she knelt by his side.

Aiden let out a cough as he sat up to greet her. "Don't be alarmed, sister. They say it won't be fatal."

Tears began to fill her eyes. "Why did you have to go and be a fool, Aiden? I can't lose you, too."

She rested her head on his chest and began to weep. He raised his hand to comfort her but paused a moment.

"I didn't realize you still cared, sister."

She lifted her head to glare at him. "How could you say such a thing? You are my flesh and blood and all I have left of our family."

His eyes turned away. "You married that Kingshelm lacka and I thought…"

"You thought what, Aiden? That I threw away all I cared about? That I abandoned my family?"

She shook her head. "Don't you see it is exactly that kind of thinking that has destroyed our people for so many years? Titus is not your enemy. He sent us…"

"He sent you to finish us," Aiden interrupted.

"He sent us to aid you. He knows the kind of monster Jorn is, and he knew you would not be able to stand against him alone."

"This aid.What comes attached to it? That we give up our cause of a free Islandia? That we should come under the banner of Kingshelm whenever he needs to call on us? An aid with a price attached. If we refused, then what?"

Lydia scrunched her face at his words. "Brother… has the world jaded you so? Yes, Titus would ask you to lay down your rebellion and in exchange you would be free to rule Valkara again, your rightful kingdom. He does not wish to be your enemy."

Aiden grew still. His eyes fixed on the ceiling in deep thought. After a moment he looked at his captains. "Leave us."

"But sir?"

"I said, leave us."

Without another word the room emptied, leaving only the Valkaran heirs behind.

"Are these his words or yours?" he asked.

"Titus and I have spoken on this many times leading up to this day. We have decided that this is what is best for the kingdom. You may rule Valkara as our forefathers have always done, so long as you keep the peace."

Aiden shifted, letting out a grunt of pain from the wound. "What was the result of the battle? How many lost?" he asked.

"Our forces remained relatively fine. Yours, however…"

"So, the captains were lying to me," he mused.

"I doubt lying is what they intended, only…" she stopped.

"Only, holding on to a dying dream," he sighed. Her silence was the answer he had now come to realize for himself.

"I suppose it was a foolish dream," he said ruefully.

"Not foolish, brother. Misguided. You desired freedom from what you perceived as corrupt rule. In many ways the old way of things had to be destroyed, but something new is rising."

He let out a faint chuckle. "You really think that?"

"I have seen too much sacrifice to believe it was all for nothing," she said.

"This world is a cruel place, sister. It takes without mercy, nothing more."

"I wouldn't be so sure, Aiden. If you look hard enough you can find beauty in it. Hints of something more, something that will take all these wrongs and make them right."

"The New Dawn? Is that what you speak? Don't tell me you believe that child's tale."

She examined her heart. Did she really believe what she was saying? Something inside her confirmed the truth she had come to believe. Yes, despite everything they now endured there would be purpose to the pain. Whatever the New Dawn may be, it would make things right at last. All they had suffered would no longer remain a sorrow in which they could never escape.

"I do, brother."

He scoffed. "There we may disagree, but I see no reason why we cannot come to terms if Kingshelm will keep their word on restoring Valkara to our family. I will need more than word though. I have seen enough of man's broken word to last the rest of my lifetime."

"Come to Kingshelm with me. Titus will confirm my words. We will march together and end this reign of Jorn's once and for all, together," she looked down at the wounded shoulder. "Maybe you should get that mended before we go."

He let out an annoyed grunt.

"One more thing, brother. Where have you kept the man named Henry? Titus asked me specifically for his release."

"He will be returned to you just as soon as we arrive safely at Kingshelm."

She gave him a nod of approval as she stood to her feet.

"Let's see what this High King has to say," Aiden said.

Lydia found herself barely able to contain the joy she felt returning to Lancelin and the others. The Leviatanas prince was busy giving orders when she came from the woods. A hopeful look filled his eyes as he saw her approach. He was accompanied by his strange companions from the Dreadwood, Zuma and Izel. Both were practically twins of dark complexion and even darker hair. They carried a look of anticipation for the news she brought.

"Please tell me we have terms," Lancelin said.

"We have terms," she said with a smile. "We will march tomorrow with Aiden and his remaining forces to Kingshelm. From there we will make plans for a final assault on Jorn.

"What convinced him to give up his rebellion?" asked Zuma.

"I'm not entirely sure. Maybe the prospect of home, the loss of so many, family?"

"Whatever it is, I am happy there can finally be peace," said Izel.

Lydia looked the two Dreadwood natives over, curious at their interest in affairs far from their home and wondered when they had arrived at the battle.

Turning to Lancelin she asked, "I didn't realize our friends here had joined us in the fight."

Lancelin grinned as he looked at Zuma and Izel. "I sent a message to them some time before we marched. Things have settled in their new homes here in the Riverlands. They joined our company a few days back on the march, wanting to help.

Zuma continued for him, "This is our home now. Since our fight with Eloy, we realize we cannot just sit idly by, shutting out the rest of the world."

"So, we came to help in any way we could," finished Izel.

"Noble of you. But why this fight?"

They looked to Lancelin. With a shrug of the shoulders he said, "I asked them. I knew they were deadly with a bow and they wanted to help."

"In our home, the clan doesn't see issues as our own. If there is a dispute, we all come together until it is solved. It has been a custom long before our time."

"Wasn't your tribe under the rule of one of the Felled Ones? How could you trust any custom with such a ruler leading you?" asked Lydia.

Izel gave her a curious smile. "No matter how vile a ruler, do not all cultures and people have things that are still admirable? Besides, this one predates even him."

The response had taken Lydia aback. Of course what the young woman said was true. Valkara's ethos revolved around a warrior culture. Strength, violence, and hot-tempers for so long had ruled the day. Yet, there was still much to admire about her kinfolk. The hardships had strengthened them against all sorts of threats. Their love of nature and song was unparalleled in Islandia. Perhaps all these things could be redeemed.

"If our discussion on culture and custom is at an end I would like to discuss the march home," said Lancelin. Lydia rolled her eyes but stood ready to listen.

"I believe the two armies should travel a good distance apart. We may have terms, but I doubt either side trusts one another. Last thing we need is some renegade starting a battle in the open plains or near a city."

"We could send delegates from each side to ensure no action is done to one another," commented Zuma.

"Hostages?" Lydia asked. "I don't know if Aiden will be too thrilled."

"It's a good thought, Zuma, but, no. Any sign of mistrust could send this spiraling toward conflict."

In that moment Lydia knew what to do. "I will march with Aiden's men. We will go ahead of Kingshelm's forces. That way, they cannot run off or strike us from behind. We can arrive quicker than our large force so negotiations can begin right away."

"Are you sure, Lydia? You'll be alone with them."

"I will be fine. Just make sure our army doesn't do anything stupid."

Lancelin gave her a nod. A messenger came darting from the camp. Lancelin stepped forward to address the man.

"What is it?" he asked.

"A word from Kingshelm, my lord," the messenger said out of breath.

"From Titus?" Lydia asked with a tinge of fear gripping her voice.

The messenger gave an affirming nod. "The High King wishes to inform you of strange visitors landing in Samudara Port. Hundreds of boats, it's said."

"What could this mean?" Lancelin asked to no one in particular.

"No one is sure, my lord, but the High King requests your return immediately and he has asked that you bring the army."

Lydia looked at the others. The joy of the day suddenly seized by a rising sense of dread that one threat was now giving way to another.

6

TITUS

A DULL HUE OF gray covered the sky. The cry of seagulls rang out above him, and his nostrils were filled with the scent of salt water. Titus found a calmness had always claimed him when he visited the sea. The sea with its endless embrace was untamable by any man. That thought struck fear into most, but for him the reminder that this world could not be hemmed in by sheer force of will brought him peace. No matter his striving, his vain attempts at glory, or his triumphs, there was always something that held greater power.

When he stared out at the sea, it was the gentle reminder that he need not think his failings would be so great as to send the world crashing down forever. There was something greater that could overcome them, much like waves crashing into the banks of sand. What may be written could be washed over, molded to fit into the purposes of that higher power. The pounding waves also raised in him the courage that, though he may fail, he must try. The race of men must use their time wisely. What is written may be molded and changed, but what will it speak to those who are able to read it? He was called a steward for a reason. While many looked to him as High King, it was the purpose of stewardship that drove him. He was pulled from his thoughts as he felt Geralt step beside him. The grizzled warrior inhaled the salt water smell.

"Never been a fan of the sea. Dry land is where I have planted my feet most of my days, and I prefer to keep them there. Give me dense evergreens and jagged rock any day," said Geralt.

Titus couldn't help but let out a bit of a chuckle.

"Something I say funny, lad?"

"It was nothing really, Geralt," Titus said with a faint smile. Internally he mused over how men could see the world so differently. Experience was the great shaper of perspective.

The old warrior let it go, but Titus could see the man's puzzled look as he searched inwardly at what could have been so funny. Titus turned his attention to the bustling port that lay to their right. He had taken some time alone by the sea before embarking on their true task. He searched for the answers and for guidance on what he should do next. No distinguishable answer came to him, but a sense of peace was all he needed. He drank in one last view of the vast expanse of water. Just off the coast floated several marvelously decorated ships of vibrant color. Their sails displayed varying symbols of their respective clans and homes. On their decks rested all manner of cargo. Some cargo was being offloaded and others were draped with tarps on deck. It was because of these ships that they had come.

"We should gather with the others and head into the city."

Geralt gave him an agreeing nod. They returned to the small envoy that had accompanied them on the journey. The envoy held a mixture of royal representatives and ambassadors. All the politicians of Kingshelm wanted to investigate Islandia's newfound arrivals. As they approached the city, Titus observed the strangeness of the place.

Samadura Port was unlike any other city, town, or dwelling in Islandia. This port had come to be the only place with connections to the outside world. The Founders had always been paranoid of outsiders, wishing to keep what they had fled far at bay. Samadura had only risen out of necessity of trade, and it soon became a magnet to all and sundry. Most of the city was built from a strange colored stone, a mixture of dark grays and deep blue. It gave the entire city a wet look, as if every inch was covered by the spray of the sea. In juxtaposition the roofs of every building were a red clay tile. Large wooden pulleys littered the ever expanding skyline before them.

The flair of the town had come from the melding of every kind of culture. Men of the south had first established the city as a fishing port. When it fell into Leviatanas' hands it began to develop into an urban center. All manner of men gathered here and thus it became, in a casual sense, the port of Islandia. As Titus and the others wandered the streets, men of all colors and creeds carried with them carts of exotic goods. Fabulous furs of creatures Titus had never seen were draped from a nearby tanner's shop.

Fish of all kinds hung in the streets, the morning catch on display for sale. Even as the Steward King's son, he had not ventured to this port often. With the import and export of so many goods from all manner of places, it had become a hard place to rule. It may have been one of his father's greatest failures, letting the port exist almost entirely independent from the rest of Islandia, but the pressures of the time had drawn his attention to other issues to govern over.

Now that left Titus in a precarious position. The High King prancing around the streets was an unfamiliar sight for many inhabitants of the city. Strange looks and ponderous glances were thrown his way. He could feel Geralt tense at his side as he, too, noticed attention being drawn to them. He was thankful to have a friend with him for this meeting.

They soon found themselves at the port. An endless array of ships sat docked along the shore. As far as he could see, wooden docks housed all kinds of sea vessels. One in particular grabbed his attention. It was a mass of crimson and gold. At its bow was a sculpture craved in the image of a leviathan. Its snarling mouth and scaled neck protruded so far that it partially covered the docks it banked against.

"That looks like a warship to me," Geralt said.

"Indeed it does," Titus said studying the behemoth.

Just as the words left his mouth a dock-master came scrambling out of the crowds to meet them.

"My lord the king, it is an honor for you to visit our dockyard. How can I best serve you?"

The dock-master showed the veneer of pleasantries, but Titus felt the man's distain for ruling authority hidden beneath his words.

"I wish to speak to the owner of these ships," Titus said motioning to the array of vessels.

"Ahhh yes, the man named Ulric. That is who you'll wish to speak with."

"Indeed, where is this, Ulric?" Titus asked.

"Right here," came a voice behind him. Titus turned to see a man standing with his hands on his hips. The man's features and skin were worn from a harsh life at sea. His thick black hair and stubbled chin colluded with his rough exterior. Piercing eyes of deep brown sunken into a chiseled face stared back at them. There was fire to those eyes and Titus wondered if it was a sense of desperation the man carried within. The garb he wore was chainmail that had a tint of bronze. Peaking out from his midnight cloak was steel plating covered in gold. Over his shoulder rested a white fox fur, an exotic animal rarely seen in Islandia. It was a paradoxical scene. The features of the man told a tale of hardship while his clothes revealed great wealth. Behind this stranger Titus could see several others who stood armed and ready.

"Ulric, High King Titus, it's a pleasure to finally meet you." Titus extended a hand to the man. Ulric took it in his own with a cracked smile.

"To meet such royalty, we are humbled."

"I wish to know why you have come to our lands and what it is you desire from us."

"Of course, High King." Ulric's eyes darted around the dock. "But I think it's best we speak of such matters elsewhere. Some of my captains and I have lodging nearby. If it suits you, my King, he can join us there."

"Lead the way," Titus said with a motion of his hand.

Ulric and his companions turned, leading them down the main road from the docks. Ulric steered them to an elaborate lodge that overlooked the vast expanse of sea. The building bested any resting place Titus had seen in all of Kingshelm, even before the fires. Every kind of ornate decor filled the place. Sculptures of beasts and men both known and unknown to him. Gold trim covered every room's frame. As they were ushered down the halls, he couldn't help but notice the painted rich hues of indigo and crimson. Around every corner a servant was never far away. Ulric lead them into his private chambers. Large sculpted doors swung open to reveal a room painted with the familiar crimson and gold of the hallways. The room's design carried a symmetry to it. Sharp lines and thoughtfully considered shapes all morphed into elaborate patterns. Thin windows stretched from the outer wall, letting the ocean air waft into the room. The song of sea birds and steady waves gently filled the room. Beneath them pillows and soft furs covered every furnishing.

Titus had never seen such lavish dwellings outside the palace walls. He looked to Geralt whose face carried a hint of distain at what he saw. Who were these men?

"I hope this is to your liking, my King?" Ulric asked as he seated himself next to a small fountain at the center of the room. Without command, a servant moved out from the shadows to offer Ulric a gla of wine.

"I am afraid I will show my ignorance, but I didn't know su place as this existed," Titus said, still marveling at the room.

"Strange? A king does not know the finest places of his own kingdom?" Ulric asked in an innocent tone, swishing his drink.

Geralt stepped forward with a protective air. "Best watch how you address the High King, outsider."

Titus rested a hand on his friend's shoulder. "What Geralt means to say is I am relatively new to the role of High King and Samadura Port has existed with some autonomy."

Ulric raised a curious eyebrow as he set his empty glass down on the servant's tray. "It is a fine place. I haven't stayed in such a dwelling in many years."

"But you have stayed in a place like this before?" Geralt asked.

Ulric jumped to his feet with a clap of his hands. "Yes, in fact where I come from... sorry, correction, where I came from, I was royalty before... well before the time of reckoning." Ulric's voice hinted at disdain.

"So, you are no longer a king?" Titus asked.

"I am afraid not. You see, much of the world beyond your shores has been under the rule of one master. Baruuk, Monstro, Zhu, Inkosi, Maluuk all these are titles of the one who has dominated people far ɑnd wide."

"The Felled One," Titus muttered.

"Ahh, so you have a name for him as well? This Felled One, as you ɛcame enraged with many of his subjects a little over a year ago. In ʒe countless rulers and peoples felt the fury of his wrath. He drove ɔm their homes and now some have washed up on your shores."

ʋou're refugees? Strangest ones I've ever seen," said Geralt.

ɡht you said it's been many years since you ruled?" Titus asked.

tive, High King," Ulric said with a gleam in his eye. "My ɪstroyed long before my birth, but my royal blood still ᵐething. I have been a member of court in a kingdom ᵻther. I grew up there all my life until Maluuk decided rn it down."

here?" Titus asked.

"As I fled with many others, we bounced around various islands and kingdoms hoping to avoid Maluuk's wrath. I began to see there were many like us, lost, unsure, and needing leadership. I was born to rule but was never given a throne. I decided to use that gift in leading a new band of people to safety. As all good rulers should."

Titus could sense the unease in Geralt at the casual certainty of this man named Ulric. A strange energy covered him and his followers.

"Ulric, what would you ask of Islandia?"

Ulric casually grabbed another glass of wine and took a sip as he paced the room. "I wish for my people to live in peace far from the rule of Maluuk. I followed a trail of rumors that spoke of a far off land that had repelled his rule."

Ulric's eyes looked probingly up from his glass. Titus felt the weight of both question and judgment in the statement. What was this man's intentions? Titus narrowed his eyes as he searched for what to say next.

"You wish for peace, but do you bring peace with you?" he asked.

"A wise question, my King. I will admit I am not always a modest man. I yearn for the finer things in life."

"That's obvious," Geralt grunted as his eyes scanned the room.

Ulric let out a faint chuckle. "Guilty, but I do not wish to take what is not mine. I come representing a new clan of men and women from all sorts of lands in the hopes of finding a place to call our own, with your permission. Whether you have some quiet farmland you wish tilled, or some enemies we could conveniently overthrow for you. We wish only to honor your rule, however it best serves you."

"I do not wish to use your people as a weapon in my hand. As for a peaceful solution, I believe we could come to an arrangement," Titus said.

Ulric jumped to his feet. "That is all we could ask for, my King."

Geralt shifted uncomfortably beside him. Titus pushed aside his unease.

"I cannot make this decision alone. I will call a council together of all the rulers in Islandia to decide what can be done."

"There may be no need for this. I have sent my men to all your lands and have heard back from at least one who has said the same as you."

"You've sent men out to all our lands?" Titus asked, trying to withhold his concern.

"I did not mean to overreach, High King. I had not understood the rule of this land until now."

"I am not concerned with hierarchy, only where your request has gone. There are others who may not seek your good fortune for free."

"We will heed only your voice from now on. I can only be thankful you responded to us first."

This complicated things, Titus thought. *If Jorn gets word from these men...*

He lifted his eyes back to Ulric. "How many have you brought with you?"

Ulric's face squinted in thought. "Counting all, close to 5,000."

"That's an army," Titus heard Geralt say under his breath.

"Are all of you so well armed and well off?" Titus asked.

Ulric let a faint smile touch his lips. "No, not all of us. We are a company filled with people from many walks of life. However, we have those who could afford to provide for such a voyage. We fled, but not without taking our coin with us."

"You bought yourself your own personal army, and we are just supposed to believe you came sailing to our lands in peace?" Geralt growled.

"Believe what you like, but we will prove our loyalty to you, High King. We do not wish to create conflict where it's not needed."

"I don't believe a word..."

Titus raised a hand cutting Geralt off. "Ulric, for now, have your people camp this side of Lake Leviathan. This land is much less occupied than it once was," the words tasted bitter as he said them.

"You and a small company of your leaders may join us on our return to Kingshelm. We can discuss your future here with a full council." His eyes shot to Geralt hoping he understood it was not his decision to make.

"You are too generous, my King," Ulric said bowing.

"We will depart tomorrow morning. I suggest you make preparations 1 the meantime."

With that, Titus bowed and moved to leave. He could feel that alt was anxious to speak with him in the absence of Ulric's listening They followed the hallway and went down a cascading stairwell reaching the door of the lodge. Once outside the doors, they back into the bustling streets. Titus felt Geralt grip his arm.

s, we cannot let them into Kingshelm!"

ipped his arm free. "Do you think this is your decision to to leave these people without a home, abandoned to that uk, wherever he may be lurking out in the wider world?"

y appeared to me, he warned me of something... a danger . It's them Titus. Can you not see that?"

v, Geralt, is that you claim to have seen Eloy. All you een from a wild binge the night before."

ls left his mouth, he regretted them. "Geralt, I..."

ing. Let us go. I only hope I am wrong."

'eralt stomped into the crowd of people, guilt his at was he to do? Leave these men and women end of days? Deep down, though, he couldn't hat Geralt may be right.

council." His eyes shot to Geralt hoping he understood it was not his decision to make.

"You are too generous, my King," Ulric said bowing.

"We will depart tomorrow morning. I suggest you make preparations in the meantime."

With that, Titus bowed and moved to leave. He could feel that Geralt was anxious to speak with him in the absence of Ulric's listening ears. They followed the hallway and went down a cascading stairwell before reaching the door of the lodge. Once outside the doors, they stepped back into the bustling streets. Titus felt Geralt grip his arm.

"Titus, we cannot let them into Kingshelm!"

Titus ripped his arm free. "Do you think this is your decision to make? Am I to leave these people without a home, abandoned to that monster Maluuk, wherever he may be lurking out in the wider world?"

"When Eloy appeared to me, he warned me of something... a danger that was coming. It's them Titus. Can you not see that?"

"What I know, Geralt, is that you claim to have seen Eloy. All you heard could have been from a wild binge the night before."

Even as the words left his mouth, he regretted them. "Geralt, I..."

"It's fine, High King. Let us go. I only hope I am wrong."

Titus watched as Geralt stomped into the crowd of people, guilt his instant companion. What was he to do? Leave these men and women to die or wander until the end of days? Deep down, though, he couldn't shake the nagging feeling that Geralt may be right.

7

IMARI

THE OBSIDIAN STONE was cold beneath his palm. He gazed at the small inscription above the sarcophagus. *Imbaku brother of Khosi Imari, defender of Khala, Honorary Title: The Rescuer.* The deep ache in his heart had never vanished. The last year was a whirlwind that kept his pain at bay, but now, in the stillness, the sorrow that once haunted him from a distance felt ever present.

"I miss you, brother," were the words that fell from his lips. He patted the cold stone once more before he took in one last view of the royal tombs. He found a slight comfort that Imbaku and his parents could rest together, their tombs only a few feet apart. So much loss, and for what? Sahra's ancient claim to the city? Was it worth his family's life for a piece of territory? He choked back the resentment growing within.

His journey to Sahra was today and bitterness had no place if he wished for successful negotiations. Stealing one last glance he turned to leave, ascending the stairs into the palace courtyard above. Impatu, now the captain of the Bomani, Imran, the commander of the city guard, and his sister awaited him. Each exchanged with him a look of solace.

"My time to depart has come," Imari said to them.

"I still don't like you going alone," Khaleena muttered.

"Are you sure I cannot accompany you, Khosi?" Impatu asked.

"I am sure my small escort of guards will work just fine. Besides, I need my finest leaders here in my absence."

None of them looked convinced, but they held their tongue regardless.

"Brother, may I have a word?"

He nodded and allowed Khaleena to pull him aside.

"Why do you insist on leaving again when such strange things are transpiring in the Kingdom? Sahra has abandoned us at every turn. Why invite them to a seat at the table now?"

He fought to keep his anger in check. "I don't just go to aid Sahra, sister. If these men have visited them, Sahra may have a powerful new ally. Besides, it wasn't just Sahra that left Islandia to her fate. In fact, Nabila even sent her own blood to fight beside us on that dreaded night."

Her face grimaced at the insinuated insult. She moved to speak again but chose to turn away, her cheeks flushed with embarrassment. Imari regretted his words even as he spoke them. He needed her as an ally, yet he found himself pushing Khaleena away more and more. For what purpose? Yes, she held resentment toward Sahra, but it was because of her love for Khala that she had endured so much.

"Khaleena I..."

"Save it, Imari. I know what you think of me."

"Khaleena, can we mend this thing between us?" he asked, lowering his voice so the others might not hear.

"Another time, perhaps, but now you have a journey to take," she said coldly. With that she turned to Lombaku who awaited her beneath the shade of a nearby pillar. Together they ascended the palace stairs.

"I don't like seeing you both like this," Impatu said as he drew near.

Imari let out a sigh. "Neither do I, friend. Perhaps it will change, just as it did with Imbaku."

He tried to give a reassuring smile but felt no room for joy. Impatu placed a hand on his shoulder. With a sorrowful heart he watched his sister disappear from sight.

"In the meantime, have the Bomani keep an eye on her and her Masisi."

"You want us to spy on her?" Impatu asked in a hushed tone.

"It's likely nothing, but too many uncertainties abound. I cannot take any chances."

"I don't like this, Khosi."

"Neither do I, Impatu."

He gave the captain of the Bomani one last embrace before moving toward Imran. He could see the unease on Impatu's face as they departed for the long journey ahead. He hated asking this of him, but the list of those he trusted grew thin and he feared unrest in Khala was only a small distance away.

He had grown accustomed to the long journey through the desert. There were endless dunes made of windswept sand. Despite its treachery one couldn't help but fall in love with the breathtaking star-filled nights. Life in the desert was a deadly and wondrous combination. He did appreciate his life not being threatened at every turn this time around. Their journey by land had taken them to the familiar port city of Wahah. A place of memories he'd rather forget.

Trade had once again resumed in the large plaza and, to his surprise, the place looked busier than ever. The cries of market vendors and travelers alike echoed in the crowded streets. Only this time, he did not hide amongst them. All manner of ships clogged the docks as they arrived to deliver and receive their goods from the capitol city of Sahra. It was on one of these vessels that he and his escort hitched a ride. They followed the red rock coast of the Sahra mountain chain westward. The jagged peaks loomed as a sinister welcome onto the high seas.

He couldn't believe his eyes as they passed one of the small islands off the coast of the mainland. Along the shores was the bustling activity of inhabitants living on its once destitute land. A small outcropping of towns now littered its rocky coast in an attempt at a new dwelling space.

"Why would anyone choose to live there," he wondered to himself.

He soon found his answer. As their vessel pulled into Sahra's port he could see that an enormous amount of growth had taken place since his departure little more than a year ago. The streets were lined with people, almost to the point of overcrowding. Even the envoy that traveled with him could not contain their shock.

"How has Sahra accomplished so much?" he heard one of his men whisper.

As they offloaded from the boat, a group of Sahra ambassadors greeted them.

"Welcome, esteemed Khosi," said one of the men as he bowed. His decorative robe jingled with small bells cleverly stitched into his ensemble.

"Greetings, royal ambassador," Imari replied.

He couldn't help but continue to gaze at the renovations made to the dock.

"I see you appreciate the vast improvements to the empire," said the ambassador.

Empire? Imari mused to himself. *Is this what you are creating, Nabila?*

"It seems Sahra has kept themselves busy," he said to the ambassador.

"Indeed. Our Queen Nabila has used her vast resources to improve the lives of many in Sahra."

"I am glad to see the royal treasuries at work for the people," he said withholding his true feelings.

"It did not all come from the coffers. The Queen devoted many resources in finding the deep source of water within the Nawafir Mountains. On discovery of a great aquifer, we have been able to do the work of ten years in one."

"It must have taken a lot of manpower?" Imari asked.

"Oh yes, indeed," confirmed the ambassador, "but with no wars or conflict we have been able to devote nearly all our manpower to such tasks."

Of course you have. While the rest of Islandia fought to keep the darkness at bay, you took advantage of our sacrifice, is what he wanted to say. Instead he found more considerate words.

"I am happy to see Sahra has been spared the wrath so many have faced."

The ambassador blushed at his words, knowing full well the meaning behind them. "Well, I suppose you will wish to see the queen now."

"I suppose so," Imari said with constrained resentment.

Don't allow the bitterness to overcome you, he repeated to himself.

They were escorted down the road that led to the city. Endless streams of merchant caravans poured out in both directions. A route that would normally take less than half a day would now consume all the day's light. He was grateful they traveled via a royal escort, enabling them to charge ahead.

Again he found himself in awe as they approached the ancient city of Sahra. Behind its dark red walls, towers with golden domes and exquisite carvings littered the sky. From them water trickled down to fountains within the city. Water which had been the scarcest resource in Sahra was now a free commodity to the people.

On top of this Imari could see the streets were full of life. No more did the cloud of dread and doom permeate the air. The watchful eyes of the Sycar had vanished and in their place freedom emerged. Trade was at an all time high, and Imari couldn't find a beggar on the streets. All of this would have been overwhelmingly great news had it not come at the expense of all others in Islandia.

While Sahra thrived, Islandia fought to stay afloat in the aftermath of the Felled Ones. After pressing through the buzz of the city, the ambassador led them into the palace walls. A buzz of activity crisscrossed between them and the palace complex. Servants carried all manner of food and goods. Delicacies that Sahra had only possessed in tales of old now were displayed as trivial items.

"Where has Sahra been able to grow such vegetation? I understand you have more water but these things cannot grow in the ground here," Imari asked.

"Very perceptive," said the ambassador. "These fruits and vegetables I believe arrived from New Valkara not a day ago. Only the finest will do," he said with a self-aggrandizing smirk.

She's trading with New Valkara? he fumed to himself. *Is there no end to this evil?*

He put on a mocking smile to the ambassador, turning the man's smirk into an uncomfortable frown. They found themselves being led into the throne room. Various streams of color painted the room from the mosaic glass above. The admiration Imari once held for the dazzling stained glass images above, now made his stomach turn. He realized the former glory they displayed had only been possible because of the labor his people endured long ago. Much like the sacrifices of Islandia had paved the way for the Sahra now before him. Maybe it was just the Sahra way.

He took in a breath as they passed by the auburn stone fixtures of the room. Everything in the room, including the throne itself, had been carved from the mountain. Even the Nawafir peaks could not escape Sahra's wrath. He knew his judgement was skewed, but his anger was getting the best of him now.

Following the ambassador, they ascended the twisting set of stairs behind the throne until they reached the lone hallway that led to the chamber of the Sulta. Imari's stomach churned. He wasn't sure he wanted to see who the woman he loved had become. More malevolent than her father, yet just as sinister. The oak doors swung open to reveal the Sulta seated at the large stone table carved from the mountain. Beside her was an attendant fixed on Nabila's words. As the door opened, a smile crossed Nabila's slender face. Her sharp features and deep brown eyes gave no sign of malice at his arrival. Her dark olive skin and silky midnight hair were the same features as the woman he loved. The curves of her body fit tight in a red sari. She stood as they entered and gave Imari and those with him a formal greeting.

"Welcome dear guests from Khala. I hope your journey faired you well," she said keeping her smile. Her dark brown eyes fixed on Imari.

"Thank you, my Sulta, it did. We can't help but see how much the splendor of Sahra has grown under your rule," he said not hinting at his true feelings. Still, he could see under the veneer of hospitality a slight twinge at his words.

"It is marvelous isn't it? Our workers have tirelessly slaved to grasp the full potential of the Nawafir water source. It has given us the freedom to stand on our own."

"Stand on your own? Interesting. I remember a whole host of men who stood on the ramparts of Kingshelm but none of them had the look of Sahra. Strange?" Before he could stop, the words had come tumbling out of his mouth.

The veneer of a smile was gone now, only a cold and calloused frown remained on Nabila's face. "I was told you came here for different reasons? Was I misled?"

Imari could feel the uncomfortable shifting of the ambassador's feet beside him. The guards at the corner of the room perked up at her words.

"I apologize, my Sulta. My desire is not to start a quarrel. It... it is good to see your face again."

Nabila's flushed cheeks faded and she coolly lowered herself back into her chair. "Have a seat then, Khosi. The rest of you, leave us."

Imari nodded to the others who had accompanied him, and in a blink they sat alone in the cold stone room with the city of Sahra visible from the window at Nabila's back.

"It all started here, in this room," Nabila mused aloud.

It had, and now Imari wasn't sure what to make of the events of that day. Sure, Fahim was a cruel tyrant but that was obvious. Now, well, he didn't know what Nabila was anymore.

"It seems like so long ago," he said.

"That it does. What brings you all the way to Sahra, Imari?"

Straight to business then, he thought.

"Strange guests have visited us recently. Outsiders from faraway lands. I wanted to know if they had come knocking on your door as well?"

"They have, not three days ago," she said with an air of disinterest.

It took all his strength to speak calmly, "And what did they say?"

"Oh Imari you must have a better bargaining face than this," she said with a smirk. "What makes you so eager to know what words they brought?"

"Because it could threaten Islandia," he said bluntly. "These men came seeking land to call their own from us. I assume they asked you the same? Did they proclaim to be refugees?"

"Yes, they requested the same from us." Her eyes stared down at the parchment filled table.

"And?"

Her eyes rose to meet his once more. She enjoyed toying with him. "Relax, my dear Imari, I told them there is no room in Sahra for outsiders. I am the same woman now as I was on that fateful day in this room. My aim is to make Sahra great, not expose her to outsiders."

"An empire," Imari said.

Nabila's face soured. "Now where did you hear that from?"

"Your loose lipped ambassador. I would advise you to find a new one. He revealed many things to me that I doubt you wish exposed."

"Do tell." Her eyes were laser focused now.

"He informed me you are trading with New Valkara. How could you do such a thing, Nabila? You know what kind of man Jorn is!"

"You think me a monster? My people need outside resources to survive. We cannot grow our own crops. Khala has cut her trade with us in half. Kingshelm has stood in disarray and Leviatanas is no more. What am I supposed to do? Yes, Jorn is vile and wicked, but he has what Sahra needs and he is willing to give it. In case you didn't notice, our population has grown dramatically. Without more resources my people would be starving in the streets."

A sound of rebuke dripped from her words. It was true Khala had cut much of its trade with Sahra. Not by any sanctions imposed by Imari but by the will of the people themselves. They had grown more than suspicious of Sahra caravans arriving at their doorstep.

The truth of her words stung but he couldn't shake the anger welling up within him. "Much of Islandia is in disarray because some of her kingdoms did not answer when their High King called."

"I thought you were going to avoid that topic?"

"How can I, Nabila, when it has driven such a wedge between us?"

Pity filled the Sulta's eyes as she examined him. She bit her plump red lips in consideration of her next words. "Not just us but your sister as well?"

He couldn't deny it. "Yes, Khaleena and I... well, let's just say, it is more than strained."

"I have a similar situation with my own blood," Nabila said staring behind him.

"Amira?"

"Yes, whatever she saw in Kingshelm changed her. She isn't as pleased with my policies as she once was."

"And this has not convinced you of my own plea?" Imari asked.

"You have said it yourself. Sahra has regained much of its splendor of old. Water has never flowed so freely in our streets. We lack nothing, need nothing, and can defend ourselves. None of this would be possible had we gone and died in your battle. Besides, you won did you not?"

"You cannot be serious, Nabila!" He rose to his feet. "Sahra needs nothing? That's why you gain supplies from the most vile kingdom in Islandia. None of this would be possible? You are correct in that. If not for all the kingdoms who died in that battle, Sahra would be nothing but a waste by the army of the Felled Ones. Not that you would know the devastation they wrought."

A voice came from the chamber door behind him. "My Queen, are you alright?"

"I am fine," Nabila replied to the guard.

"It seems this meeting of ours is over," she said in monotone.

Imari shrank as he realized his loss of composure. "I assume this means you will not join the council in Kingshelm on the matter of these outsiders?"

A tiny flicker of anger and pain burned in her eyes as she looked at him. "Fear not, dear Khosi. You need not fret about us allying with these 'outsiders.' None outside our walls are welcome."

None, even him. The message was clear behind veiled words.

"Nabila…"

She called her guard back into the room and with a wave of the hand dismissed him. "Farewell, my love."

He left the chamber in silence. None of his escort dared to disturb him. The conversation rolled in his mind a thousand times. Each image flickered by. He wished he could change it all. This was his love. Could things not be mended between them? Was Sahra truly to blame, or did he project his own fear and pain onto their failure? Questions without an answer. He was pulled form his thoughts when a voice caught his attention as he passed through the throne room.

"Greetings, Imari." From behind a pillar's shadow appeared the face of Amira.

"Amira, I assumed you would not be here any longer."

"So she told you, huh? I may disagree with my sister, but I cannot abandon Sahra."

All he could muster was a sad smile at the royal sister.

"I want to go with you," said Amira.

"Go with me?"

"To the council in Kingshelm. My sister may not care about these outsiders but something does not sit well with me."

"Kingshelm really did change you," Imari said with a faint smile.

"I do not wish to talk about that night," Amira said, turning her head as if to ward off the memory, "but I do seek to know more about these outsiders. So what do you say, Khosi?"

"I could use a few more allies in Sahra. You may join us."

A look of joyous surprise crossed her face. "That makes things easier."

"What do you mean?" he asked.

"Well, now I don't have to sneak into your caravan," she said with a smirk.

It dawned on him that the Sycar may be gone, but standing before him was its last remnant. "Very well, we set off tomorrow. You can stay with us this evening."

As he turned he couldn't help but grin at finding at least one ally among so much uncertainty.

8

LYDIA

T HE TOWER OF Kingshelm's royal keep stood as a beacon welcoming her home. Somewhere inside, her beloved awaited. Too much time had passed since she last entered the halls of her new home. Kingshelm had become a place of comfort and safety to her in a world full of chaos. Not since the killing of her father, King Doran, had she had a place to call home. Finally, she felt like she had a sanctuary, a home, once again. She could feel the tension in her brother as they approached the city. For him it would be a reminder of the atrocities done to him and Brayan.

She understood his unease at such a return. On her other side was Lancelin. He carried a calm demeanor as he waited to give his report to Titus. A half-victory had been won and soon they could deliver the final blow to Jorn. Something bothered her, though. The news of strangers coming in from the outside world brought a certain dread. Nothing she had encountered beyond Islandia had brought peace to their land. Why should this group be any different?

The small company of army commanders and Aiden's captains passed under the whitewashed walls of Kingshelm. The ground shuddered as the large wooden gate closed behind, sealing them within its vaunted defenses. The armies had agreed to stay some distance out from the city until a truce had been hashed out and battle plans made ready.

Kingshelm reflected little of its former glory. Hovels sprung up at random, creating their own varying districts. Each carried a unique flavor to them. The majority of refugees who had returned now lived in humble shacks cluttered with debris. As one ventured nearer the palace, the living spaces improved. Renewed structures rose from the ashes of the old. Their clay brick roofs and plastered walls pocketed half empty streets. It would take decades for the city to return to its former glory, and perhaps it never would. But maybe that was the point. Walls and roofs could be rebuilt, the lives within them couldn't. She was stirred from her musings as the palace wall came into view. With giddy haste she entered into its welcoming embrace.

A vast garden had sprung to life in the space before the fortress. White fountains surrounded by vivid color adorned the grounds. A smell of spring filled the air, a pleasing aroma to all who entered the complex. A small unit of guards stood at their post to greet them. Waiting at their head was her love. He wore a dark gray tunic that bore the symbol of the High King. A roaring lion, proud and fierce. His hair was freshly trimmed at the sides with its wavy brown locks grown long on the top. His light green eyes stirred at the sight of her. An expression of unconfined joy illuminated his handsome face.

Without a word, he stepped forward to embrace her. Wrapping her in his arms he squeezed her tightly, ignoring all others. For only a blink she felt they could melt away beyond all that surrounded them. The woes, fears, and future nothing but a distant dream. Just as quickly, she was torn from that fantasy as Titus pulled away. He planted a gentle kiss on her forward.

"I missed you," he said.

"Same," she said, her Valkaran accent breaking through.

Titus turned his eyes to the other guests and back to her. "There is much I need to speak with you about, but first." He moved to embrace Lancelin. The two shared the joy of old friends united after a chasm of time had passed. Titus moved to Aiden and extended a formal handshake. At first Aiden only stared at the extended palm, but Lydia caught his eyes. With a look of agitated persuasion he took it.

Titus' eyes lit with recognition at the other guest who had joined them. "Henry!" he cried as he fell on the man.

The long lost defender of Kingshelm had returned, albeit a bit worse for wear at that. He had endured much during his captivity. His face was now decorated with a scraggly beard and had been worn by exposure to the elements. The tunic that he wore hung like rags on his thin frame. She could see the look of anger flare up in Titus' eyes as he examined the man, but just as quickly he tucked his true emotions away.

"It's good to have you back, Henry," Titus said placing a hand of comfort on his shoulder.

"It's... it's good to be back, my King," Henry fought back the tears forming in his eyes. Lydia reflected on the sacrifice he had made so they could return to Kingshelm. A price, she wondered, if he had come to regret.

Titus clapped his hands and a host of servants came pouring from the shadows. "Get this man cleaned and in the finest clothes available. Then bring him to me. I am sure there is much we both can share with each other."

Lydia took note of her king's effort not to stare at her brother. He was doing his best to hold the tensions of this meeting at bay.

Titus continued, "Tonight we will have a royal dinner, then a council together. There are pressing matters for all of us to discuss."

With that, he waved his hand and the host of servants descended on them, ushering each to their respective quarters. Aiden gave their proddings an unsure glance. Titus raised his hand to stop them.

"I will escort this guest and his companions myself."

Aiden leered but Lydia could see he would rather face Titus than a handful of pushy servants. Henry and the other captains who had joined them were ushered off, leaving the small company of Titus, Aiden, Lancelin, and herself behind. A light breeze wafted through the courtyard cooling the sweat that had accumulated on her neck. Despite nature's best effort, she could still feel the tension thick in the air.

"Place looks even better than when we departed, friend," Lancelin said trying to break the awkward silence.

"Thanks, Lancelin. Many have worked hard to restore our home," Titus said looking at Aiden.

Her brother let out a grunt, "If you ask me, it looked better burnt."

"Aiden!" she snapped, but Titus raised a hand to calm her.

"You can speak freely here as long as all of us are allowed to do so," Titus said.

Aiden gave a shrug of the shoulders, allowing another moment of awkward silence.

"You said you would come in cooperation," Lancelin snarled, lifting an accusing finger.

"Cooperation is different than consideration. This place still reeks of disillusioned narcissism. Obscene palace beauty, decadent dinners, and fine clothes. What have you really changed?"

"Step inside these palace walls and see for yourself. Kingshelm is no longer a place of extreme wealth. What resources we have are being used to keep people alive in the streets. As for our hosting you, it is only out of the highest honor for our guests that we put on such an evening. Perhaps you should remove the lens of pessimism from your eyes."

Aiden turned his gaze to her as if seeking an answer to the validity of Titus' claims.

"It is true, brother. All our resources have been devoted to bringing the city back to life as well as raising up a force to stand against Jorn. You will not find the lavish tastes displayed from your last visit."

Aiden nodded for the king to lead the way, content with his sister's reply. Titus turned abruptly and started for the palace entrance. Aiden soon followed. Lancelin turned to her with rolled eyes. "Great start."

"Give it time. He may come around yet," she said.

As they entered the complex of halls and interweaving courtyards, she took note of her brother's eyes. They darted to and fro as if inspecting every inch of the place. White, pristine walls carried no beautiful tapestries, no fine decor, only white washed stone. All the gold furnishings had been stripped away for more practical metals. At last, they reached the large waiting room outside the throne room with its twin ascending stairs. It lay bare as if emptied of occupancy.

"So, your words are proven true. Is the grand tour over?" asked Aiden as he stood with arms crossed in the center of the room.

"Yes, it is. Your room is just down the hall. Lancelin, care to escort our guest to his chambers?" Titus asked withholding his growing frustration. He could not hide such things from her, though. She could see it in his eyes. Lancelin sighed at the command and motioned for Aiden to follow. The Valkaran royalty scowled but obeyed, leaving them in the stillness of the vast room.

Titus turned to her, a tender smile painted on his face. It was the face that she had grown to love. The one that could melt away everything else. She collapsed into his arms, weariness overtaking her. She was unsure if it was the long journey, the stress, or the never-ending conflicts that had taken their toll. Perhaps it was all of them. With one swift motion he lifted her off her feet.

"Please, Titus, I am not a damsel in distress."

"I know." His lips met hers in a passionate kiss. In a blur she found herself carried away to their chambers. Long journeys and time apart brought deeper meaning to moments of intimacy shared between lovers. She lay wrapped in the bed's linen sheets, her head nestled against his chest. She listened to the soft beating of his heart, the rhythmic breath of his lungs.

"There is so much weighing on me," Titus said, breaking the silence. "Too much…"

She twisted around to stare up into his eyes. "You do not have to carry it all alone, you know?"

He gave her a loving glance. "I know. But I fear as king much has fallen to me that I do not have the answer for. Am I to be a rigid ruler that allows no others but our own to dwell among us, or do I open the gates and allow anyone and everyone to come to our lands? They say that Maluuk rules all others in the world. Should we not be a beacon of hope for them? But then Geralt claims Eloy warned of treachery…"

"Geralt?" She sat up at the mention of the name. "When have you seen Geralt? What do you mean Eloy warned him? Before his passing?" she asked.

Titus let out a faint chuckle. "There is much I still need to tell you."

A flood washed over her at all that had transpired. The man who had become like a father to her now restored from the pit he had chosen to wallow in. The mysterious sighting of Eloy and these strange men. She understood why Titus could be so torn. She laid back down with a crash. Her red curls splayed across the pillow.

"I am sorry to weigh you down with all this," Titus said looking at her.

"I am your High Queen, your burdens are my own. The words of Eloy, why does Geralt lend them to these men? Could a threat not come from Jorn or even Sahra at this point?"

"It is why I have struggled as well. Even with your brother Aiden," he confessed.

Aiden…she did not want to think of him as the one with treachery in his heart, but she could not deny his hostility. He could see the tension in her face and moved his hand to caress her cheek.

"Don't fret love, we will discover the truth soon enough."

She clasped his hand in her own. What could they do in the midst of such a tide? How could one find truth in the midst of so many voices? She felt sleep begin to pull at her and, before she knew, it a dreamless slumber overcame her.

Later, she found herself roaming the halls of the famous palace imagining what it would have looked like before its burning. Her stroll was leading to her actual purpose, to see the man who had been her guardian all her life. The last time she had seen him, he was in a drunken disarray. He had cursed them all for continuing life as normal after all they had endured. His tirade had hit closer to home than she'd liked to admit. But that was what mankind does. They retreat to what they know when times are uncertain.

She stood before the door of his room, rattling the door with a faint knock. She heard the man's infamous grunt call out from behind the door. Hinges creaked as the wooden door opened. His eyes grew wide as he looked at the familiar face. With Geralt's version of an invite he silently motioned for her to step inside. His face had weathered since she last saw him. Lines stretched from long nights and hard days. He wore an informal tunic of bronze and gold. But it was his eyes that caught her. Within them was a joy she had never seen before. A smile stretched across his face.

"Well, look who it is. Here I thought the High Queen had forgotten about her old guard dog."

"Even an old dog has to be cared for," she said smirking at him.

"How are you, lass?"

She let out a tired sigh. "There have been better days," she admitted, "but I hear you have had quite the change. I see you've even cut your hair." She raised a hand to the short strands.

"I was due for some grooming. Titus talked with you about me, huh?"

"He tells me you've had strange visions."

"I'm guessing he told you they were drunken ones. Am I correct?" he asked in guarded tone.

"Not necessarily. He doesn't know what to make of them."

"What do you think?"

She paused, resting her hand on her chin. "I think there is no way you are the man standing before me without something drastic happening to you."

He let out a hoarse laugh. "You're not wrong, but that doesn't mean you believe me, that what I encountered was real."

She peered into his eyes. "Geralt, more than ever, I have to believe that there is something more that can come from all that has happened to us. What you said about us all just returning back to normal... you we were right."

"I was drunk," he said.

"You were and how you said it is another matter, but your words were true enough. We can't just go back to the way things were. Otherwise, all that was paid for was just to keep the status quo. I can't believe Eloy sacrificed what he did for that."

"You're talking about the New Dawn aren't you, lass?" he said it as if he hadn't thought it a possibility until now.

"Maybe that is why you had your vision. Maybe something is coming. Something that is going to shake us all from our sleep."

A slight grin crossed his face. "Glad to see you're still thinking, lass."

She could feel a blush fill her cheeks. "We will see if my words prove true. There is another matter about to take place. My brother Aiden has come and Titus is expected to restore Valkara to him in a royal hearing. Will you be present?"

"Think I'm going to stay away from any royal hearings for now. The last time I went it didn't fair well for anyone. I prefer not to be a distraction," he said with a wink.

"Very well, just this once I'll let you off the hook. But I am in need of a royal body guard. The ones I have now couldn't best me, let alone the best Valkara has to offer."

"The best, huh? High praise coming from you."

"You're not that old yet. Give it a few years, then I might give you a run at it," she said.

"If it pleases my Queen," he said with a mock bow.

"Enough. I expect you to report for duty after this meeting. You'll be a busy man. I know it will take some time for you to get used to that again."

"Are you going to continue to insult me or go to your meeting?" he asked.

"I suppose I've abused you enough." With that she turned to leave but was stopped by his parting words.

"It's good to see you again, lass." His voice carried sincerity that reached far beyond the casual phrase.

Without looking back she replied, "You too, Geralt."

With that she stepped into the hallway, unable to repress the smile creeping across her face. With Geralt's return she couldn't help but feel a little bit of the world was being made right. She found herself humming a favorite childhood tune as she mused at the empty walls once more. Perhaps the New Dawn was coming after all, and each restoration in the present was a small hint of that coming glory.

The throne room was lit by a kaleidoscope of color shining down from the stained glass atop the vaunted hall. A small council had been drawn with various members of importance gathered. Atop the throne sat Titus, his face set in stone as he listened to the events that had transpired near the Forest's Edge. The royal crown weighed heavy on his head this morning.

The High King leaned back breathing deeply as Lancelin finished the report. Lydia scanned the audience taking in their reaction from her small throne just below him. A mix of unease, dread, and ambition filled the crowd. Each of them carried emotions that threatened to pull the hearing into the depths of turmoil.

"Thank you, Lancelin. I have heard enough of your report. Aiden, I would like to hear your proposal. Lydia has informed me what Kingshelm has offered upon her request, but, before we come to any agreement, I need to know your intentions."

Aiden stepped before the throne, an air of confidence bordering on arrogance exuded from him.

How he could carry himself in such a way with his forces so diminished was beyond her. Lydia watched him carefully.

Aiden rubbed his wounded shoulder as he waited for Titus to speak once more.

"Son and heir of King Doran, the terms we present are these. As long as Valkara remains true to the High King's throne and stands with the kingdoms of Islandia as a united kingdom, the throne and all territories of Valkara shall be restored to you in this I swear by royal oath."

Lydia glanced at the royal recorder writing down Titus' words with fervor.

"As a seal to this promise we will send the full force of our army to accompany you, along with your own men, to dethrone the usurper Jorn and restore Valkara to you. On this I swear my royal oath. Does the true heir of Valkara accept these terms?"

"I would be foolish not to!" blurted Aiden with a childish grin.

The royal court erupted in disgust at his response. Suddenly Lydia felt the sinking feeling that she had made a mistake in trusting her brother, but then he caught her by surprise.

"I have no love for your throne, as it is well known, High King. Kingshelm has brought many dark nights to Valkara, but... my movement was about more than my personal feelings. Men have fought with me, died for me, in the hopes of having a kingdom to call their own again. If you are offering that, I cannot refuse and I will do all I can to maintain it."

The room grew silent as they awaited the High King's response. Titus stared down at Aiden, intently weighing the man in his mind. Finally, his eyes flickered as he ended his examination.

"I only have one more request. Henry, please step forth."

The loyal agent of Kingshelm broke from the crowd in the room. The man's face was now clean shaven, giving him the appearance of years shed. His sandy blonde hair was combed back, and his blue eyes had returned to life. He carried a new sense of dignity as he strode to the center of the room.

"Yes, my lord?" he asked as he approached the throne.

"I am sorry to place you in such a position, but you were this man's captive for more than a year. What do you say of him? Will he keep his oath?"

All eyes fell on the returned man. Lydia looked to her brother instead. A glimpse of unease covered Aiden's face. Not many in the room had seen Henry before his restoration, but any who had would know his answer.

Henry licked his lips as he chose his words carefully. "I have always served the High King faithfully, my lord. I have given my life in service to this kingdom. I have spent many sleepless nights in the open country. I have known fear, loneliness, and hunger for the throne."

His eyes turned to Aiden. "My time spent in the captivity of this man is shaped by all those things. I have served the throne faithfully to this day. If restoration of Valkara to this man will serve the realm best, I see no way I can stand between it."

The tension in the room fell at his words. Lydia realized that the man before her was of the noblest kind. History is often remembered by kings and tyrants, but it is those who faithfully serve that often make history what it is. Here was one of those men. She knew what his words must have cost in the vein of personal revenge, and yet he was willing to forgo his own justice.

She could see this revelation dawn on Titus as well. He rose in his seat and with a booming voice declared, "If there are no objections, then by the integrity of this court it shall be so. Valkara will be restored to Aiden and we will march on Jorn as soon as it is possible. With this decree the council is dismissed."

The room erupted into the sound of undistinguishable voices. All of them she was sure were weighing the results of the day. She moved up the few steps to the throne. A weary look painted Titus' face. She could feel the presence of Lancelin arrive just behind her.

"When do you want us to make preparations to march?" he asked.

"There is one more matter that must be resolved before I send the army as far as Valkara. They should arrive tomorrow," Titus said.

"The outsiders?" Lydia asked.

He nodded. "Maybe then we will finally have the answers we seek."

"Or more questions," Lancelin chuckled.

Titus let out a weary sigh. "Indeed…"

9

TITUS

THE DINING HALL clamored with sounds of silverware on plates. Titus surveyed the room filled with hundreds of delegates, all belonging to the outsiders. Ulric sat at their head, all smiles as he devoured his steaming meal. Lydia and Lancelin, along with a dozen delegates from Kingshelm, sat eyeing the new arrivals with suspicion. Titus could see Geralt standing off in the corner of the room, hidden amongst the crowd. Geralt's keen eyes scanned each face in search of any form of treachery. He had taken his new role of head royal guard in stride.

Above the noise Ulric stood and beckoned for Titus to sit among them. The audacity of the act to invite the High King to his own table could be seen on the Kingshelm's delegates' faces. Titus let it roll off of him, giving the difference of culture as Ulric's excuse. He seated himself next to Lydia who quickly clutched his hand. Slicking back his jet black hair, Ulric gave him a childish grin as he sat.

"I must say the hospitality of Kingshelm is not lacking! Although I was a bit worried by the look of the place on our way in."

"Watch your tongue. Do I need to remind you that you are a guest here?" said Lancelin.

"It's all right, Lancelin," Titus said gesturing to his friend. "These men are not accustomed to our ways."

"Yes, sorry, where are my manners, High King? It has been awhile since I sat amongst royalty. The sea, it changes a man."

A shared smile crossed the faces of the men around him.

"When I suggested you bring your leading men, I assumed a dozen," Titus said as he surveyed the dining hall. More than a hundred men sat clustered in the vast hall. Each of them with a unique style of clothing and language.

"Ahh yes, again I must apologize, High King. Like I mentioned, we all hail from many different lands. I may be royalty, but I am no king. When I brought the proposal that we should confer with you about a possible stay here, the list of representation grew until…well, you can see for yourself," Ulric said motioning to the room.

"You mentioned you are all from various lands. Where exactly do you hail from? And how do you know our speech?" asked Lancelin.

"May I answer this one, my lord?" the man sitting next to Ulric asked.

"Go on, Cedric, we are all free men here," Ulric said patting the scrappy looking man on the back.

"Our company encompasses men from all over the world. As far as the open plains of Rasku to the dry and barren earth of Gurun. Men from frozen lands and scorching deserts. Some hail from the dense jungles of Kaskar and Mascar. My own boots carry the snow of Northland with me. And, do you see those men over there?" Cedric leaned over the table pointing to a group with narrow eyes and smaller stature.

"They hail from a land called Osaka. Renowned for its legendary blades. Tempered steel with a slight curve to their swords, and their armor! Large shield plates placed on the shoulders with beautiful artistry crafted into the plating. The helmets hold the face of demons to frighten their enemies."

"Enough, Cedric. They don't need to know about your admiration of the Osaka," Ulric said rolling his eyes.

Cedric's gray eyes shot him a sideways glance. "As you can see, I am an admirer. As for us, we understand one another well enough. Your language is as old as they come. Sure, there is some differences in dialect but the Edonian mother tongue is the gift given to all from the old empire."

Titus shot the others a look of surprise at Cedric's words about Edonia. Before he could ask more, Lancelin pressed another question.

"What about you?" Lancelin asked lifting his chin toward Ulric.

The man shifted in his seat as if the question stirred unwanted memories.

"I came from the continent of Edonia, land of the once proud empire. It has long passed those glory days. A millennia has come and gone since that time. My father ruled a small kingdom on the northern end of the continent. A realm left in the aftermath of Edonia's fall. He ruled for some time until a rival took it from him. My family fled as refugees to Northland after. Thus, I was born in a foreign land but grew up in a royal court."

Cedric chimed in again, "I was one of many royal attendants in the Northland. When my masters fell to Maluuk, I fled with prince Ulric to safety. We eventually ended up at a place called Mascar."

Ulric broke in, "Apparently many other kingdoms had suffered what we had and fled to one of the few remaining havens left untouched. Soon, even Mascar came under assault."

"How did you end up here?" Lancelin prodded.

"Did your High King not tell you?" Ulric asked a bit exasperated. "We followed a trail of rumors that led us back here. In fact, these rumors had grown long before our journey. Strange tales of men invading the ghost city of Edonia had reached our ears some years ago."

"So you know of the city of Edonia?" Titus asked.

"Know it? It was practically home at one point. Although ruined long before my time. No one dared enter that foul place."

"Except for Eloy," commented Lancelin.

"Yes, this High King you speak of. I wish I could have met him. A brave man to enter that city."

Titus noticed a strange mood fell over Ulric as he spoke. Edonia meant something to the man but he couldn't discern what.

"We wish he was still here as well," Titus said.

"I hear he played some part in the matter of stopping Maluuk. Is that correct?" Ulric asked.

"He did. It was his sacrifice that saved us from Maluuk's forces. Yet, we are still dealing with the remains ourselves. Soon, we will take care of Maluuk's last servant, Jorn, once and…"

Titus raised a hand to cut Lancelin off. He could feel Lydia squeeze his hand, a sign of her unease.

"What exactly is it you are looking for Ulric?" Lydia asked.

Ulric's eyes darted between them. "We only wish to serve in any way we can. Perhaps we can assist with this Jorn you speak of?"

Titus shook his head. "It is a matter best discussed at a later time. When we all have decided on the decision of your staying here."

He could feel Lydia sit back in her seat, yet tension still gripped her. Even Lancelin who had spoken absent-mindedly now could sense the gravity of his mistake. At all costs these men must not know of Jorn. Titus feared if the council's decision was to expel these refugees they might turn to their enemy.

Thankfully, Ulric decided to let the matter go. "When do you think the rest of your council will arrive?" he asked.

"I have been given word that Imari will head this way in two days time. As for the rest of the kingdoms, you have them here," Titus said motioning to Lydia and Lancelin.

"Ahhh, thus the probing by you," Ulric said with a smile toward Lancelin.

"I had to know what kind of men I may be letting into our kingdom," Lancelin said.

"Understandable. I hope you found your answer," Ulric said.

"We should let our guests rest. They have traveled a long way just to arrive at Islandia," Titus proclaimed.

"One last question," Lydia said, her eyes fixed on Ulric.

"You have mentioned that all other men around the world serve Maluuk. Was this not the same for you? Or did you somehow earn his clemency all these years?"

It wasn't just a probing question, but a dagger that pierced through the fog. Even as she asked it, Titus felt himself recoil and yet it, too, had weighed on his mind. He had been too afraid or maybe unwilling to know the truth. In that moment he felt both admiration for Lydia and shame on himself for not reaching for this truth sooner. The question did not faze Ulric.

"Yes, we served as a reluctant slave obeys a master. What could we do when all the world is under his authority?"

"You could have stood against him, regardless," Lydia said, not pulling her punches.

"Perhaps you are right," Ulric sighed. "We had never known any to stand against him and win. That is why we are here now. To make up for our past failings. Besides all that, look at us. Do we look like the servants of Maluuk?"

Ulric leaned over the table drawing near to them. "Look into my eyes. Do they carry a silver sheen? Does my skin look clammy and pale? No, we are not servants of that dreaded fiend."

He slumped back into his chair. Cedric stared at his companion, a look of surprised admiration on his face.

"Very well Ulric. We apologize if we are a bit cautious, but you understand why we would take care not to allow the servants of Maluuk into our midst," Titus said as he stood, placing a hand on Lydia's shoulder.

Ulric's eyes stayed unflinchingly on Lydia. "I fully understand, High King. One cannot be too careful."

An uncomfortable silence hung in the air. Titus cleared his throat, "Lydia, I think it's best we let our guests relax for a time. There can be more questions later."

She rose to her feet without a word and turned to the door. Geralt stepped out from the shadows to follow close behind. Titus turned back to Lancelin, Ulric, and Cedric. "Gentlemen."

He turned with a bow and quickly followed after Lydia who had already taken several strides to leave. He caught her by the arm in the hall just outside the dining room. She whirled around on him.

"I know what you are going to say, Titus, but I don't trust them and neither should you!"

"That's not what I was going to say. What I wanted to say was thank you."

She blinked at him in amazement. Geralt behind her carried a self-satisfied grin at the response.

"What... what for?" she stammered.

"For doing what I was not brave enough to do."

She gave him a sheepish nod as her cheeks reddened. "Sorry about snapping at you."

He embraced her, kissing her forehead. "All is forgiven. Although I think I will retire to our room for a moment. There is much to reflect on and a lot to consider."

"Very well, I believe Geralt and I were going to have a sparring match," she said looking up at his grizzled face.

"News to me," Geralt grunted.

"I need to blow off some steam."

"Very well, when you are done you can meet me in our room," Titus said with a wiry smile.

"Keep it together over there, High King," she teased.

"Enough. Talk to each other like that when I'm not around," Geralt said, rolling his eyes.

"Very well. See you soon, my love." She leaned over, leaving him with a kiss on his cheek. He watched as she and Geralt strolled down the corridor. He couldn't help but smile as he reflected on how truly grateful he was for her.

He made his way through the winding paths of the palace until he reached their room. With care he closed the door behind him after he entered. The lunch had tired him and he wished for silence to think before the council would begin in the next few days. He approached a small wash basin in the corner of the room. That's when a sudden voice boomed behind him.

"Titus."

He turned, half expecting an attendant, when he was struck to the ground in terror and awe. Before him stood Eloy. His eyes of bronze gleamed and his thick black beard curled in the form of a welcoming smile. Titus was unsure if he should bow or cower at the sight.

"Don't be afraid, friend. It is truly me," Eloy said.

"How..." was all he could get to leave his lips.

"I don't have much time with you, but know that the power of Maluuk is overthrown. His gift has been wrestled from him and given to a new master. That answer must suffice for you now."

Titus could only nod his head. Eloy reached out a comforting hand to help raise him to his feet. As he stood, he felt small compared to his High King. Something had changed in the man. He still bore the olive skin of his Sahra roots. His features shared commonality with the man he had come to know, but something more radiated from him. It took him back to the revealing of Dawn Bringer on the eve of the great battle against the Felled Ones. It was in this man's presence a new reality began to break in. The world around him grew richer and deeper in his company.

"I need to speak with you about these visitors," Eloy said breaking Titus from his awe.

"Yes, my King. I gladly receive your council."

"Ahh, so now you seek it, do you? Did Geralt's warning not stir you?" Eloy said with a playful smile.

A tinge of guilt filled him as he remembered Geralt's words of warning in Samadura. "I... I failed to believe him, my King. I did not know if his words were true or who they spoke of."

"It cannot be changed now. A path has been set and you must reveal these men for what they truly are."

"You do not plan to stay?" Titus asked, disappointed.

"The time hasn't come yet. Soon, all this pain, all this world has endured, will be made right. But that time hasn't arrived. Maluuk has one last plan he must enact before he is condemned for good."

"I don't understand, Eloy."

The High King smiled and placed a hand on his shoulder. "I know, my friend, but soon it will be made clear."

A tint of sorrow filled his face as he stared into Titus' eyes.

"What is it, my King?" Titus asked.

"There is still much pain to be endured before the end. I wish it was not this way, but the call to victory is difficult and full of sacrifice."

"I can answer it, Eloy, just help me, help me know what to do to serve the kingdom as you have."

Eloy gripped his shoulder. "You will, my dear friend, and in the end we will be victorious. I leave you with this. Draw a council as soon as you can. You must expose these visitors for who they truly are. You may not have heeded my warning before, but do not delay in doing so now or I fear much more will be lost."

"I will, my lord, I will call them out and demand they tell me what they truly intend."

"Very good, my friend." Before Titus could say another word, Eloy vanished before his eyes. He stood stunned for a moment. His mind reeling from the encounter. Immediately the doubts came creeping in. Had it been real? Was this induced by all the stress he was under, his mind groping for a way to cope? No, it had been real and he knew what he must do.

He burst from his room, found a nearby attendant, and ordered him to send word to all who still remained in the palace. They were to gather in the throne room for an emergency council. Without so much as a question, the man scrambled to grab others in spreading the word. Titus wished he could deliver the word to Lydia himself, but this was urgent. He returned to his room briefly to strap Dawn Bringer around his waist. One didn't walk into the lion's den unprepared.

A host of delegates gathered before him as he sat upon the High King's throne. The ebony lions splayed their menacing prowess to the empty room. A door opening caused him to glance over his shoulder. Both Lydia and Geralt had arrived, each harbored a look of concern. His eyes met Lydia's, and he mustered a weak smile. She conjured up her own fragile reply and then quizzed him with a look. Raising a hand, he motioned for her to stay back and observe. His gaze slowly drifted to those in front of him. Ulric and his captain, Cedric, stood before several dozen of these "outsiders." Taking the proper precautions Titus had made sure all of them were disarmed as they entered the room. A host of guards had been given the order to discreetly place themselves at the exits in case anything were to happen. Now, it was time for a confession.

"Thank you for gathering on such short notice," he said, his voice echoing through the hollow room.

"Is this about the battle with this Jorn fellow? Did something happen?" Ulric asked.

Interesting that he brings that up again, Titus thought to himself.

"No, it is a different matter. I want to know the truth. Who are you really?" he asked.

"I've told you, High King, we are..."

"I know what you've told me," Titus interrupted. "Now, I want the truth."

Out of the corner of his eye, he caught Lancelin shuffling in below him. His loyal friend stood prepared. He wore his jade armor that practically fit like a second skin. He could see the jade eyes fixed on Ulric and his companions, ready to spring to action on the High King's word. All the air felt as if it had been sucked out of the room. An eerie silence hovered over them all. Each could feel the weight of this moment.

"The truth?" Ulric asked. "Is it the truth you seek or a reason to mistrust us?"

"Perhaps they are one and the same," Titus countered.

"Would the High King indulge me in something?"

"Go on."

"Come look at my arm," Ulric said beginning to roll up his sleeve.

"Titus, I wouldn't..." Lancelin began to caution before Titus stopped him with a hand.

Silently he descended the throne's stairs passing through the squad of black marble lions on each side. Their stone strength no longer able to shield him. He stepped forward until he was only a few feet away from Ulric's outstretched arm. Staring he saw what looked to be a branded crescent moon on dark leathery skin.

"Do you know what that is?" Ulric asked.

"Yes… Eloy spoke of a king from Edonia who had made it his symbol. He was a follower of Maluuk." Titus raised his eyes, looking at Ulric with suspicion.

Ulric kept his arm extended as he spoke. "Maluuk has claimed all of us as his slaves. He tortures and kills those who don't bow to him. My father, all our fathers, have been under his rule whether by choice or coercion."

"So, you belong to him?" Titus said, snarling. His hand fell to Dawn Bringer, while keeping his eyes locked onto Ulric's.

"As if we have a choice," Ulric snorted in disdain.

"There is always a choice."

"So easy for you to say in your faraway lands, tucked away from the rest of the world."

"We faced the same monster as you. The only difference between us is we did not bow."

Ulric slowly shook his head as his extended arm retreated. With delicate care he began to cover his brand once more.

"You see, Titus, that's the thing. If you stand long enough eventually you have to bend the knee."

Ulric's eyes hardened as he scanned the room. "All of us were like you once. Bold, proud, eager to do what we believed was right. In the end it didn't matter. Power was what mattered and Maluuk had it. We came to the conclusion that all men have to serve a master. We gave up looking for a benevolent one."

Titus' jaw tightened. "You weren't fleeing Maluuk, you were sent by him. So, why have you really come to our home?"

"Perceptive, High King. We have traveled land and sea, desert and jungle, frigid terrain and all manner of threats to deliver a message."

"What message is that?" Titus growled.

A faint smile crept onto Ulric's face. "Maluuk sends you a gift."

Titus blinked. Something felt wrong. A sudden agonizing pain radiated from his abdomen. slowly he lowered his hand. As he drew it up he found it was stained with blood. As he forced himself to look he saw the cold steel of a hidden dagger lay buried into his side. He fell to a knee as his strength waned. He could hear muffled cries behind him as those he loved began to realize what had been done.

He looked up at the gloating Ulric. Buried behind the man's eyes lay a hint of sympathy. Titus mustered up his remaining strength to grab Dawn Bringer, but felt the pull of the blade from his side. It shot another flare of crippling pain through his body. In a flash he found himself collapsing to the floor.

Ulric's voice floated over him as if in a distant dream, "I'm sorry it came to this, but you understand we all have a master we must answer to."

He watched as the man bent down beside him. In the distance he could just make out a shadow rushing from the throne. He fought to regain some semblance of the situation but it was all beginning to blur. Try as he might he couldn't make out what the voices surrounding him said. They melded into a tired droning in his ears. His vision clouded with a veil of red violence. More and more it became a fogged curtain of crimson until all turned to black.

10

LANCELIN

H
E FIXED HIS gaze on the outsider named Ulric. Titus had summoned them all to the throne room for an urgent meeting. Dread haunted him over such an abrupt call. He felt his mind racing to determine what it could mean. Again and again he returned to these strangers. Who were they, really? Flexing his hands he stared once more at this stranger, this "king" of the outsiders.

Titus sat calmly on his throne as he awaited the arrival of Lydia and Geralt. As if on cue, a door behind him swung open revealing the pair. Lancelin found his attention pulled back to Titus as the High King rose from his throne.

"Thank you for gathering on such short notice," proclaimed Titus.

"Is this about the battle with this Jorn fellow? Did something happen?" asked Ulric.

"This man has a little too much concern for Jorn," Lancelin grumbled to himself.

"No, it is a different matter. I want to know the truth. Who are you really?"

"I've told the High King we are…"

"I know what you've told me," Titus interrupted. "Now I want the truth."

What was Titus doing? Lancelin felt himself stepping toward this Ulric, his hand ready to grip Dawn's Deliverer. Just as he put his foot forward he noticed Titus wave him off. Begrudgingly he stepped back and scanned the room. Every face shared a look of dread. He took special note of Lydia whose eyes never left Titus.

"Would the High King indulge me in something?"

"Titus I wouldn't…" he cautioned.

Titus ignored his warning and stepped forward to meet Ulric. He watched as Ulric extended his arm out to the High King. Instinctively Lancelin felt his hand lower to his sword hilt once more. He strained to hear as Ulric now proclaimed their true intent.

Then something horrid happened. Before he could move, speak, or stop it he watched as Titus stumbled to his knees. Something was wrong! Instantly he withdrew the blade at his hip. An echoed response joined him from the other guards. Slowly, Titus crashed in a cascade of red to the floor as a small dagger was ripped from his abdomen. Fury overtook him and he rushed forward to cut this traitorous Ulric down. Ulric in response bent down unsheathing Dawn Bringer.

"Your filth does not deserve to touch such a blade!" Lancelin cried out.

Ulric's eyes now met his with a look of arrogance. Ulric ignored him and turned briefly to face his own men.

"Men of the world, the time is now!"

In response, a loud clamoring of weapons being drawn filled the hall. An order rang out to fire. He watched as each outsider revealed beneath their cloaks a hidden weapon, an array of projectile weapons he had never seen before. They flung out their bolts at a startling pace.

The hail of fire ripped through the squadron of guards descending on them. With a rapid motion the strange weapons were drawn back to fire once more.

"Crossbows! Fire!" came the order again. More guards fell to the deadly weapons. Lancelin turned to see Lydia and Geralt close behind him. With a motion of the hand he waved them off.

"Turn back! You cannot survive this!" he shouted.

"I will not abandon him!" Lydia said, rage burning in her eyes. Geralt, on the other hand, could see their fate if they chose to stay. He pulled at the young queen's arm.

"Come, lass."

He knew words would not persuade her as she fought his grip.

"What of you!" she cried pointing a finger at Lancelin.

He held Dawn's Deliverer up for her to see. "I have the only weapon that can stop these fiends."

In the background he could hear the clacking of the crossbows winding up for their next volley.

"Go!" he barked, taking one last look at his friends. He fought the overwhelming sorrow threatening to take him. This was likely his final hour, but what greater honor than to spend it in defense of his friends. He heard the rush of retreating feet behind him, knowing they had heeded his advice. His eyes now fixed on Ulric who wielded Dawn Bringer.

"Wipe that smile off your face, prince. Your friends will be ours soon enough," said Ulric.

"That depends," said Lancelin.

"On what?" snarled Ulric.

"How good you are with a sword." He did not hesitate. He sent a flurry of controlled blows at Ulric. Each one sent sparks flying as the two blades touched. He summoned all his training to fight the battle in his mind. He must not lose control of his emotions, even now. They exchanged strikes as Ulric continued to back his way toward his men. Several ran to accompany him, but he dismissed them with a hand.

"He's mine. Take care of the others."

Lancelin pressed his advantage, feigning low and slashing high. Ulric dodged the true strike and countered with his own. The impact nearly robbed Lancelin of his footing, but years of training and muscle memory helped him regain composure. The flash of the specially imbued steel filled the room. The violence around them morphed into a huddled mass of quiet spectators. Both guard and outsider alike gawked at the skill of the swordsmen and the quality of the blades.

Finally, Lancelin saw his opening. Ulric overreached on a counter and left his flank exposed. With a flick of his wrist Lancelin sent the fine edge of his sword across the exposed shoulder, tearing through hidden plating and flesh.

With a grimace of pain Ulric withdrew, letting his arm hang limp. He gave a curt nod to those who stood encircling them.

As Lancelin stopped to take in the scene, he knew it was over. Every guard lay dead and he stood surrounded by a host of archers. With a sigh he lifted his blade to take one last shot at the man who had caused so much pain. Without warning, a hail of arrows came raining down. Many of Ulric's forces carried the look of surprise as they fell to the ground in a pile of corpses. Lancelin looked to see Zuma and Izel with two dozen archers that had crept into the room. Each of them drew their strings back to unleash another volley of death.

Cedric barked the order to return fire. Darts covered the throne room as both sides unleashed their fury. More than a dozen of those who had come to rescue him had been cut down by the deadly accuracy of the crossbows. He could see the smile on Ulric's face as the tide turned once more. Those left with Zuma and Izel cried out, brandishing swords as they charged at the reloading archers. The result was a crashing of foes in a tide of chaotic battle. Lancelin joined in, cutting down any who stood in his way. Ulric moved parallel, striking down Kingshelm's guardians with ease.

The thought passed through Lancelin's mind that he promised himself never to use his Dawn Blade against men. With each blow he delivered he couldn't help but feel a tinge of regret that it had come to this. Even if these men acted as monsters, he wished no man to face this fate. Yet, this was the way of Maluuk, creating enemies where there need not be, stirring hatred for those who could live in peace.

Corpses fell until only a few remained standing. That's when he saw Ulric move to strike Izel. In a gesture of sacrificial bravery, Zuma jumped in front of her, taking the blow onto himself. It rent him free of his sword arm and right leg as he crumpled to the ground. Izel screeched at the sight, dropping her weapon in a desperate sob. In his distraction, Lancelin didn't see the foe creeping up behind him. With the hilt of his blade the intruder sent a blow crashing down onto the back of Lancelin's head.

The impact blackened his vision. When he came to a gloating Ulric stood over him. Behind him the few remaining outsiders held Izel captive as she shed quiet tears. Zuma lay gasping for his last breath on the floor, his eyes turned to stare at Izel and the men holding her.

"Bind them," Ulric ordered. His glance turned to Zuma. "Put him out of his misery." Ulric gestured with a jerk of the head.

Izel screamed in defiance as two of Ulric's men approached with weapons in hand to the maimed form. She broke an arm free but was greeted with a strike across the face that left her in a sobbing heap.

"You don't need to," muttered Lancelin before he was cut off.

"I don't need to what?" snapped Ulric. "Do you see how many of my friends lay dead on the floor? All because of your stupid king?"

He brushed the two men to the side. "Move. I'll do this myself."

He hovered over the broken Zuma, bloodied and battered on the cold marble floor. The stains of his injury painted the beautiful patterned mosaic into a deathly crimson beneath him. Zuma stared up defiantly at his would-be executioner.

"Take heart, Izel." Zuma's eyes flickered over to Lancelin before returning to Ulric. "You too, Lancelin. I die with courage against these monsters. Soon, I will join in the same honor as our High King." His tone was saturated with disgust for the imposters that stood over him.

Our High King, Lancelin thought, but the reflection was interrupted by the thrust of the executioner's blade. A wail echoed out from Izel before she was knocked unconscious in order to silence her.

Ulric turned his attention to Zuma's corpse and barked an order, "Throw his remains in the river along with the High King. No need to enshrine them for others to rally against us."

"It is too late for that," hissed Lancelin.

"Ahh, you think your friends will escape? Our army is not as far from your city as you might think," Ulric said with a self-assured smile.

"You've been planning this treachery all along, then? Well, go on, finish me. I don't care to see your short lived reign."

"I am afraid you misunderstand our plans, young kingdom-less prince. I need you alive for now. You are going to show me the whereabouts of a certain cave. I was hoping to discover it with a little less bloodshed at the beginning, but, I suppose, it would have happened sooner or later."

"If you think I am helping you you're…"

"Oh, you will be helping me. Otherwise she will share the same fate as your friend on the floor there," Ulric said motioning to Izel. "And please, don't feign your ignorance of who she is. I saw how you were distracted by these two. Just know I killed the young man as a warning that I mean what I say. She will die if you do not help us, and, trust me, I will find that cave."

Lancelin slumped his head. "It's in Leviatanas. That's where we will need to head."

"Ahh, a bit of a homecoming for you, then? Very well, I will call on you when the time comes to march. Cedric."

At the order, Cedric sent a fist crashing into his face. The last vision of Ulric's smile faded into dark oblivion.

Time was an illusion now. Darkness filled every crevice in the space that housed him. Even when they had pulled him out of the dark cell, he was only greeted with more gloom. In the transition of time, he had been taken out of the city walls. Treachery upon treachery had led these men at every turn. Whether by bribery or threat, they found a way to escape and now…Kingshelm was hemmed in by the force of thousands. Each legion a masquerade of culture. The Osaka bore the fine distinctions Cedric had admired, their armor ebony with a blood red crescent moon. In fact, the entire army bore this symbol. This was the mark of their true master, the one that united the world, and in that unity destroyed it.

He was paraded through the besieging army's camp as a prize that would lead them to their ultimate goal, one that still eluded him. A few stray words here and there hinted of a "revival" but he was unsure what it could mean. Grief threatened to overtake him as the images of Titus and Zuma flashed before his eyes. Behind them he could still see the limp body of Eloy marred beyond recognition. Is this what it meant to be his servant? Would they all be chosen for a life of destitution while evil reigned?

He had no answers and only an ever-growing stream of questions. These questions remained inside the hollow shell he called himself. He did not doubt his decision to join Eloy over Maluuk. He knew he would rather die for the true High King than become a puppet to the parody. He only feared that the parody might have the final say after all. In these darkest moments he remembered Geralt's vision. How he hoped beyond hope the man's visions were more than a drunken stupor. Could such a thing be true? When he looked within himself, all he saw was doubt. Yet he would not let the spark within him die.

The following day Ulric gave the command for them to march. They traveled by land around the southern edge of Lake Leviathan. In a steady march they advanced up the thin strip of land known as The Spine. How he wished for words to say to Izel who accompanied them, but what could he say? What could be done to reverse the horror that had taken place. Besides, the pain in his own heart felt too great a burden to overcome.

It didn't take long before they reached the first of many ruins. He couldn't turn his gaze from the rubble that was once Levia Landing. The town in its former glory had carried valuable trade from Kingshelm. It, along with all other cities in Leviatanas' territory, had been leveled when Maluuk first marched his army little more than a year ago. Each day of their journey northward was a reminder of the devastation that was wrought onto his home. The barren roads and burnt villages all cried for a sense of justice that never found an answer.

Is this truly all there is? Will the strong and corrupt always win? he wondered. Like the towns, he felt his cry was shouted out into an empty void.

As they neared the end of the long journey north they passed the port of Jezero. Its ruins were a monument in the far off distance. The place was a reminder of his failings long ago, how he too could have been like this Ulric who served Maluuk. As they passed by, spring rains began to open from the heavens. The small band of captains led by Ulric pushed forward, soaked to the bone. Lancelin and Izel served as their disheveled guides. Their captors neither spoke nor acknowledged them unless it was about the road ahead. Mere morsels of food were given as a measure to keep them going. The endless marching finally ended when at last they reached the crossroads, the barely treaded path into the mountains to their left and the smooth road to Leviatanas straight ahead. All stopped when Lancelin motioned the way down the remote road.

"We will go to Leviatanas first," Ulric said.

"Then you will be making your journey longer," Lancelin complained.

"But you see, young prince, it's exactly the road we must take. There is something there that we need, and you are going to show us."

Dread filled him. The truth was he had not returned to his home since the day of its doom. To return was too painful, too horrendous a thought that he had buried it deep within his soul. Even the possibility of seeing his father and mother... what the Felled Ones might have done to them, to all of them who called Leviatanas home.

"I can wait here. Just tell me what you need, and I can give you direction," he said lifelessly.

A look of recognition crossed Ulric's face. He realized the young prince feared his home. "No, I think it best you come with us. Don't you want to see your father and mother again?"

Lancelin swallowed hard, knowing he would have no choice but to obey. Onward they went, past the meadows filled with trickling streams. Past the rotting corpses of both village and villager. They followed that dreaded road until the very walls of Leviatanas loomed before them. The city coiled upward to the top of the mountain chain it rested on. The once proud city of shining domes and fluttering banners now stood an abandoned haunt. Mold and vegetation were its only living inhabitants. Tattered fabric swayed gently under an ashen sky. He grit his teeth at the swelling agony in his chest. Every step closer, every breath, was leading him to face a reality he fought to avoid.

They passed through the gates that hung on their hinges in disarray. Wild jackals scattered into abandoned homes as the scent of intruders flooded their nostrils. Tattered remains of victims long dead lay in the streets. An eerie silence, broken only by a haunting breeze, greeted them. They ascended the spiral roads until they stood before the palace gates. Flashes of that fateful day flashed before his eyes. The same doubtful journey that he carried now. Yet that day something had broken into his reality. Eloy had restored his father, and all the gloom that had enslaved the city was overthrown. Now, standing before the gate once more he couldn't help but feel the painful irony of the moment.

Would Eloy somehow break into this dreaded scene and change everything? Doubt nagged at him that the High King was dead. He had done all he could to stand against this evil. Had it really not been enough to overthrow Maluuk?

The gates creaked open as two of Ulric's men cleared the way. Inside the palace walls a last stand had been made by the few faithful guards that had remained until the end. They lay slaughtered in a careless heap before the throne room doors. Each and every one of them paying the ultimate price to protect his father. He watched with numbness as Cedric and a few others thoughtlessly kicked their corpses aside to clear a path into the great hall.

The moment had come. He would have to face his father and mother. As they entered into the desolate space nothing but a faint pale light illuminated the room from the four slitted windows behind the throne. The once spotless white walls were now grimy and stained. Invading vines had slithered up the walls and punctured one of the windows. The rain and elements had taken their course. It was not the state of the room that brought him sorrow, however. Hung from the balcony used for his father's council swayed two bodies. Both nothing more than skeletons covered in rotted clothes. On each of their heads was a crown.

He fell to his knees as the emotions overtook him. His vision was blurred by hot tears and he could sense the vomit rising in his throat. Why had he not come before? Why had he not given them the proper burial they deserved? He had failed them, he had failed them all by bringing all this to Islandia in the first place. He heard a voice call to him. It sounded like the voice of Eloy. He looked up startled, but found it was only Ulric.

"Balzara. Where is his body?" Ulric asked.

Lancelin shook his head as if in a daze, "I... I don't remember."

Ulric let out an annoyed sigh. "You best try to remember otherwise we string this girl up there with them," Ulric said pointing at his parents.

Balzara... a name he hadn't considered since that day.

A vision flashed before his eyes. Standing before the throne in the restored state of the great hall was Eloy. His face cemented with a smile.

"I told you, didn't I?" Eloy said.

"You told me... you told me what?" Lancelin mumbled.

"You would see it. You will see the day."

"What day are you talking about!" Lancelin cried in hysteria.

But the vision was gone and he was back in the damp, moldy throne room.

"What's he going on about?" Cedric asked.

Ulric squinted at him, and Lancelin could see fear within his eyes. "We should leave this place. It has a foul stench."

The others in the group shuffled nervously at his words.

"Now I'll ask one more time. Where is Balzara's body?"

What was this vision about? Lancelin's mind raced to absorb what he had seen. *Had it been real or just a memory?* He could feel something had shifted within him. His waning strength now felt a measure of restoration, as if new life had filled his tired soul. He stood to his feet with the knowledge that he must press on. He took one last look at his parents, at their lifeless bones suspended above. With one final bow of reverence he turned to Ulric.

"Follow me."

He led them back outside into a small unmarked graveyard reserved for those most dreaded in society. Rain came cascading down once more as they began to dig up the grave.

"Bloody rain," complained one of the captains.

"Shut up and dig. It's a blessing you won't have to dig up the hard winter ground," Ulric said with a smirk.

The man grumbled and took the shovel in hand for his turn to dig. Ulric turned to Lancelin as the next round of digging began.

"Must have been hard seeing your parents back there."

He was taken back by the offhanded comment. "Don't even speak of them, you snake!"

Ulric sighed. "I faintly remember my father's court as a child. Grand visitors, marvelous feasts, and, more importantly, his comforting presence. It was all so... wonderful. That is until a rival kingdom received a mysterious donation of weapons. Not long after, my father rejected a man named Maluuk... and his gift."

"Why are you telling me this?" Lancelin asked.

Ulric's gaze wandered back from the men digging to fix on him. "Because no matter how loyal, how kind, or how benevolent of a ruler you are, Maluuk always wins..."

Before Lancelin could respond, a crescendo of chatter rose from the diggers. Amongst the mud and muck they pulled up the bones of the dead charlatan. Something caught Lancelin's eye that he had never noticed before. A small, silver amulet was wrapped around the wrist of Balzara. Cedric stepped forward and took the decayed arm in his hand. With one swift motion he snapped the bones in half, retrieving the amulet.

Ulric took the amulet, giving it a careful inspection. Lancelin could see a shining gem in the shape of a crimson crescent moon set in dark stone.

"What is that?" he asked.

Ulric gave him a cautious eye before tucking it into his tunic. "What we came here for. Now are you going to lead us to this cave, or do we have to get violent?"

Lancelin looked over at the disheveled and tired face of Izel. She stood exhausted and downcast in the grip of a soldier.

"You know more about these matters than you are letting on. How would you know of Balzara unless Maluuk had told you? Why do you even need us to find this cave? Your master dwelled there himself at one time."

Ulric's face turned to a snarl. "We may know what to look for, but I have never traveled these lands. Nor do I know all my master's ways, so either lead the way or watch us slaughter your friend."

There was menace behind the words, Lancelin knew, but something else lay there too. Resentment. Ulric was just another puppet. For the first time he could see that the man standing before him was not unlike him when he first encountered the powers Balzara held. Only Ulric had come to believe there was no other choice but to serve this monster Maluuk.

"You don't have to do this, Ulric. There is another way."

"What did you say to me, dog?" Ulric asked as he sent Lancelin to his knees with a kick. A crack of thunder rang out with a burst of rage.

"I was once like you. Stuck serving a master I despised for purposes I deemed noble. What does he hold over you? A loved one? A promise of power? A better world in the end? Open your eyes, Maluuk leaves nothing but destruction in his wake. Do you think he won't lead you down the same path when this is over?"

"Shut up!" This time it was a knee that sent Lancelin reeling in the mud. A faint squeak of protest could be heard from Izel. Rising to his feet, he raised a hand of comfort toward her.

"You know it's true, Ulric. I see it in your eyes. You don't want to do this, but you think there is no way out. I thought the same until… him."

"You don't know me. What difference does it make? We both serve a master and one of them is dead. I'd rather keep my life than wallow in the mud."

"It makes all the difference," Lancelin muttered. "Do you not see what becomes of Maluuk's servants? Corrupt monsters that feed on their fellow man. What kind of gift is that!"

Ulric stood silent in the dying light. His chiseled face beaded with drops of rain. Behind his eyes a hint of doubt stirred, but it disappeared as quickly as it had come.

"Bind and gag him until we reach the mountain pass. I don't want to see him again until he's needed, understood?"

Cedric nodded and moved toward Lancelin with a quickened pace. He felt pity for this man. He had a glimpse of being free, but chose the shackles instead.

Another dull day loomed overhead. The sky was the pale gray of sorrow without tears. The scraping of rock underfoot echoed off the jagged cliffs surrounding them. Lancelin stood at the head of their party leading Ulric and his men to the cavern they desired. The cave was a place he had no desire to see again, but neither was Leviatanas. In all of this he had accepted there would be many such things he dreaded to face but must do so despite his resistance.

The haunted valley opened in front of him. The gnarled, leafless trees still stood sentinel in the silent pass. The mouth of the cave welcomed them with its familiar jagged teeth. His captors stopped in quiet reverence and awe of the place. Ulric stepped forward as the first to break the stupor that clung to them.

"Light some torches," he ordered to a few of the men standing near their supplies.

They scrambled through a pack and assembled the needed light. Without waiting for the others, he motioned for Cedric to withdraw Dawn's Deliverer and follow him. The two men set forth. The faint light radiating off the Dawn Blades disappeared in the dark of the cave.

What could these men want with this cave? Lancelin pondered. His eyes caught sight of Izel being dismounted from her horse. They had kept him away from her for most of their journey. Ulric was smart and took no unneeded risks. The young woman from the Dreadwood looked road weary. Her eyes a dull red behind dark bags. Despite the lack of privacy, she mourned the loss of Zuma day and night. He felt a pang of guilt. If it wasn't for him she would never be here enduring all this.

He shot her a comforting smile as their eyes locked. She mustered up all the strength she had, yet it only produced a twitching of the lip. He was jerked from the moment by a tug on his restraints.

"Come on. Time to get moving," ordered the guard assigned to him.

With a less than patient pull at his bindings, Lancelin began his march with the rest of the party into the depths of the cave. The damp and cool air saturated all it touched, flooding his mind with memories of where his journey had started. This was where he had brought this wretched plague on Islandia. Perhaps it was here that he could end it.

Time dragged on with the rhythmic march through the darkness before them. Only when they reached the large cavern did they regroup with Ulric and Cedric. The two men had been up to something strange. In fact, the whole cavern had a new appearance. All around symbols blazed with blue light. Lancelin followed the trail they laid until his eyes settled on a symbol shaped like a rune encrusted door. Across its face lay mysterious symbols he could not decipher. He could see all along the symbol's edges a sharp line of cracks spread like a spider's web. They stretched out beyond, encompassing the chamber.

What happened here? he wondered.

Ulric and Cedric stood irritated at its sight. With a chalky substance they diligently worked at marking a symbol of their own onto the stone floor. Their drawing was circular in shape, its edges were filled with mystical and dark icons and symbols. Lancelin could only grasp half of what was written, but, from what he could decipher, it was some sort of conjuring. The mystery began to click in his mind.

"What are you planning?" he snapped.

Ulric impatiently looked up at him from his work. "You marched them all the way in here? For what, so you could march them back out?" The irritation was barely restrained in his voice.

The guard in charge of Lancelin stumbled over his words, "I wasn't sure... I didn't... well I wasn't sure if you'd want us to leave them alone."

Ulric sighed. "You didn't want to miss the ceremony? That it? Well, don't worry it almost didn't happen at all."

"What do you mean?" asked another of Ulric's men who bore the Osaka armor. "We traveled all this way for nothing?"

Cedric rose to his feet and dusted off his hands. "He said 'almost.' You see that symbol on the wall?" he asked.

The man nodded.

"Well, that was the source of Maluuk's gift. Someone has destroyed it."

A sudden fear fell over them all.

"You mean to tell us someone has the power to do that?" asked the Osaka armored man. Lancelin couldn't help but notice the trembling in his voice.

"Maluuk's rage toward these Islandians makes much more sense now, doesn't it?" Ulric hissed. "He would have no power here if we were not lucky enough to capture this."

Ulric raised up Dawn Bringer. The light from the blade illuminated the entire cavern. For the first time Lancelin could see the full scale of the cave. Cold, dark stone stretched beyond sight. In its depths pools of water sat still, a source of frigid cold older than recorded time. This was an ancient and hollow place. One that gave the feeling of being outside the bounds of time itself.

Ulric lowered the sword and stared intently at it. "The king of the Dawn Blades. Whoever wields this holds the rights to the High King's throne and, with that, the sway over all this land."

Lancelin narrowed his eyes. "What are you implying?"

Ulric turned to him as if he had forgotten the captive was with them. "You have heard more than you needed already, young prince. Cedric, take him and the girl back outside and make sure there is no one to warn of what is coming."

Cedric nodded and motioned for the guards to follow. Lancelin pulled at his bindings but nothing would give. He was forced to march.

He glanced one last time over his shoulder to see the somber face of Ulric fixed on them. It dawned on him that maybe this man was jealous of their fate, to escape the grip of his dreaded master. For that Lancelin could have pity, but for whatever the man had planned, it must come to an end.

All throughout the march his mind raced for a way to escape, but to no avail. Even as the light outside the cave blinded their eyes, he fought for any opportunity he could find, but none came. He and Izel were made to kneel among the dead trees. The white dirt and dust beneath him would likely be the last thing he would ever see. He could hear the sobs of Izel next to him as she was forced to the ground. Coldness filled the guard's eyes as he stared down at them.

In his peripheral vision, Lancelin could see Cedric's boots beside him. "Any final words you would like to share, prince? It's not everyday that we execute royalty. I suppose we could at least honor you with a parting speech."

The others laughed at the mockery. Lancelin lifted his gaze from the ground to breathe in his final living moments when something among the trees caught his eye. A figure dressed in white armor walked in a confident stride before him. His jaw dropped and his eyes rested on the face of Eloy. Cedric took note of his shocked expression.

"What do you think you see? Some of your friends coming to rescue you? Did you sneak out a message, you wretch?" Cedric turned his gaze but saw nothing.

Eloy gave a confident nod, and in that moment Lancelin felt his restraints loosen. He knew what to do. As his captors still gazed around them in confusion, Lancelin leapt to his feet and threw himself again the unsuspecting Cedric. The two of them crashed to the ground, throwing up a cloud of dust and dirt. Lancelin felt his restraints fall and he broke his arms free to reach for Dawn's Deliverer in its sheath on Cedric's waist. The captain of the outsiders was afforded no more than a shocked gasp before the blade was plunged into his chest.

Not waiting for the others to react, Lancelin rose to his feet with blade in hand. Wielding two precise strikes, Lancelin watched the other guards fall, headless. Izel looked in shock as her captors were slain. Lancelin moved swiftly to cut her free. With an extended hand he helped her to her feet.

"How...?" was all she muttered.

A grin crossed his face and he looked to the empty space once occupied by Eloy. "The true High King has returned."

Not waiting for a response, he spoke again, "Izel, gather two horses. We must journey to regroup with the others."

"What about you? What are you going to do?" she asked.

"Finish this," he said as he turned to the mouth of the cave.

She gave a nod of approval and scurried to the horses tied nearby. He found renewed strength as he rushed through the damp tunnel. Dawn's Deliverer lit his way until he reached the chamber opening. He stopped in his tracks and sheathed the blade as he crept into the massive cavern. Ulric and the others now stood around the strange symbol he had drawn earlier. Placed in the middle of the circle was a flickering blue flame. All gathered swayed to a rhythmic hum that reverberated out into the vast space.

Ulric stepped forward, his face illuminated by the faint blue light. "Great Maluuk, born from this cavern eons ago, we beckon thee."

"Come, master," echoed the others.

"We offer you this amulet carried by your servant Balzara. With it we beckon your hallowed presence to come forth to reclaim the gift that has been stolen," Ulric chanted as he threw the amulet in the fire. A puff of smoke arose that grew into a thick mist around them.

"May your presence lead us back to restoration," the others chanted.

Ulric unsheathed Dawn Bringer and held the sword high so all could see. "With this blade we hold the authority of this kingdom."

"May Maluuk reign in all lands," cried the others.

The dark mist began to swirl around the blade, gathering steam until it encompassed the sword in a torrent of black mist.

"With this authority we invite you, our lord, to reign in these lands. We invite you to seek your revenge upon those who cast you out. With this blade we now usher you forth here and now!"

Ulric slammed the sword into the growing blue flame, sending its embers flashing across the symbol. The others wailed in a breathless gasp. The room grew dark as all but the faint glow of the blue symbols lit the chamber. In the deafening silence a thick smoke began to roll out from the primordial lakes. Soon it claimed the entire cavern, shifting among all those in the circle until it culminated where the fire once burned. The faint blue of the room turned to a sickly green as a figure slowly emerged from the smoke.

Lancelin blinked to see more clearly. In the midst of the circle stood a man of regal features. His pale skin was wrapped in the hard casing of ebony armor stamped with a blood red crescent moon. On his shoulders draped a royal garment of silver and black. His chestnut hair was adorned with a majestic crown encrusted with all manner of gems. All this was a sign of a king to be honored, even worshiped, but Lancelin could see in the cold silver eyes the malice laced within them. This was Maluuk, The Lord of the Felled Ones.

Maluuk gripped Dawn Bringer and with one strong thrust raised it above his head. To Lancelin's dismay, it had been transformed into an agent of darkness. Where there was once golden light shining from its edges, now in its place glowed a sickly haze. A thick cloud of darkness swirled around the midnight colored blade.

"Welcome, High King Maluuk," all cried in unison.

A devilish grin crept onto Maluuk's face. In that moment countless eyes filled the surrounding darkness. Silver slits shone like dying stars in the night sky. The army of the Felled Ones had returned and Lancelin knew he had no choice but to flee. Turning without a second thought, he rushed down the winding tunnel.

The return of dread and confusion filled his mind. How could this be? Had he not seen Eloy return? Had Eloy not rescued him? Why then would he let Maluuk return? Was his sacrifice for nothing? All this and more raced through his mind, but he knew he must warn the others if they stood a chance of survival. Maybe there was no chance at all. But he clung to the hope that if Maluuk had returned, so could Eloy.

11

GERALT

EVEN AS THE throne room door slammed behind them, Geralt couldn't help but feel guilty for leaving Lancelin behind. But, he had a job to do and he would fulfill his duty at all costs. He looked down at Lydia, the young woman who had become like a daughter to him. It took all his strength to pull her the few steps forward down the hall. Even with all his strength, she managed to break free, collapsing to the floor.

With overwhelming grief, she drenched the stone beneath her with her tears. He reached a hand to pull her up, but she turned away, vomiting. He swallowed, unsure of what to do. Lydia wiped her mouth and stared up at him.

"I know that we need to go." She stood to her feet, shaking.

He gave her an approving nod. What strength she had to muster for this moment he could not comprehend, but they had to keep moving. They rushed through the halls in a breathless gasp. Outside the sound of thunder cracked in the air. Geralt stopped to look out a nearby window. The sky was crystal blue. What was that sound? Another crashing noise rang in his ears.

"Come lass, I don't like the sound of that."

"Where are we going, Geralt? Are we not safe in our own palace?" she asked.

He paused for a moment. In all his rushing, he had not thought through where they should go, only away from here. His mind trained and honed by years of war came swelling to one conclusion.

"We need to get to the army and inform your brother of what has transpired. With their backing, we can march against these fiends."

Her red and puffy eyes gave him a tired stare.

"What is it, lass?" he asked.

"I'm tired of war, Geralt. I am tired of violence and evil. When will it end?"

He fought back the lump in his throat at her words. With an outstretched arm he pulled her against his chest. "I don't know, lass, but we have to keep fighting. You hear me?"

He felt the gentle bobbing of her head brush against him. With care he pulled away looking her in the eyes. "We will mourn soon, I promise."

A sudden sound of footsteps resounded down the hall, coming in their direction.

"Get ready," he growled as he withdrew his sword. Lydia followed his example but they were greeted with a pleasant surprise. A squadron of archers came rushing toward them and at their head was Zuma and Izel.

"We heard sounds of violence. What has happened?" they asked.

Where to begin? Geralt thought.

Before he could say a word Lydia stepped forward to speak, "Treachery has been done to Kingshelm. The High King is dead, and soon Lancelin will join him if you don't hurry to the throne room."

A mix of shock and grief filled them.

"We will go at once," said Zuma.

Izel nodded and the entire squadron hurried to the throne room. Lydia caught Zuma by the arm before he could follow. "Thank you for serving us so well."

"Of course. Kingshelm is our home now, and we will not allow our friends to be harmed."

With that Lydia released his arm, and he was off to what fate Geralt was unsure. She stood staring at the troops as they disappeared around the corner.

"I should be with them, Geralt. I should be defending Titus' body from those monsters."

"No, what you need to do is survive because, if we have a kingdom left after this, it's going to need a ruler."

She turned to him, grief starting to fill her eyes again, "Me? This kingdom doesn't need me. It needs..."

"I need you," Geralt snapped. "Like you, I have lost everyone I ever cared about, everyone except you."

A timid smile crossed her face. "You going soft on me?" she asked with a pathetic sniffle.

"If that's what it takes to get you to survive, fine," he said choking back his own pitiful reply.

Her eyes sharpened as she regained her composure. "Let's go."

Once again, they set off through the disheveled halls. Servants and members of the royal court floundered around seeking answers for the ensuing chaos. The sounds of impact had picked up tempo outside the palace walls. In the midst of the chaos Henry spotted them and came racing to their side.

"My Queen, are you well?" he asked.

Geralt could see her bite her lip in restraint. "No, I am not, but we can explain more in detail when we join the army."

"Join the army? What has happened?" he asked, searching both of their eyes.

Geralt extended a hand to the man's shoulder. "Titus is gone. These outsiders have betrayed us and we must get to the army as quickly as possible. Do you know the route to the hidden tunnels beneath the palace?"

"Of course. It is the job of the royal guards to know."

"Good, then lead the way."

Without another word, Henry motioned for them to follow. Even with all his training in the art of subterfuge Geralt could see the faint touch of disbelief cross Henry's face. They rounded a corner that took them to a small room bare of any decor except for a single rug on the floor. Beneath it rested a covering that, once removed, revealed a staircase that spiraled downward. It led them deep beneath the earth. Geralt imagined more than one life had been paid for such a structural endeavor. The cool air of deep earth settled over him, bringing a chill across his sweat soaked back. Henry led them, torch in hand, until they reached the bottom. In the underground tunnel a faint light in the distance greeted them like a pinhole amidst a sheet of darkness.

"That way," Henry said, directing with his head.

With the faint flickering of the torch the three of them hastily made their way to the secret exit. As the small shimmer of light grew, Geralt could see it would lead them just outside the city wall on the southwestern end of Kingshelm. The blinding light of the sun welcomed them from the tunnel exit. Tucked away under the shadow of the large stone wall of the city floated a small paddle boat.

Henry quickly loosed it from its bindings and ushered them in. Just within the edges of Geralt's vision he could see the source of the thunderous noise from earlier. A great host of men had begun to surround the city from its eastern side. Large catapults flung heaps of stone against the whitewashed walls. The banks of the Terras River were all that kept the invaders at bay, and soon even that would not stop them.

"A siege?" murmured Henry in confusion. "How could they muster one so quickly?"

"They couldn't," Geralt said, "unless they had planned one all along."

"You mean to say these outsiders had planned to attack us this whole time?"

"Why not? Get your men inside the city in a gesture of peace. Then have your army trail you a few days behind. Coordinate the timing of the attack and you have yourself the perfect element of surprise."

"With no army in the city to defend it." Henry said, his voice fading.

"Stop the boat!" came the voice of Lydia as she pointed at something in the water. Her sudden outburst had shaken both Geralt and Henry from their sullen stupor. He followed the line drawn from Lydia's pointing finger to an object floating in the distance. It was a corpse.

"Steer the boat to him now!" Lydia ordered.

Without question, Henry turned to bring them near the floating body. With a gasp of sorrow they realized it was Titus. Lydia scrambled to bring him into the boat and nearly capsized them. Geralt placed a steadying hand on her shoulder, but she would not be stopped. With the frenzy of a devastated lover she pulled the corpse of Titus onboard, gently laying his drenched head in her lap. Tears poured from her eyes as she stroked his wet hair. Geralt could feel the sting of tears begin to fill his own eyes at the sight of the dead king.

His skin had grown pale and his muscles grew tense with rigor mortis beginning to settle in. The High King's face had settled into a look of contentment. The white tunic he wore was tarnished by the stain of blood that had flowed from his wound. It stretched up his torso until it reached the lion embroidered on his chest. This was no way to see the king. Geralt turned his eyes to Lydia who sat silently holding her love. But he could see the look of sorrow had vanished from her eyes as she drank in the sight. In its place was one of scorn and rage.

Road weary and drained from grief, the encampment brought some semblance of joy to all of them. They had paddled along the Terras River a few miles until they thought it was safe to disembark. From there they had walked the tiring journey north until they had encountered a merchant willing to spare a cart for the dead king. They reached the encampment that evening. Several scouts rode out to greet them and were taken aback once they discovered who they were.

Their eyes revealed the horror of what they saw. Geralt could see they tried their best at showing royal reverence, but every now and then he caught them stealing a glance at Titus' corpse. It wasn't long before the trio was ushered into the camp. A host of commanders and captains emerged from their tents to greet them. By now all those Geralt had known were dead. The men became a list of nameless faces that stood before him. Thankfully Lydia knew them all and played the formality of queen while internally she remained the weeping spouse.

They had decided that a plan of action would be drawn together that evening, but first... first they must bury the king. The ceremony was done in haste. As evening settled in, he found it was only Lydia and himself who remained at the humble grave. She had picked out a spot under an ancient oak tree in the open plain. Its branches had come into a full spring bloom and life once again teemed among its branches.

Beneath its splayed branches rested High King Titus. His final resting place was marked by a small mound beneath the mighty oak. Just above, Lydia had lovingly carved out of its bark a small symbol to honor the grave. The Morning Star now watched over him. The symbol of life that felt so distant from their reality. Lydia knelt beneath the tangle of branches letting the full weight of her tears flow that she wished for no others to see. In a hushed tone he could hear her sharing her parting words with Titus.

"I have walked with you to the end of our road, my love... and it was too short." She drew in a deep breath. "Why must I walk it alone in our darkest hour?"

Slowly, she rose to her feet and brushed off her knees. With red eyes she turned to Geralt.

"Do you wish to mourn alone, my Queen?" he asked.

"I have mourned enough, Geralt. I don't have tears left to shed. Now is the time to act."

He gave an agreeing nod. They stood to return to camp and meet with the council to discuss their next move. As they entered into the camp an escort of guards led them to the tent of meeting. Inside, the faint light of flickering torches illuminated the faces of the commanders who stood ready to begin. Lydia had put on a firm face as she stood before these men. Geralt could see she would not back down to them, even in a moment of tragedy.

"Gentlemen, I have called this council in order for us to determine the fate of Islandia. This is not an exaggeration. The very kingdom is at stake because of these outsiders. Kingshelm as we speak has come under siege. No doubt word will reach Jorn shortly of what has transpired."

"What then do you suggest, my Queen?" asked a commander Geralt didn't know.

"I know what she should do," came the voice of Aiden abruptly. "She should keep her promises."

"You would demand the queen to help your cause in the midst of all this madness?" Henry asked.

"It is not my cause. It is our cause. Jorn is still a threat and I would argue an even greater one now that he has others who will align with him. I have been informed that these men answer to Maluuk. Is this not the same master that Jorn serves? Who is to say he isn't planning to march and join forces with them as we speak. We cannot possibly stand against both armies. Not with our numbers as dwindled as they are."

Lydia's face was hard as stone. Geralt knew the truth in her brother's words, but many in the room would dismiss it as self-seeking.

"My Queen, may I suggest we gather our forces with Khala? Imari has proven to be faithful to answer to the High King. Together, we would have a force large enough to take on these outsiders," Henry suggested.

"But not large enough to face both Jorn and this new army. Either way we must divide their forces," argued Aiden.

"By dividing our own? How will we stand against these outsiders when half our army is stranded in Valkara?" Henry protested.

"Enough, both of you," Lydia cried. Geralt could see behind her emerald eyes the weighing of their words.

"Commander, how many men do we still have remaining in our army?" she asked.

"At least 3,000 men of Kingshelm and another 2,000 of Leviatanas, my lady," he replied.

"Brother, how many of your own remain?"

Aiden narrowed his eyes in suspicion but conceded his answer to her. "600 uninjured fighting men."

"600 and you expect us to send our forces with yours pulling so little weight?" Henry asked.

"Henry, enough," Lydia said, raising a hand to silence him. "I understand your hesitation to work with my brother. I carry my own as well." She shot Aiden a hardened glance. "But he is right. Jorn will not go away, and if we do not deal with him now he will only grow stronger. He is the weaker head of this monster and, if we can lop it off, we should."

A smile crept onto Aiden's face at her words. "Don't get too cocky, brother. The true fight will be against these outsiders. That's why I am only sending half our force to march on Valkara."

"Half? We may not even match Jorn's remaining army with that number. You would be sending us to a slaughter against Valkara's defenses."

She turned a sharp eye to him. "We need to maintain a force large enough to stand against Ulric and his men. The force I give will be sufficient. If it helps, I will accompany you."

"My Queen, I highly suggest you stay with the larger force…" Henry said before being cut off once more.

"I will take my protector to keep me safe." Her eyes shifted to look at Geralt. "He has never failed me after all these years, and I don't suspect he will now. That is, if he is willing to return to Valkara."

He knew the answer before she asked. "Of course, my Queen."

"Then, by decree of the High Queen, I fulfill the promise of Kingshelm to march with Aiden's men to retake Valkara for the family of Doran. In my stead I leave Henry, loyal and faithful servant of Kingshelm as High Commander of my armies. You will lead them south to regroup with Imari and the Khalans. Together we will wipe out this plague that has befallen our lands."

"High Queen… I am honored," said Henry kneeling.

"Rise, Henry, you may wait to thank me when this is all over."

"It is my honor to serve, my Queen. I will make ready the army at once, with your leave."

"Go." With that command Henry dismissed himself from the tent. The rest of the commanders presently followed after him.

Aiden's jade eyes fixed on Lydia with a piercing gaze when all had been dismissed.

"Careful how you look at your queen," Geralt warned.

"Ahh Geralt, how you have risen among the ranks. Mighty fine of you to be so concerned for my family."

"Silence, Aiden! Geralt has been faithful to me more than my own blood. I would watch how you speak to him in my presence," Lydia snapped.

Aiden ignored the remark. "You know this is a massacre you are sending us to? Jorn will have more than men awaiting us. Dark arts are now performed in Valkara."

"What we have will suffice. Just be ready to win yourself a throne," she said giving him a wave to dismiss him. With reluctance, he turned from the tent.

"A bold move," Geralt said.

Lydia turned her eyes to him revealing the vulnerability hidden beneath the bravado she adorned. "I'm just glad you are going with me."

"Of course, my Queen. It's time we finish this."

12

IMARI

KHALEENA HAD MADE sure that her displeasure was shown at Imari's allowance of Amira into Khala. At least for now she must bow to the will of the Khosi. Some time had passed since his visit to Sahra, and the daily tolls of leadership had preoccupied his time. Amira had chosen to help where she could. Her skill as a warrior came in handy for training the new ranks of the Bomani. In the beginning they looked at her with suspicion, but she had proven her worth. His mind returned to the present as he overlooked the throne room. A host of ambassadors and tradesmen stood on the mosaic patterned floor, flanked on the side by royal banners. The people had brought with them a new round of pleas for him to consider.

Encircling the room stood a company of proven Bomani recruits. Their leader, Impatu, had placed himself at the foot of the throne. Opposite him was his sister, Khaleena, arrayed in a splendid leopard skin robe. He found himself staring up at the hanging gardens above.

Their glistening leaves reflected a palate of colors from the sunlight shining overhead. A royal court member broke his daydreaming once more with a tired yawn.

"Did you hear me, my Khosi? Crop yields are…"

The tradesmen was cut off by the door of the throne room being flung open. A royal messenger rested his hand against the doorframe, straining to speak the urgent message.

"An… an… army approaches Khala, my Khosi," the messenger said between breaths.

Imari found himself rising from the throne, but before he could speak Khaleena asked, "Is it Sahra? Have they decided to march on us?"

"No, this army comes from the north. It… it looks like Kingshelm," answered the messenger.

Imari shot Khelaana a cold look for speaking out of place. "Send an emissary out to meet them. I assume they come in peace, but let us be sure."

The messenger inhaled his breath and scurried away with his new orders.

"Impatu, gather the Bomani at the main gate. Inform Imamu to warn the city guard."

"It will be done, Khosi," bowed Impatu.

He descended the throne steps when Khaleena caught his arm. "You don't plan to let another foreign force into the city do you, brother?"

He pulled his arm free from her grip. "I will do whatever is best for the kingdom."

He saw the watchful eyes of Amira tucked within the shadows of the room and wondered what she made of the news. He felt a tinge of guilt rise in him at what other task he had given the old Sycar. She had a gift in espionage and he had asked her to use it. He didn't trust his sister's motives any longer. With the Masisi now dwelling in the city, she had the force to make a move if she pleased. No news of betrayal could be found, but tensions seemed to grow every day between them now on how Khala should be run.

He wasted no time in securing a camel to take him to the city gate. An entourage of Bomani stood awaiting his departure. With their protection, he moved out into the streets. The city had been able to return to some semblance of normal but scars still marred her beauty. If they were not found on the surrounding sandstone buildings, they would be manifested in the Khalan themselves. Unsure eyes and blank faces looked out at the Khosi passing by. A sense of unease and uncertainty filled the people. How he wished it could be cured, but time looked to be the only solvent for their wounds. He only hoped things were mendable with Nabila.

One step at a time, he thought.

He took in a breath to soak in his wonderful home. Every refreshing fountain, each vendor's display, and every home that was occupied by the people in his care. He must remember who he was fighting for. Soon, the city sights vanished and the towering defenses dominated his view. Before long a lone rider came up to the walls of Khala. A grin crossed Imari's face at the sight of his old friend. He quickly made his way down the ramparts to the city gate. The large wooden doors creaked open revealing the lone knight from Kingshelm.

"Henry, you are alive!" he exclaimed as they embraced.

"It is good to see you too, Khosi. I only wish it wasn't under such circumstances."

"It is strange that on your return you bring an army with you," Imari said.

The look in Henry's eyes spoke of the dire words he would need to speak next. "Imari, the High King Titus is dead."

Even as Henry spoke, Imari could feel a numbing sensation wash over him. How could this be? Who could have…

"The outsiders who arrived at Samudara Port did this. They have come to conquer Islandia."

The vision of treasures placed before him by the man named Cedric flashed in his mind. He felt the tightening of his fists at the confident smiles and honey dipped promises they had given.

"What happened?" he asked.

"They came to Kingshelm under the guise of peace. High King Titus, by some revelation, called them to speak their true intentions, and in that confrontation he was slain. Shortly after, these outsiders placed Kingshelm under siege. It looks as if this had been their plan all along, and it gets worse."

"How so?" Imari asked.

"We believe these men are servants of Maluuk. He is using them to exact his revenge. Lydia and Geralt have led a force against New Valkara in hopes of destroying them before these two foes can unite."

Imari looked over Henry's shoulder at the army with their banners flapping in the distance. "Why have you brought your army here? Should it not be in Kingshelm?"

A look of quiet unease flashed across Henry's face. "Well, my Khosi... we had hoped that Khala would join us to expel these men from Islandia. Our numbers have dwindled and we thought with your help..."

"With our help you could spill more Khalan blood for a Kingshelm cause?" came the voice of Khaleena behind them.

Imari turned to see his sister, hands on hips, carrying a look of disgust.

"Don't tell me you plan to drag our people into another war, Imari."

"Khosi, I would not come here if it wasn't dire. The battle can be won with ease if Khala joins our forces."

"How many men do you think we have?" Khaleena asked. "Can a thousand truly turn the tide?"

"It can. Beside numbers, it is the vaunted Bomani we are speaking of. By skill alone they outmatch any man two to one."

"Our Bomani are but boys now, led by a boy who has fought in a handful of battles. They no longer are the thing of legend," Khaleeana said, restraining her displeasure.

"Khaleena, enough!" Imari shouted. "Do you believe you have the authority to speak for me?"

"I speak for our people. Someone must. Look around, Imari. They are fearful, fearful of being dragged into another fight that is not their own. If you call on their sons to fight and die again you will have a revolt."

"And who would be its leader?" he seethed.

It was in that moment he noticed all the eyes of his Bomani guard that had fallen on them. Each carrying a weight of shock and fear at the bickering of their leaders. Imari swallowed the lump in his throat before speaking.

"Henry, I must think on our decision. You and your army are welcome to camp outside our walls. Food and water will be provided at a fair price."

"Khosi, if we lose, they will march on your walls next," Henry said with desperation.

"A shell of their forces which we can dispatch," Khaleena said in response.

All Imari could do was sigh. He was tired, tired of fighting tooth and nail with his sister. Tired of war and among all this, the news of his friend's death had already been drowned out.

"I... I need to think," he muttered. Not waiting for a reply he turned to face the palace. Barely holding back the swelling of tears, he warded off the blurred faces around him. All of them wondering what could place their Khosi in such a state. Once inside the palace, he scrambled to his quarters. In a reckless flurry he scrounged together what he needed to travel to 'the place.' It had become an oasis of solitude for him long before he had been honored as Khosi. It was there he must retreat if he was to work through the clutter of voices that hounded his mind. A voice emerged from the dark of his room, startling him.

"Where are you planning to go?" asked Amira as she emerged from the shadows.

"A place of refuge. Just for a day or so. I need to think all this through."

"Khaleena will take advantage of your absence. You must know this. She may even speak of a mental break in you."

"Perhaps it is breaking," he sighed. "I am tired, Amira. Tired in a way that cannot be fixed with all this noise around me. I will be gone only a few days. I trust Khala will not collapse in such little time."

"What about Henry?" she asked.

How could it be explained to him the ever growing division between Khaleena and himself? Imari thought.

"Have Impatu prepare as if we are marching to war. In the meantime, would you speak to Henry for me?"

"What would you have me say?"

"Explain to him what is truly happening in Khala. That things are not as simple as he had hoped."

"It will be done," Amira said bowing.

"Thank you, Amira. Little did I know of the allies I still had in Sahra."

"Ally Khosi, I believe I may be the only one in Sahra who sees things in a similar way."

"Indeed," he said sullenly. He reached inside his tunic and pulled out a small, white dagger. Its edges radiated with golden light.

"What's this?" Amira asked.

"I want you to have it. It has brought me hope in times where I have been in dire need of it. Perhaps it can help you now."

Without a word Amira nodded and tucked the small dagger underneath her own cloak. With a somber smile she slipped back into the shadows, dismissing herself from his presence. Imari found himself staring at his stash of supplies that he had kept for such a journey. He only hoped it would bring him the wisdom he needed.

The rolling dunes of sand sent fragments of glistening specks across an azure sky. Beyond the tides of sand, waves from the Islandic Ocean crashed against the pebbled coast. No cloud could be seen in the sky. Imari found himself among a long abandoned cluster of buildings. At one time they had been built to rival the great port of Samudara. The project had failed, but in its wake, the abandoned site had become an oasis for many a Khosi.

He inhaled, allowing the smell of salt water to fill his lungs. A gust of sea wind swept up another swell of warm sand as the wind rippled off the dune before him. This was his place of solitude, of rest. It was here he had learned to reflect on all that had happened to his family after their murder those many years ago.

It was here he had retreated, once more searching for answers that eluded him. In quiet meditation he strolled down to the beach. White foam formed at the surface of the crashing tide. Beneath his feet the sand radiated the heat of the midday sun. He felt the calming rhythm of the ocean wash over him. With the sand beneath him and the waves around him, he searched his mind for the revelation he needed. He relayed every option, every move, and yet... nothing. The answer would not come, no matter how hard he fought to find it.

He knew the Khalans would rebel at the call of another war horn. His sister was right in that regard. They had grown restless and weary of bloody battle. How could he reconcile that with the loss of his friend? He owed Kingshelm for the very kingdom restored to him, but had he not repaid his debt? Was it a debt? They were the grand throne that all must answer to but the true High King was gone. He loved Titus like a brother, but all knew whose throne it really was.

Then there was Nabila. He was stirred from his thoughts as the sound of hooves drew near. Almost all had forgotten about this place. Only royalty had kept its memory alive. Royalty. It dawned on him who his visitor was just as her face peeked over a dune above the beachfront.

Khaleena and her trusted warrior Lombaku steered their camels down the steep dune toward him.

"I came here to be alone, Khaleena."

"I know why you came," she said, a hint of dread in her voice.

"Then why do you disturb me?" he asked as she dismounted before him.

She drew in a deep breath as her gaze met his. "It is time, Imari, for you to step down as Khosi."

So it was true, he thought. *She desired the throne after all.*

"You have a good heart, brother, but that heart has failed in serving the interests of our people."

"So why did you come here to tell me this, and why bring him?" he asked pointing a finger at the hulking figure of Lombaku.

Khaleena shot Lombaku a glance. "I need you to return to Khala and proclaim you have passed on your rule to me. I prefer you did so peacefully but, if not..."

"But why here, sister? Why not wait for my return? Do you even desire my return to the city at all?" he asked.

A look of sorrow passed over her face. "I thought you deserved to hear this in privacy. Besides, your return is urgent. Impatu has ordered the fighting men to assemble. Soon the city will be in an uproar."

"He did so on my orders, Khaleena."

"So you would create the riots yourself, then abandon your people?" she snapped.

"You don't understand the stakes, Khaleena. You haven't seen what the servants of Maluuk are capable of."

"I know full well what they are capable of," she said pulling the collar of her shirt to reveal her scars. "Don't you dare question me on such matters."

"I can't just abandon Kingshelm. The price that Eloy paid to save us..."

"You see this is the true root of the issue! This Eloy. You claim he is so grand, so great, yet Khala has not seen his benefits. Why should I not have the privilege to meet this High King?"

"Perhaps we should change that," came a voice behind her.

The three of them turned. Their expressions turned to awe and fear as they gazed upon the man standing beside them on the beach. He wore royal attire bleached white. His brown eyes narrowed, sending small creases across his olive skin as he smiled.

"E... Eloy," Imari said, stumbling at the sight. "How?"

Khaleena stood wide-eyed, staring at the High King. Fear and terror caused her body to tremble.

"You have no need to fear, Khaleena. I am not a tyrant like those whose hands you have fallen into before."

Khaleena could find no words as her eyes remained fixed on Eloy. Finally, she mustered up the strength to speak, "Is that truly him, Imari?"

"It is, though I can hardly believe it myself," he replied.

Eloy's gaze turned to him. "You doubted what Geralt told you? Even after the dagger I gave him?"

"My King, you must understand the insanity of the claim! From Geralt, no less."

"It is typically those least expected who make all the difference. But who the messenger is should not concern those who receive the message." Imari felt the small rebuke but it did not hamper his amazement. Here was Eloy in the flesh before him, but suddenly his mind was flooded with a question.

"High King, I tremble at asking such a thing to a man of your... power. But, if you have returned, why has all this happened? Why has Titus been killed and Kingshelm besieged? Are you here to save us now?"

As the words left his lips, tears suddenly streamed down Eloy's face. To Imari it felt like an intrusion to a depth of sorrow only this man could feel. In his presence reality somehow became more so, and Imari could sense even Eloy's grief was held within a fuller reality than he could comprehend. Its richness held a nuance that no mortal man could grasp.

"It is one of the great sorrows that has passed in an age full of them," Eloy said. "I am afraid the night has not yet reached its peak."

"What are these cryptic words of yours?" Khaleena asked. "Have you not come to defend your people?"

"Khaleena, do you know who you speak to in this way?" Imari scolded.

Eloy gave her a gentle smile as he raised a hand to Imari. "Princess of Khala, you speak with boldness and truth."

"What kind of king am I is your real question. One who will bring the weight of judgment upon his enemies and one who will extend life to those who call him friend."

"Life? What kind of life? Was this Titus your friend? Because I see no life in him?"

The insult bounced off the High King with no effect. Instead, Eloy stood silent, his eyes peering at her as if searching the depths of her being. It made Khaleena squirm, the feeling of her heart being laid bare before this man.

"You believe Imari is not fit for Khala. You came here to end his reign one way or another did you not?"

She stood mute as Eloy continued, "It is Sahra that has wounded you, indeed those that rule Sahra. They have taken your sense of dignity. They have stripped you of peace and now you cannot live peacefully with your world or yourself."

Her head shook unsteadily, yet Imari could see her body was frozen even as she looked to turn and run away.

"You think that by shutting everyone out you can protect yourself, you can find peace. But, you know it is those you love who you need the most. You are chained by your pain and you cannot escape."

Tears streaked down her cheeks and Imari could see she barely concealed her sobs. Still, Eloy pressed forward.

"I can break those chains."

"How," she said in the faintest whisper.

"Let go. Let go of all the hurt."

"I can't. Where will it go if I don't hold onto it? When will the justice come? Who will fight for Imbaku, my parents, me?" she questioned at the top of her lungs.

Slowly, Eloy moved to her as she slumped to the ground. "I will, Khaleena. Soon, very soon, all this evil and this pain, everything will be dealt with. The New Dawn is coming, and in its rays the night will be vanquished."

"How can this be?" she said, looking up at him with tear-filled eyes.

"There is a gift that belongs to me. I will share it with all who call me friend," he said.

"Can I... can I..."

"Yes, Khaleena you can."

She wrapped her arms around him in reckless abandon. Lombaku stepped away in shock at the sight. Imari knew more than words had touched Khaleena. Deep within all the torment, all the pain, something had broken and in its place, life had sprung once more. Eloy helped raise her to her feet.

"Imari," he said.

He felt himself standing at attention at the call of Eloy. "Yes, High King."

"You have come seeking answers on what to do, and I have come to tell you. Take your forces and those of Kingshelm and go to Sahra."

"Sahra, my lord? You must be..." but he stopped before finishing. How could he say such an absurdity to this man?

"Yes, my King."

"Very good. There is dark news you will find on your return, but take heart. The dark of night may come..."

"But the dawn will follow," Imari said, finishing Eloy's words. "It is the ancient proverb."

"I am glad you know it," Eloy smiled. "I must go, but there is still unfinished business here." His eyes motioned to Khaleena.

"I understand," Imari said turning to his sister. As he went to return his gaze to the High King, Eloy was gone. The moments easily could have been taken as a dream if the residue of his presence had not so drastically changed them.

Khaleena's eyes raised to meet his. "Brother."

"I know, Khaleena."

She shook her head. "What I have done… you are a worthy Khosi."

Imari swallowed, fighting the emotions that threatened to overtake him.

"Do you remember that day on the boat? When we were returning home for the first time?" she asked.

"Of course."

"Could you ever trust me like that again?"

He smiled as he knew the old Khaleena had returned. *Not the old,* he thought. That would overlook all she had overcome. This was his sister reborn.

"I would have it no other way."

13

LYDIA

ALKARA WAS NOT far now. The sound of late spring snow crunched under Lydia's feet, indicating the last grasps of a Valkaran winter clinging to life. Before her was the picture of a pristine wonderland of snow-crusted woods. The pine and spruce trees stood clotted with the white substance. Everything was just as she remembered from her childhood days exploring these same woods. That was, until they neared the city.

She could hear the gasps of horror from those marching behind her. Even her brother who had been accustomed to all manner of gruesome sights stopped in his tracks. Along the road on either side hung the corpses of men. Their rotting flesh was erected on wooden poles that traced the path to the city. Some whose tattered clothes remained bore the symbol of a ram, others a lion. These men had been taken captive in their fight near Forest's Edge.

Carrion birds circled overhead, ready to pick apart the remaining flesh of the bodies that ushered them home. Even the most battle-hardened of the group turned aside at the horrendous sight. Yet the memory of those haunting dead eyes would not leave them. Jorn's message was clear: no mercy, no quarter, no return for those who tread these lands.

Lydia turned and saw the fire in Aiden's eyes. Such violence would not deter him, it only fueled his hatred. With a cool nod he motioned for them to continue. On and on the nightmare ushered them until the peaks of the Valkaran fortress came into view over needled tree tops.

A hoarse voice caused her to jump as it choked out a warning from above. One of the men crucified clung to his last breath of life. His skin was crusted and cracked from long exposure to the elements. His blood red eyes hauntingly stared at those who passed by. The stench from his naked and rotting flesh induced a feeling of vomit at the back of her throat. The dying man drew in a final breath, his bare ribs throbbed from the effort of his last words.

"Turn... back," he moaned with fading strength. "Turn back," he said again before his head slumped in a sickly motion.

She turned away in horror, fighting back the sheer vileness of it all. Just as it began to overwhelm her, a hand clasped her shoulder. She jerked from its grip in fear until she met the eyes of Geralt. He glanced at the hanging man and then back at her.

"You alright, lass?" he asked.

She shook her head. "No, but let's just finish this."

She forced herself to stomp forward in the ankle deep snow, ignoring the remaining atrocities along the road. Soon her home, Valkara, lay before them. The dark stone of the city sat nestled into The Crowns Mountain chain. Its buildings and walls sat sleepily under a blanket of snow. All was still. No bird sang, no wind blew, no sign of life could be heard behind the city's walls. She felt Aiden move beside her.

"It's time, sister. Time to take back our home," he said with the grin of a warrior.

For the first time, she felt uneasy about coming here. Until this moment it had felt clear. They could finally slay the monster that had destroyed their family. She could get some sort of satisfaction for all the pain she had endured, but now an ill feeling came over her. Would this truly satisfy her? It wouldn't bring Titus back, or her father, or Brayan, or Nara, or her mother? All of them were gone, and like the city she once called home felt empty and void. She could feel the waiting eyes of Aiden.

"Yes, it is," was all she could muster.

With an eager smile he turned to the officers behind them. "Begin cutting down the tree line. Build ladders and rams. We will begin our siege when the work is done."

As her brother left to help give the order to the other men, Geralt came to her side once more.

"Something is off in the city," he said. He stared suspiciously at the emptied walls.

"You feel it, too?" she asked.

He let out a sigh. "Best help with the preparation. Not much we can do about it now."

He stepped away, leaving her alone in the snow filled clearing. Her eyes lingered in one last look at the city she once called home. For good or ill this place would never be the same. Turning, she found a nearby captain. He gave her the task of stripping the felled trees that would be turned into weapons of war. He handed her a small axe made of wood and iron. She approached the tree line with axe in hand and set to work.

The afternoon and evening were filled with the sounds of collapsing trees and the thud of axes. It amazed her what a few thousand men could accomplish in less than a day. Dozens of ladders and several rams had been fastened to conquer the New Valkaran defenses. Even with all the noise, no activity could be seen or heard from within the city walls.

"What was Jorn doing in there?" she thought.

Many wondered if Jorn and his men were even in the city. Rumors of ambushes or disease spread across the camp, but Aiden was convinced the man was there. When the sun faded from view his belief was realized. It started as a low rumble, but soon broke out into a bellow of deep and dark menace. A horn sounded from behind the walls, one of unnatural and devilish origins.

"Men! Prepare for battle!" came the echo down the line. Soldiers scrambled into formation, each taking with them a ladder for their respective company. Small, dark figures scurried to line the ramparts above. Dark armor engraved with the mark of a silver fox flickered in the dying light of the sun. The men of New Valkara wore the familiar mockery of the ancient battle helmets. The mask once made to honor the ancient king Odain now resembled a snarling fox.

The backdrop to the drawn battle lines depicted a sun of deep orange and crimson fading over the treetops. The men beside her stirred, anxiously awaiting the first order that would break the silence. As the sky darkened, one by one the archers along the wall engulfed their arrows in flame. Soon, a string of dancing light illuminated the haunting forms on the wall. Without warning or cry the flaming arrows filled the sky. For a brief moment their sinister light exposed the battlefield below and transformed the blanket of snow into fire. As the arrows sank into shield, armor, and flesh, the order was given to charge.

With a roaring battle cry, the forces of Kingshelm, Leviatanas, and Aiden rushed forward with shields overhead. Another volley came soaring and, with it, more lay dead on the snowy clearing. Finally the first of their forces reached the walls. With hooks they anchored their ladders and began the deadly ascent. Lydia led a force of her own to the main gate. Its iron capped wood was ready for the battering it would soon face.

They reached the protection of the wall's arch just as the next volley of flaming arrows poured out. She shouted the order to begin their barrage. Thunder reverberated off the walls as the wooden ram tipped with iron smashed into the gate. Its greeting was met with a slight bending of iron and cracking of wood. Again it sent its greeting and was met with even more give.

Her ears perked up as a bubbling sound churned above her. As she looked she could see the rims of cast iron pots being poured over slitted openings.

"Oil!" she screamed throwing herself out from under the covering of the gate just in time. As she recovered, the sight of molten pitch rained down. Men screamed in agony as the blazing hot ooze engulfed them. In a terrorizing scene two flaming arrows zipped downward, lighting all entrapped in the inferno. Every one of them now gone in the blink of an eye.

She felt a firm hand lift her to her feet. The gaze of Geralt met hers. "Are you mad? What makes you think it was a good idea to go with the ram?" he asked.

She stared at him stunned, still mortified by the smell of burning flesh.

"I couldn't ask our men to do what I would not," she muttered.

Geralt didn't reply but lifted his eyes to the ramparts above. The hail of arrows had ceased and in its place was the ringing of swords.

"Come, your brother has forged a path up the walls," Geralt said.

"What of the gate?"

Both looked at the flames that climbed up the dark stone.

"It will be some time before that fire dies down and another ram can be sent. This is our best bet."

She nodded in agreement and followed him to a nearby ladder. The shouts of men sounded out into the field. Their cries of agony and rage were the horrific symphony of the night.

How long must it be the song of their age? Lydia thought as she placed one hand in front of the other. Geralt disappeared over the parapet above. Steel on steel rang in her ears and a body came tumbling over the edge beside her. She watched as the corpse lifelessly plunged to the ground with a thump. It had been one of Jorn's men. Yet the sight brought her no peace.

Now it was her turn to reach the ramparts. With a turning of her hips and a push off the ladder she landed in the midst of chaos. Men on both sides fought vigorously for every inch of ground. Steel met flesh in a bloody dance of blades. She could see Geralt just ahead cutting his way toward Aiden. She chased after him and took care with her footing on the bloody and oil-soaked ground. Bodies from both sides lay strewn about in a ghastly array, a tripping hazard waiting to take another with them to the grave by a deadly fall off the wall.

With carefully placed feet Lydia darted across the path. Sword held high, she repelled the blades of any who dared to assault her. One of Jorn's men took his chance and found himself on the terrifying end of a trip to the ground. Another swiped at her legs, hoping to sweep her off her feet. She quickly jumped, dodging the blow, and sent a counter blow crashing down onto the man's helmet. The strike cut through the helmet and mask leaving a scar across its surface and a marred face beneath.

She pressed forward until she found herself just behind Geralt and Aiden. They stood at the front cutting a way forward. For a brief moment, she looked out at the city. Besides the defenders awaiting them at the bottom of the wall, it sat silent and void of life.

"Where have all the people gone?" she wondered.

A flash of steel broke her thoughts as the threatening silver entered her vision. With raised sword she deflected the blow. Before she could counter, Geralt thrust his sword into the attacker's side and, with the kick of his boot, sent him toppling over the edge. Eyes wide with terror, she gave him a grateful nod.

"Come, press the attack! We've almost won the gate!" cried Aiden.

The order sent a jolt of energy through the men as they pressed all the more to overcome the city's defenders. That final push was all they needed to vanquish the remaining forces on the wall. What remained of their enemy retreated to the streets below. Lydia found herself above the gate next to her brother, once again staring out at the vacant city.

"What has he done?" she sighed.

"He will pay with his life for all the blood he has shed in our home," Aiden snarled. "Come, sister, let's finish this."

She grabbed her brother's shoulder before he could walk away. "Aiden, this has to be more than revenge. This fight is to see Valkara restored and peace brought to Islandia again."

He shrugged her hand away. "We will have peace when all the monsters are slain."

With that he gave the order to push the attack. Their forces poured from the wall and flooded the streets below. The time had come to take the fight into the city of Valkara. She watched Jorn's men continue to retreat deeper and deeper into the heart of her home. She felt the calming presence of Geralt move beside her as she stared out at the scene.

"Not a pretty sight," he said.

"I never wanted to see a city at war again."

The grizzled warrior let out a sigh. "Come, lass, it will be over soon."

As they descended to the streets an eerie calm had settled where they stood. The fighting had moved near the keep itself and in its wake were left the bodies of the dead soldiers scattered outside the empty dwellings.

"Where are all the people?" Lydia asked, bewildered.

Geralt remained silent at her question. They pressed forward into the heart of the city but still, no signs of life could be found. The sounds of fighting drew near as her family's fortress came into view. A slight movement in an adjacent alleyway caught her eye. Huddled in the shadow of the buildings was a decrepit creature. Its ash colored skin clung to its bones. The creature's hair was tattered and stringy. Haunted eyes gazed at her. Beneath their pools Lydia could see awe and terror.

She took a step closer, drawing Geralt's vision to the wretched thing.

"Lydia," he warned but she waved him off. The creature shuddered and shriveled at discovery but sat paralyzed at her approach. Tears burst from Lydia's eyes when realization dawned on her. This was no creature or beast. It was a young woman. Her bony frame shivered as Lydia knelt beside her.

"You're Princess Lydia," croaked the woman.

"I am. What has happened to you? Where are the others in the city?" She asked.

The woman shuddered and turned away, closing her eyes. "You've come to rescue us? Yes, rescue. You can tell her. It's safe," the woman mumbled to herself.

Lydia extended a hand to the woman but pulled it back as she began to shriek, "Gone! All gone! The men taken for labor, the woman slaves or worse… and the garden. The garden is a terrible place. Do not go to the garden."

"What's in the garden?" asked Lydia.

But the woman closed her eyes and groaned. All she repeated in a haunting tone was, "The garden, the garden." She rocked back and forth in a state of terror.

"Come, lass, we should go," Geralt said, placing a hand on Lydia's shoulder.

Lydia bit her lip feeling the pangs of guilt at what had been done to her people.

"I failed them Geralt," she cried. "I left them to die and suffer under this monster."

"You cannot change the past, but we can stop him now!" he said pulling her up. His face softened into compassion as he looked her in the eyes.

"You did not fail them, Lydia. There was nothing in your power that could have prevented this monster, Jorn. But now we have the chance to stop him forever."

She wiped away her tears and took in a breath. He gave her a faint smile. "You have grown to be more than I could have imagined."

"Come, Geralt, enough. You're getting soft on me again," she sniffed.

They turned to leave. She couldn't help but steal one last glance at the woman who sat rocking and muttering to herself.

"I am so sorry," she said softly. The woman could not hear her, but she knew what they must do. This was for more than just her own family. It was for all the lives Jorn had destroyed.

As they approached the keep's walls, she could see the last of Jorn's forces melting away. The cracking of a battering ram thundered against wood and she could see the fortress would soon be theirs. Aiden waited near the gate, his foot impatiently bouncing off the cold stone. He turned to greet them with an eager smile as they approached.

"We've done it. Valkara is ours! Their forces have turned to nothing. All that remains is to cut the head off the snake. Fitting we get to strip him off the throne in the throne room itself."

Another crack echoed out, and this time it was followed by the shattering of wood. Men rushed forward prying the doors off their hinges. Troops began to flood the fortress complex only stopping to allow the three of them through. As they entered, they were taken aback at the reaction of their soldiers. Some turned back and others bent retching.

What is it?" barked Aiden to no reply.

"The gardens..." muttered Lydia.

"What do you?" but before he could finish she had already dashed ahead.

As she broke past the wall of soldiers she met the abominable sight. Where there once was a beautiful garden with a marvelous fountain, now stood... she shook her head. For in its place altars of various stones and sizes had been erected. Strange symbols marred and deformed the scenery. But it was what lay on the alters that sent a shiver up her spine. Bodies, countless bodies, lay strewn and naked atop the vile stones. Their entrails hung loose from their sides and where they once had eyes now rested hollow sockets.

Then she saw the rest. Thousands upon thousands of bones stacked beside the walls. The ground revealed by torch light was stained crimson from the countless dead. Men, women, even children had not been kept back from the horrendous ritual. Aiden came beside her, his mouth open at the scene.

"What... what is this?" he said, barely able to release the words.

"The sacrifice," said Geralt as he came beside them.

"The what?" Aiden asked.

"This is what it means to serve the master known as Maluuk," Geralt said, jaw clenched at the gruesome sight.

"This is for the Felled Ones?" Aiden asked, astounded.

Lydia turned to him, her cheeks flushed. "Do you see now why we had to stand against such a beast? Eloy died not a trivial death, but to stop this!" she said pointing a finger at the awful scene.

Aiden gulped as he surveyed the horror. "Let's... let's just go deal with Jorn."

He moved forward in silence toward the keep. His gaze was careful to avoid the wretchedness that surrounded them. Geralt turned to face her. "Be careful, Lydia. Jorn will not go down without a fight. Something tells me he has more in store for us than we know."

This was a warning she took to heart. Slowly the full measure of their forces trickled into the royal complex. Each new man who entered was taken aback by what they saw. With caution they moved forward covering every inch until they reached the throne room doors. They found no resistance as they covered the courtyard, only the haunting view of the grizzly sacrifices.

Aiden, with sword in hand, pushed open the throne room door. It was dark inside with only the light of the moon shining through vaulted windows illuminated the oak interior. The space had been laid bare. All but the carved pillars and elevated throne remained. Atop it sat a man dressed in midnight armor, a blood red moon painted across his chest. His chainmail wrapped where his right arm used to be. Across his lap lay the ancient Dawn Blade of Valkara known as Dawnbreaker. It glowed a sickly green and black smoke swished around its edges.

"Children of Doran, you have finally returned home," Jorn said smiling. His silver eyes lit by moonlight made her shudder. It brought her back to that horrid night. The night Nara had been slain, the night this monster had done his best to slay her too.

"Silence, Jorn. Your voice has been heard enough in these lands! Come give me your neck, so I can end this," shouted Aiden.

"Ever confident you are, boy. I suppose you believe you have won a battle, and that makes you think you could be king?"

"I will cut you down where you sit!" Aiden cried.

Lydia placed a hand on her brother. "Silence, Aiden, he has hidden treachery for those who act brashly."

"Astute, little Valkaran. If only I had slain you that night instead of your feeble sister."

She let the rage wash over her so that it might not fog her mind. For she would need all her wits to defeat this foe. Jorn raised the Dawn Blade in his hand.

"I don't think you will find me as easily slain as you would like, even maimed as I am. Thanks to you," Jorn said pointing the tip of the blade toward Geralt who stood leering at him.

His eyes settled back onto Lydia and her brother. "I suppose you think you've won. Seeing as my army is destroyed and only I remain. But it isn't the enemy you know that you should fear."

Jorn rose to his feet, and as he did silver eyes filled the dark void behind him. Suddenly on their flanks even more silver orbs appeared. All of them carried a seething hatred beneath.

"What is this?" Aiden asked taking a step back.

Casually Jorn descended the steps of the throne until he was only a few feet away. "It is the enemy you don't know. Or rather, *you* don't know, Aiden. Some of you are acquainted," he said sneering.

"How is this possible? Eloy..." stuttered Lydia before Jorn interrupted.

"Your High King failed! Maluuk and his army have returned with vengeance on their mind. Thanks to our little foreign friends. I heard they did a number on your lover."

"Enough!" shouted Aiden as he rushed forward with a wild swing of his axe.

Jorn lifted the corrupted Dawn Blade with ease, breaking the axe in two. Aiden did not relent. He ducked out of the way of Jorn's counter sending several furious blows with a hidden dagger. Jorn weaved his way free of the assault and with a flick of his wrist sent the small blade across the floor.

"Attack them!" ordered Jorn. Out of the shadows the host of deformed beasts burst. The men accompanying them rushed to meet their foes, but Lydia knew they stood no chance. Even as the men unsheathed their second swords known as Light Bringers, it would not be enough. Behind the throne a dark mist suddenly permeated the walls. From it more and more of the creatures poured out.

Many of them she recognized. The deformed shapes of a wolf-like beast. Spidery creatures that moved with deadly speed. Long clawed monstrosities in the form of men but skin pulled tight with faces like skulls. Even the wide mouthed creatures with razor sharp teeth had returned. It was a nightmare relived, only those she needed by her side the most were gone.

Out of the corner of her eye she could see Jorn moving toward her. Aiden now lay on the floor gripping his leg from a blow she had not seen. The sneering monster raised his sword to strike her down. With agile speed she dodged the incoming blow and sent her boot crashing into his knee. With a howl of pain Jorn dropped to the ground, the grip on his sword loosening. She took the chance to reach for the weapon but found he had recovered too quickly.

Jorn sent the blade upward with a backhanded swing. She could feel the cold bite of steel across her chest and glide past her cheek. All was a blur as she was tossed onto her back. She heard a voice cry out her name over the clamor of battle. Time slowed and her vision grew fuzzy.

Had this been how Titus felt in the end? Cold? Alone?

She no longer fought her fate. Rest, she could finally rest. But the finishing blow didn't come. With all her remaining strength she rose, leaning on her elbow. With a speed she had never seen in a swordsman, Geralt had jumped between her and Jorn. With deadly precision, he sent Jorn retreating even as he swung the Dawn Blade. With intense focus Geralt skirted each blow until he had driven Jorn back to the stairs of the throne.

She could see the panic in Jorn's eyes. This was the vaunted warrior that tales spoke of. She had never seen anyone move with such controlled strength. In his retreat, Jorn stumbled on the steps he had neglected to see. It sent him floundering onto his back. The Dawn Blade betrayed his grip, landing a few feet away. He raised a pitiful hand to Geralt.

"Mercy... mercy, you must..."

Without word the sword in Geralt's hand slide between steel plating, penetrating the chainmail beneath until it reached the heart. With a cry of gurgled pain Jorn spoke his last. Geralt, in silence stepped away from the corpse and picked up the Dawn Blade nearby. At the touch of his hand the mist dissipated and the green glow vanished. The black blade slowly morphed into the cool dark steel of its true form. A subtle light of pure golden hues began to radiate at the edges. He quickly moved to her side.

"Are you all right?" he asked.

She sat up examining the gash in the leather armor. Only a small cut grazed her skin. Reaching a hand to her face she felt the mark on her cheek.

"I'm fine, just a scratch."

Geralt offered her the hilt of the Dawn Blade.

"I believe this belongs to you," he said.

"Geralt you saved us... I."

He couldn't help but fight back the tears in his eyes. "I was given a task, lass. By a man I respected long ago. To keep his children safe. I failed at that task until this day."

She choked back the lump in her throat as the reality around them settled in. "Geralt, I cannot thank you enough, but you should keep that blade until we can escape."

His eyes focused again in a way that shocked her. How easily he could switch to a warrior at a moments call. He nodded and gripped the sword. Aiden hobbled to his feet drawing both their attention.

"Aiden!" Lydia cried.

"Save it, sister. We've got to go."

Geralt rolled his eyes. "Help him. I'll hold these beasts off. We need to make it to the escape tunnel."

Lydia chuckled silently to herself. More than once that tunnel had come in handy. She ran to Aiden's side, taking his arm around her shoulders.

"Come on, don't be dead weight," she chided as they scrambled forward. Any of the Felled Ones that neared them Geralt cut down with ease. Dawnbreaker sang in its restored form. As they retreated from the palace, their forces followed like a tide receding from the shore. A growing number of them fell as the dark army gave chase.

Through the streets they fled. Lydia glanced at the now empty alleyway where the strange woman once sat. The place was vacant, leaving her to wonder about the woman's fate. She shook her head. What would any of their fates be by the end of this. The monstrosities rained down curses on the retreating army. Their malicious intent filling them with unparalleled speed.

As she looked over her shoulder, she wondered if they would have any army by the end of this. Following Geralt they rounded a corner where a small exit lay tucked into the frame of the city wall. While the remainder of their forces retreated to the main gate and the ramparts, they slipped away down the quiet side street. With a kick Geralt sent the door flying off its hinges. With a waving hand he ushered them in. Bursting through the exit they stumbled onto the snow covered clearing.

The once white sheet was now a crimson stained horror. Mud and the remains of battle churned into a sludge of destitution. Trampling through it they reached the adjacent tree line. Just behind them the first stragglers of the army came bursting out from the city. Some braved jumping the dangerous heights off the wall, while others could be heard screaming from within the city. All fled before the coming terror.

Searching they found a nearby stable boy clutching a pair of horses.

"Where are the others?" Geralt asked.

The stable boy gulped. "They fled when they heard the army retreating, me and a few others are all that remain."

"Cowards," hissed Aiden.

"Geralt where are we going?" she asked.

"Khala?"

"We can't make it that far. Not with the pace we will need."

"That's not where we should go," interrupted the stable boy said.

All three turned to the bold young man. He blushed at their stares but continued, "I mean, word was just received but an hour ago. The Khalans along with the rest of the army march to Sahra. They sent word of a foul army joining with the outsiders. In the message they said we should meet them there to make our stand."

"Sahra it is then," Geralt said. "Mount up, you two. We have a long way to go."

Aiden raised a hand to halt them. "I need to say this before we go."

"Quick about it," Geralt said.

Aiden nodded. "I'm sorry I didn't come to Kingshelm's aid. I... I didn't realize what the threat truly was." His eyes turned to Geralt. "Thank you, Geralt, for serving our family all these years."

He gave him a nod of thanks as he pulled himself up onto his horse. Lydia turned to her brother and gave him a tired smile.

"We can't change the past, Aiden. What's done is done, but we can still do something about the future. Maybe in Sahra we can bring this all to an end."

He grunted as he mounted. "You still believe in the New Dawn, sister? After all that has happened?"

She mulled over his words, knowing the road she had traveled. "I have no choice but to believe. It's the only hope we have."

With that she spurred her horse on into the night knowing they had a long road ahead.

14

IMARI

A RARE GRAY SKY hung over the desert as they approached Khala. Something unnatural and foreboding was felt in its presence. Before Khala, the forces of Kingshelm and Leviatanas gathered. Dust rose from the host of men who eager for answers. As they passed by the camp Imari could sense something had changed in the mood of the men from when he had last seen them. That's when the flying of royal banners caught his attention. A small company bearing the colors of Khala came streaming toward them.

"Something has happened," said Khaleena.

"Mhmmm," grunted Lombaku in agreement.

The small band reached them on the outskirts of the city. Impatu, Imamu, Henry, Amira, and, to his surprise, Lancelin were there.

"Prince of Leviatanas, where have you come from?" Imari asked.

"Khosi, it is always an honor. Forgive me for the lack of courtesy, but I bring urgent news," Lancelin said. The other's faces with him told a grim tale.

"What could it be now?"

Henry's eyes darted to Lancelin. Fear flooded them that he could not keep hidden.

Lancelin cleared his throat before speaking, "I was taken captive by the outsiders. They forced me to lead them to the cave you, Henry, and I all dared to tread not long ago," he paused, trembling at his next words.

"By some dark ritual they have brought Maluuk back, along with his army. It will not be long before they arrive. Izel, who has accompanied me, can attest to this news."

Imari sat frozen. Eloy had warned him of dark news, but this? How could they stand against this? His mind returned to the serenity of the High King's face. Somehow Eloy knew this would happen, yet he did not fear what would become of them?

Imari shifted his gaze to each of them. "This is dire news indeed, but I know what we must do."

Henry blinked in astonishment. "You do?"

"We will head west to Sahra. We can make our stand there."

Imari noticed Amira's eyes briefly flicker to Khaleena.

"My brother is right. We have spoken to Eloy and..."

"You have what?" Lancelin said, interrupting.

"He came to us in the desert. I don't know how to explain it, only that he changed me. There had been things... terrible things done to me and somehow he knew. Yet..." Khaleena said.

"It's all right, Khaleena. What has happened is for you and him to know," Imari said, placing a hand on her back. "But his command to me was to lead our armies to Sahra."

"You know what my sister will think with an army marching to our home," Amira said.

Imari cast his gaze downward. "I know, but I have to believe Eloy would send us there for a reason."

"How do you know you didn't just see a mirage?" Henry asked. "How do we know this can be trusted? It is more than a great risk

to walk our armies through the desert to fight a battle when we have walls and fortifications right here."

This time it was Lancelin who spoke up, "Imari tells the truth. There has been more than one who has seen our High King." He gave Imari a reassuring nod. "If Eloy has decreed it, then we will take our forces to Sahra."

Without protest Henry bowed in obedience. "Very well, then."

"It is settled?" asked Imari.

"If this is to be our plan, let me ride ahead. Perhaps I can help persuade my sister of the danger that encroaches on us all," Amira said.

"We will meet you at the Grand Wall," Imari said with an approving nod.

"The wall?" Amira asked.

"It was there our ancestors repelled these foul creatures once. Who's to say we cannot do it again?"

A fateful glance was shared between them knowing that the future of Islandia rested in their care. Imari cleared his throat before issuing the order, "We make our final stand together. Prepare the armies to march."

"One last thing, Khosi," said Henry.

"Yes?"

"Queen Lydia led half our force to New Valkara to depose of Jorn. I told them to gather with us here when they were victorious."

"Send out a messenger bird with new orders. Have them meet us at The Grand Wall."

"I will at once."

With that they dispersed to prepare for the journey ahead. As the others shrank in the distance, he turned to Khaleena. His eyes betrayed the anxiety that gripped him not only for their journey but what awaited them in Sahra. Would Nabila finally stand with them? Or would they be facing two armies instead of one? Khaleena seemed to know his thoughts and placed a comforting hand on his back.

"Whatever we face, brother, we will do it together."

They exchanged a somber look. "It is good to have you at my side once more, sister."

"Don't get soft on me, Khosi. I still need a hardened warrior when we face these hordes of darkness."

"Don't worry yourself, sister. You will have one," he said with eyes ablaze.

Amira had left them with details of a secret path used by the Sycar through the Endless Wastes. The path had led their company through the parched land of red clay and rock in record time. All among them gawked at the depth of the chasm that lay in the heart of the wastes. A void that scarred the land, reminding all who would gaze upon it what it had cost their ancestors to stand against these Felled Ones. He reflected once more on both the danger and beauty of such a place. Chiseled arches of stone stood as markers along their path. Their towering pillars of stone were an ominous companion to the void below. Mesas of tremendous splendor dotted the red horizon ahead, guiding them further into the wastes.

Such a place would consume even the hardiest of warriors carrying an adequate supply of water. After all their careful measurement the constant threat of low supplies still prowled at the back of their minds. Yet, the threat chasing them surpassed all others. It was the catalyst needed to keep them pressing through this valley of death.

The barren rock held no trace of life except for the occasional shrub or a patch of cacti. Even the sighting of a small lizard or snake was a rarity in such a place. He fought the constant reminder of thirst clinging to the back of his throat. It was evident in the eyes of all that the journey was taking its toll. As the cycle of starry heavens and blazing sun continued on their unending path those below started to lose heart.

Even if we arrive at the wall in time, will we still have the strength of a fighting force? he wondered.

He could sense in the nightly meetings between Henry, Lancelin, and Khaleena that all of them feared what this journey would do to morale. On the fifth day hope broke through the dire journey. The edge of a dark structure peaked over the crowded skyline of mesas. As they drew closer, the full grandeur of the Grand Wall came into view. Its presence dominated the open valley before it. The sandstone surface built deep into the Sahra Mountains stretched westward far beyond Imari's vision. Massive towers stood as sentinels against any foreign invader. On their ramparts something new had caught Imari's eye. Each tower was now equipped with large ballistas. Each held within their drawstrings bolts of devastating size. Alongside these, trebuchets lined alternating segments of the wall.

"Nabila has made some upgrades since our last visit," Khaleena said, striding up beside him.

"More for us to use against The Felled Ones," he said. He kept to himself the fear that the defenses might be used against them. Khaleena shared this hidden thought not in words but in a look.

Slowly their army filed out from the cover of the mesa filled landscape and into the daunting shadow of the Grand Wall. Above, Imari could just make out the scurrying activity of Sahra soldiers. He desperately hoped Amira had reached her sister in time to prevent a response from the defenses. A horn bellowed out into the gray sky from behind the wall. Lancelin and Henry simultaneously raised a hand to halt the army at their back. This was the moment of truth.

The loud creaking of a gate sounded out into the valley. From beneath the fortification a small party came riding forth to meet them. While Imari could not distinguish who the riders were, he had a feeling he knew. Soon the royal decor displayed on the mounts spoke of one person. Nabila. The small band stopped a short distance away, waiting for Imari and the others to ride forward to meet them.

As they approached, a royal guard proclaimed, "All hail the Sulta of Sahra. Who rides forth to speak with her wise council?"

The radiant Sulta sat on a gold encrusted horse of bronze coloring. She adorned herself in her favorite crimson sari embroidered with gold. Jewels of dazzling splendor hung loosely from a chain around her head. The crimson lips he loved did not part in a smile at the sight of him. The warriors escorting her wore the golden turbans of the elite city guard, their dark faces like stone. Their warhorses beneath stood like tanks covered in shining armor of rose gold complexion. Beside Nabila was Amira, her olive skin wrapped in simple black cloth, a solemn look covering her face.

"It is Khosi Imari and with him Khaleena, princess of Khala, the esteemed prince Lancelin, and Henry commander of Kingshelm."

Nabila prodded her mount forward. "And why does the Khosi along with his esteemed guests bring an army to our sacred lands?"

"Enough, Nabila!" Imari cried. "You know exactly why we have come."

"You will not speak to the Sulta in such a way you Khalan dog!" One of the royal guards barked.

Nabila raised a hand to silence him.

The same old roads of mistrust and prejudice will be the death of us, he thought before Nabila spoke again.

"Amira has informed me of the threat. Although, this sounds like a danger to Kingshelm, not our own people. We have no quarrel with these outsiders."

"Nabila, this is far more than some outsiders. The Felled Ones have returned and they march on our heels. If we do not stand together we will all die!"

"No!" she snapped. "You have brought this enemy to our doorstep to make it our concern, but you will be marching in the opposite direction very soon." A coldness Imari had never seen filled her eyes as she spoke.

"So you would doom us all?" Imari asked.

"You have doomed yourselves by coming here. I cannot be held to account for your poor leadership."

Imari looked back at the host behind him. It was not only soldiers who accompanied him, thousands upon thousands of Khalans had left their homes because of the trust they had placed in him. He knew already there was no Khala for them to return to. It was either the defenses of the Grand Wall or death.

"We will not turn back."

"Then I cannot be responsible for what happens next."

"I know you, Nabila, and you would never drench your hands in the blood of women and children. If you give the order to attack us, that is exactly what you will be doing."

He could see the tension within her eyes, the fight for who she wanted to be and what her kingdom demanded of her. The question was, who would win? She bit her lip before speaking again.

"You may have one night to rest. Then you and your army must leave these lands. If you do not… then I cannot say what might happen." She turned to leave, casting a glance at her sister.

"Come, Amira."

Amira turned, rage burning within her dark eyes. "No, sister, I will not."

Nabila whirled to face her. "Do not be foolish, sister. You belong to Sahra."

"No, I belong to those who have not forgotten what is truly important." Amira moved her horse toward Imari and the others.

"Ishmar stop her!" Nabila ordered. The royal guard ushered his horse forward but was stopped by Amira's voice.

"Ishmar, we both know what I can do to you. Do not try to stop me."

The guard looked nervously at his Sulta and breathed a sigh of relief when Nabila waved him off.

"Fine, sister, if you wish to perish with them, go."

"We will all perish sooner or later. I wish to do so with my integrity intact," Amira said coolly.

Nabila turned in silence and beckoned her guard to follow.

"Now what?" Henry asked.

"I'm… I'm not sure…" Imari muttered.

The camp broke into a frenzied panic at the news of Sahra's rejection. Voices rang out from all the assembly.

"We left everything to come here!"

"Where will we go?"

"You've led us to our doom! At least we had walls to defend in Khala!"

It took everything within him not to run and hide, but he was their Khosi and the task belonged to no other.

"We will not leave! Sahra must know that they belong to the same kingdom as us. We will make our stand here."

A voice cried out once more from the crowd, "So we let them stab our backs while we wait to be slaughtered by these outsiders?"

"How do you know Sahra hasn't been in on this plot the whole time?" inquired another.

He searched and could find no answer. "We will speak more on this in the morning. Until then, trust that we will find a solution."

Grumbling washed over the crowd, but all in attendance knew there were no other options. It was stand here or die. Perhaps both would be upon them soon. As he stepped away from the dispersing crowd, Lancelin approached him with the Dreadwood girl named Izel at his side.

"Imari, a word?" Lancelin asked.

Imari gave him a tired nod. "What is it, Lancelin?"

The Leviatanas prince motioned to Izel.

"Esteemed Khosi, I wish to share a story with you," she said.

"We have many pressing matters…"

"It's relevant to us," interrupted Lancelin on her behalf.

"Sorry, I'm just tired. Go on," Imari said rubbing his forehead.

Izel showed no sign of offense as she continued, "In my home when the Sombrios arrived, our people were divided. Some families served him, while others resisted."

"What did you do to come together?" Imari asked.

"We didn't," she said with a sternness in her eyes. "And it was because of that many became enslaved to these Felled Ones. Those that didn't… we lived on the run like hunted animals."

Izel let the silence hang between them a moment before continuing. "I do not know the quarrel between your peoples but if you allow it to stop you from standing against what is coming, all of Islandia will be enslaved."

"We must do something, Imari. Can we gain another audience with Nabila? Surely there is something that can convince her?" Lancelin pleaded.

He felt the weight of doubt fill his mind.

"I will see if I can speak with her in private. Maybe I can convince her of some sort of action."

Both Lancelin and Izel smiled at his words, but they felt hollow even as they left his lips. With a polite nod he retreated to his tent. He took care not to catch the stray eyes of those around. The last thing he wanted was to field more questions he had no answers to. With a breath of relief he pushed back the flap of his tent and entered the sanctuary in relief. Attendants hesitantly approached him seeing the worn expression he carried. Behind them stood Impatu, waiting to be summoned.

"I am fine," Imari said waving off the attendants. With begrudging steps he moved toward Impatu.

"My Khosi… that cannot have been easy."

"If words could express," he replied shrinking into a nearby chair. The dim evening sky cloaked the pale sand colored tent in shadow. Flickering torches danced on the canvas sheets and the quiet yawns of neighboring occupants pierced through the thin fabric. All was quiet now, if only his mind could enter the silent chorus. Impatu shuffled awkwardly, unsure of what to say.

"Lost for advice my friend? That is unlike you," he said, letting out a tired chuckle.

"The shadow of fear and confusion grows thick over us all, my Khosi."

The somber words from the typically cheerful Impatu left him feeling cold. What could he do?

He had no confidence in the attempt, but he made sure to keep his promise. A messenger was sent, but even as the evening sky faded to black no word had returned from Sahra. The camp had grown silent as many had retired to sleep. Some he imagined collapsed from the taxing journey they had finished and some for the journey they envisioned ahead.

Sleep eluded him, however. The anxiety of what tomorrow would bring gripped him. Why had Eloy asked him to journey to Sahra? Would they not have been safer in Khala? Deep down he knew the Grand Wall may be the only fortification in all of Islandia that could hold the Felled Ones at bay, and yet his faith in defenses and weapons waned. Such tools had their limits. They sowed only seeds of destruction in the end, leaving death as their lasting mark. What weapons of war could overcome the agents of death itself?

The wind rustled against the canvas covering beside him. Only it wasn't the wind. He sat up with a jolt, Daybreaker in hand. As the sheet of the tent peeled backward it revealed the olive face of Amira.

"What is it?" he asked.

"Word has returned from Nabila. She will speak to you," she said in a hushed tone.

"Will you be coming with?" he asked.

She nodded. "Maybe together we can convince her that this is madness."

"Before we go, I must grab one thing." He shot to his feet. Ushering her to follow they moved discreetly through the camp, avoiding any unneeded attention. At a heavily guarded tent he finally stopped.

"What is it you want from there?" Amira asked.

"You'll see," he said with a knowing look on his face.

He pushed back the tent flap and revealed a room full of various armor and weaponry. The familiar personable face of Henry turned from his work to greet them. His muscled arms stopped their work of sharpening his sword.

"What can I help you with, Khosi?"

"I need the blade I asked you to keep for me while we journeyed."

Without a word Henry moved to a chest that rested near the tent's frame. With the turn of a key he had pulled from his tunic, the chest opened. He lifted the crimson scabbard with reverence from the container. Slowly he turned and extended Dawn's Light to Imari. Imari took the scimitar in hand and faced Amira.

"Khosi, I…"

"This sword belongs to your family. Maybe with this gift Nabila will see we are allies in this war against a common enemy. Much like our ancestors who stood at this same precipice so long ago."

"Best of luck," Henry said turning back to his work.

Imari smiled at the awestruck Amira.

"How could you trust us with such a weapon after everything?"

"Sometimes it takes faith to see the possibility of reconciliation where others cannot."

Without another word he turned to exit the tent. The dark of night had taken its place in the heavens. A dazzling array of stars filled the

sky. Their shining gems illuminated the dark path until they reached
the great shadow that blotted out all around it. The Grand Wall stood
as a towering menace in the night. Its ramparts and towers seemed to
be a great beast that loomed overhead. The feeling of smallness was
never more prevalent to him.

A crack pierced the impenetrable depths and sent a sliver of light
bursting out from the base of the wall. A host of guards came forth
to usher them into the belly of the beast. They were escorted up a
torchlit set of stone stairs until they came to a small oak door. A pair
of guards opened it to reveal a square room filled with simple decor.
Nabila stood over a table covered in maps. Her gaze rose to meet them
as they were ushered in. She raised a hand for them to step forward
and with a look dismissed the guards. As the door shut behind them
she began to speak.

"You wished to see me?" Nabila asked.

Imari swallowed knowing each word was precious. "I did."

"Then speak." Her captivating face showed no patience for flattery
or persuasion. Only a cool calculation lay beneath her dark eyes.

"First, I have a gift." He motioned to Amira who stepped forward
unbuckling the Dawn Blade at her hip.

"Dawn's Light returned to its proper home," he said.

Nabila clasped her hand around the decorated hilt and withdrew
the sword from its scabbard. A smile crossed her face at the restored
blade. No longer did a black mist haunt its frame. Instead a radiant hue
of golden light painted the edges. Reverently she sheathed the drawn
blade and placed it on the table.

"A very fine gift indeed."

"It is the same blade used by our ancestors when they stood together
against this same threat here on this wall."

Nabila's eyes narrowed. "A symbolic gesture then?"

"Nabila, my love, if there is still any warmth between us, then
please listen to me."

"There is…" she said looking down at Dawn's Light. She sent a slender finger tracing the intricate hilt. Slowly her dark eyes rose to meet his. "That's why I must do this."

"Do what?"

The door burst open behind them as a squadron of guards piled into the room armed to the teeth.

"What are you doing, sister?" Amira growled.

"You two are the only family I have left. I won't lose you both because you insist on fighting for a lost cause."

"So, what? You're holding us captive?"

"Yes, for your protection."

"Nabila! Every man, woman, and child out there will die if you do not let them in behind this wall!" he cried.

"They are not my responsibility, and now you are free of them as well."

"Sister, do not let our people's prejudice blind you to what is right. You know this is evil!"

"What of my sister, Nabila?" Imari pleaded.

The Sulta turned away as a small tear rolled down her cheek. "Please, both of you, if you do not wish for bloodshed surrender peacefully."

Imari felt the guard behind him move to grab Daybreaker from his grip. It was a second that would decide the future of all. In that blink of a moment he released the spear.

"I will not resort to violence to stop violence," he said. "But know this, Nabila, every one of them outside that wall whose blood is shed is on your hands."

She remained silent with her back turned to them. The tug of the guard told him it was time to go. Where, he could only guess, but everything within him dreaded what was to come.

15: PART 1

LANCELIN

A N OMINOUS WALL of dark clouds filled the north and eastern sky. Like a stalking predator it moved in silence, inching ever closer. As he surveyed the horizon something caught his eye. A small flash of movement. They barreled forward at astonishing speed straight toward their encampment. With uncertainty gripping his mind he knew he must act. The early morning hours left many still clinging to sleep in their tents, but he knew he could count on Henry, Khaleena, and Izel to be awake. Sure enough they sat pouring over a small map discussing a plan to retreat toward the Dreadwood to make a final stand.

"I saw a group moving toward us from the north," he said bursting into the tent out of breath.

"Do you think it could be our forces from the north?" asked Henry as he shot up from his seat.

"I have a feeling," Lancelin smiled.

Imari's strange absence had been another blow to the beleaguered group. Any good news was welcome. All of them rushed to the edges of the camp, eagerly awaiting a friendly arrival. Their new found hope faded as the remnant of Kingshelm and Leviatanas forces drew near. It was not an army numbering in the thousands that arrived. What remained was only a ragtag group of soldiers numbering in the hundreds. As the meager host reached the camp, Lancelin could see every face carried the look of sheer exhaustion. Gaunt horses snorted and collapsed as they were finally given the order to rest. Many slumped off their steeds in weary relief.

Lancelin scanned each face searching for the High Queen or Geralt. Henry's voice came calling for them to gather to him. Lancelin brushed past those filing into the camp until he reached the source of the voice. He was taken aback at the sight. Lydia had arrived along with her trusted guardian and brother. Each of them sapped of all their strength.

A streak marred her leather plated armor and a large gash had formed across her cheek. Geralt's weathered face looked relatively the same, but his eyes revealed the look of a road weary traveler. Aiden was in the worst shape of the three. An injury to his leg left him barely able to walk. His disheveled locks and half-closed eyes told a story all their own. Lancelin found himself rushing to the three of them, wrapping each of them in a warm embrace.

"Lancelin, you're alive?" Lydia asked with astonishment.

"It's a long story, my Queen. I can explain it later."

"Good, because we are short on time," Geralt said in his typical grumpy tone.

"Why… why are you all camped outside the wall?" Lydia asked. She could barely restrain the weariness in her voice.

Henry shared a solemn glance with Lancelin and the now approaching Khaleena.

"Nabila has decided not to allow us passage beyond the wall," Khaleena said.

"What?" Geralt snapped.

"So we came all this way?" Aiden asked before stopping himself with a pathetic chuckle.

"What was her reasoning?" Lydia asked.

"She claimed this was our fight and that we have brought our war to their realm. Same Sahra shuka as always," Khaleena replied.

"What happened to the army?" Henry asked looking at the remainder of their forces.

"This is it. Jorn is dead, but he somehow was able to summon the Felled Ones again. We didn't stand a chance," Geralt said.

"I can explain how that was possible later. It's part of the long story," said Lancelin. "How much time do we have before they arrive?"

"Time? There is no time," Geralt said forebodingly.

"You mean..." Henry's voice trailed off.

"Our route to the Dreadwood is gone," Izel said as she appeared behind them.

"There is no road beyond this place. They have us surrounded. It was the Grand Wall or nothing," Aiden said, disheartened.

"So, what is the plan?" Geralt asked staring into each of their eyes. "There has to be a plan."

All looked downcast, for every plan, every hope had vanished.

"It's best you get any rest you can. If what you say is true, you may not have another chance," Henry advised.

The mood surrounding the camp was grim as the dark clouds continued their slow crawl forward. Lancelin found himself wandering aimlessly through the gloomy looks and frantic faces of the men. The sun now rose over the crest of the horizon, signaling the time had come for a decision. To their backs the daunting wall threatened to cut them down with darts and stone. Before them the forces of darkness gathered to tear them to pieces with claw and fang. Either way, doom stared them in the face.

As if stirring from a dream, he found himself standing before Henry and Geralt who stooped over yet another map.

"It's our only chance. We send all our forces at once to the gate and break our way into the wall," Henry said stroking his chin.

"A lot of people will die," Geralt commented soberly.

"No matter what we do, many will die. But it's the difference between all of us and most of us."

The grizzled warrior let out a sigh. "So be it. I'll go tell some of the men to throw together something we can batter the gate with."

"We move on the hour. It's best we catch them by surprise," Henry said. Geralt turned to leave at the order. As he passed Lancelin, he placed a hand on his shoulder sharing a look of concern.

"So that's the plan?" Lancelin asked.

Henry's face turned defensive. "It's the best we have."

"Then we will make it work. What would you have me do?"

"Speak with those close to you. It may be the last time you do."

Lancelin's mind reeled at the words. For some reason the imminent doom that approached took on a new reality at the finality of Henry's advice.

"Of course," he said, bowing.

Henry stared at the map of open plains and the Grand Wall they would soon be pressing upon. Lancelin could see a nervous twitch of a finger as Henry tapped away. The man's eyes searched for any other answer. He left him to scour for a solution. Only a short list remained of those he wished to speak with one last time. The queen had become a dear friend of his over the last year, even if they didn't always see eye to eye. Then there was Izel. She had endured more by his side than most he knew. These two were all that remained.

Sure there was Geralt, but he was never one for sentimental farewells, and Imari dwelled in the very place they would soon storm. Many of the captains and commanders of Leviatanas' forces were either killed or so new he barely could recall their names. A deep sorrow settled over his heart at such a short list. Where once the kingdom was a place of many beloved and cherished friends, it had now become a barren waste of bones and dust. For a moment he questioned why he still fought for such a place, but the figure of Eloy passing between the dead trees flashed across his mind.

The High King... the one he desired to speak with more than any other. The man who had forgiven him, restored him, called him, and died for him. Could he truly be alive? The miraculous breaking of his bonds could be explained no other way, but, if he was alive, how could they be in such a place?

A recollection came flooding to his mind, a proverb written from an ancient scribe. "The desert is a place of trial, the wasteland a place to discover the truth." Where they stood was a trial indeed. He understood the barren places being a test but the last part of the phrase always confused him. How could one discover truth in a place like this? To his great surprise something inside him seemed to answer back. *We find the truth of who we are and what we trust in the darkest places.* He gripped that thought, knowing what he must trust. If Imari had encountered Eloy and he had brought them here there must be a reason. In this he found renewed strength as he went to find Izel among the tents.

She was mending a wound of a small child when he found her. The boy's leg had been sliced against the jagged rock of the surrounding terrain. As he watched her work he couldn't help but admire the tender care with which she treated the wound. Here was a woman who had lost everything and everyone she ever cared for and yet she pressed on. Suddenly the beauty and courage of this women opened before him. As if with new eyes he saw who this young Dreadwood woman was all along. It wasn't just this boy. Countless times she had risked her life for him. Whether it was the Dreadwood, The Forest's Edge, or Kingshelm when he needed someone, she had been there. She looked up at him, tucking away a black strand of her hair that had fallen loose. Her caramel eyes stared quizzically back into his own.

"Can I help you, Lancelin?" she asked.

Her words shook him from his gawking. A flush of heat rushed up his neck at the discovery of his stare. "Uh, yes, actually. May I join you?"

She patted the ground next to her and turned to the young boy she had been tending. "It will heal, just stay off it as much as you can for the next few days, okay? And make sure to apply the herbs I gave your mother."

"Thank you," sniffled the boy as he scurried away.

Lancelin couldn't bring himself to think what fate awaited the injured and fragile when they made their assault. He watched as the little boy scampered back to his tent with new strength. He fought back the haunting images of war and death that raced through his mind. At its center lay a crippled boy, a victim of it all.

"Are you going to sit?" asked Izel.

He gave her a weak smile as he plopped to the ground.

"Henry wants us to make an assault on the wall within the hour. The hope is that at least a few can make it behind the defenses before the Felled Ones arrive."

Izel sat up straight in disbelief. "And what of those who are not fighting men? What will happen to them? Besides that, if we break down the very gates we will need to protect us, what will keep us safe? Is Henry mad?"

He lifted a hand to calm her. "He's desperate. We all are. I don't like the plan either, but what choice do we have?"

Izel bit her lip as she sank back to the ground. "None." He could see the tears begin to well up in her eyes. "Why is this world so cruel, Lancelin? Why must the innocent be treated so?"

Gently he placed his arm around her. "I don't know."

A silent moment washed over them. It was finally time to share their grief without shame or reserve, for they knew it was likely their last. After some time he spoke again.

"I am sorry I brought you and Zuma into all this. If it wasn't for me..."

She placed a finger to his lips. "You did not bring anything on us, Lancelin. If it was not for you we would still be in the Dreadwood, enslaved to that monster. That is why Zuma gave his life for you."

"I don't deserve..."

"None of us do, but that should not stop us, should it?" she said with a faint smile. "I will not give up until my last breath. I cannot. I won't let them win without a fight."

"Neither will I," he said as he took her hand in his. They watched in companionable silence as the storm clouds drew ever closer.

GERALT:

The troops had been rallied and only one task remained for him. He couldn't miss the High Queen's red hair in a crowd. She stood giving encouragement to the men being suited for arms. As he approached she greeted him with a smile and motioned for him to follow. She stopped between a cluster of tents away from the gathering noise as all mustered for their coming assault.

"I'm glad you found me before..." she couldn't bring herself to finish.

"This might not be the end, lass."

"Stop, Geralt. When did you become an optimist," she said with a feigned chuckle.

He searched for words but none came.

"I'm sorry. You were trying to be kind."

"It's all right, lass. Never easy, this part of battle. In the thick of it there isn't time to think, but before... well you have nothing to do but think. To think of all you could lose. That it might just be you who doesn't walk away."

"Geralt."

"I... love you, lass. Like my own kin. There has been no greater pleasure than to serve you. I just want... I just don't want to do this without letting you know."

"Oh, Geralt," she said as she fell on his neck. She fought to speak but the sobs had overcome her.

He gently pulled her away. "Come. It's time."

She let out a weak sniff as she wiped away her tears. "Aiden has gathered with the front line. I told him he was a Valkaran fool with his injury, but he won't stand for anyone else taking the risk."

"He's bullheaded, but behind it he's got heart."

She gave him a fragile smirk. "Ya got that right," she said letting her thick Valkaran accent ring true.

In reflection, he found he had come to admire that accent after all. It was the sound of a proud and strong people. Quick to anger, easy to upset, yet hardy and true. He was proud to fight one last time at their side.

"I believe this belongs to you," he said unbuckling Dawnbreaker from his waist and handing it to her. She took the sword in hand, feeling its weight with a few measured swings.

"I will use it well," she said sheathing the blade. With one last hug they parted. Lydia to her duties as High Queen and him to the front of the fight.

Shuffling through the last of the remaining tents he found his place among the front lines of the assault. The princess Khaleena stood exhorting the Bomani around her. Her thick black braids were wound tightly in a bun atop her head. Her sharp featured face stern and ready for war. Of all the Khalans she was the last one he would want to face in battle. The Bomani surrounding her carried passion in their eyes. The lack of fear in them took him aback. Khaleena turned to welcome him into their ranks.

"I'm glad to see the Khalans show no signs of fear for our coming task," he said.

A young Khalan warrior, lean with muscle and sharp features stepped forward. "It is not that we do not fear. All men face fear in battle. It's that we have learned what to do with it."

"The name given to me is Impatu," the young Khalan said, extending a hand.

Geralt exchanged the courtesy, grasping Impatu's forearm in the typical Khalan fashion.

"Glad we have you on our side," Geralt said looking Khaleena and Impatu in the eyes.

"They have my brother. If Nabila thinks she can keep the Khosi captive without a fight from the Bomani…."

"She would be making a fatal mistake," Impatu said finishing her sentence.

"Best of luck to you when things start," Geralt said.

"We have more than luck on our side. We have skill," Khaleena said, smirking.

She and Impatu gave a courteous nod before turning to finish giving their instructions to the fighting men. Geralt continued to wander until he found Henry barking out orders and making the final adjustments to the first wave of men who would descend upon the wall. Many pieces of wood, metal, and leather had been thrown together for shielding against the onslaught of projectiles they would soon face. Even women and children had been armed with anything they could use to fend off an attack. Henry's eyes could not mask the fear and anxiety that lay beneath them as he approached.

"Geralt."

"Henry."

"It's almost time," Henry said nervously.

Geralt placed a reassuring hand on his shoulder. "Calm yourself, commander. This will not be easy no matter what we do. Whatever happens isn't your fault."

"Sorry, friend, I can't think that way."

Geralt let out a chuckle. "Neither can I. So let's win, all right?"

Henry gave him a solemn nod. Suddenly a deep and deafening roar shattered the silence. Each man around them threw their hands up to their ears trying to blunt the sound. As it finally died away Geralt turned toward the horizon. Covering its edge as far as he could see stood an endless horde of dark figures. The storm clouds that had slowly followed them now rested over the foul army. More Felled Ones than Geralt imagined possible stood ready for battle.

"Battle lines!" Henry shouted.

Darting in front of their army was a rider on a white horse. Her fire kissed hair flowing with power and strength behind her. In a nervous rush all settled into their assigned positions. With a roaring voice High Queen Lydia rallied them.

"Men of Islandia, we face our hour of doom! Doom behind us and doom before us! But we have faced the dark night already. We have tasted fear in every measure, yet here we are. Let us go now, not as those who fear the darkness, but those who carry the light. Join me now in our doom and glory! Men of Islandia!"

The response filled the air, "A lion's roar they hear. They fear his cry. They fear to die. They know the men of Eloy are here!"

He couldn't help but allow the grin to sneak onto his face. "Now that's a speech, lass."

With one last shout the battle lines charged toward the Grand Wall. A wave of doomed men and women ready to die.

IMARI:

The door of his prison swung open blinding him with the invading light. As he blinked away the temporary blindness Nabila focused into view.

"What is it you want?" he snarled.

"I'm saving your life, Imari. The least you can do is show some gratitude."

He stopped trying to fight her, realizing it was to no avail.

"Come," she said motioning for him to step out of the cell. He stepped out into the dim and dank stone hallway. The faint creak of a door a few cells down revealed Amira being pulled from her imprisonment as well.

"What is it now, sister?" Amira asked as she was marched toward them.

"I want you to see why I have done what I've done." Without another word Nabila ordered the guards beside her to march them forward. Down the dark inner chambers of the wall they walked until they were led to a room with a small slit that peered outside the wall. The early morning sun barely pierced through the ever growing mass of clouds in the sky. As they were made to stare out onto the plains, they could see tiny dots moving into formation.

"Your friends are moving against us, so it would seem there is more to your coming here than you let on," Nabila said, examining them.

"They move on you because you have given them no choice!" Imari snapped.

"Regardless, they leave us no choice but to fire upon them."

"Nabila, this isn't you! You know this is wrong. Don't let the pressure of your people steer you to evil."

"Not all of us think as they do," Amira added.

"I... have no choice," Nabila said, showing the first sign of the burden she carried.

"Who cares what the bureaucrats or the mob think, Nabila! There won't be any of them left if we don't stand together now," Amira pleaded.

"They won't see it that way. When all we worked for will be exposed to outsiders."

"You mean, when we won't be able to horde it all for ourselves?" Amira asked pointedly.

"How long have the people of Sahra lived under the shadow of oppression? How long have they suffered because of our family? Finally they have hope. Children can play in the streets without fear, water flows freely, the people live with a new sense of life. Because of us! Now you want me to risk all that again, for what?"

"You will lose it regardless if you do not stand with us. You may even lose more than that. Is Sahra's riches worth your very being?" Imari asked.

"You think me a monster like my father don't you, Imari? That I would slay any who stood in the way of my power? I am not my father, but I am no fool either. Your people had ample time to flee from here. They chose to stay, and now they will endure the consequence."

"Could they really flee?" Imari asked directing his head to the slitted window.

With narrowed eyes Nabila stared out at the horizon. Suddenly her eyes shot open in shock as she rushed to the window's frame for a closer look. A vast host of dark specters stretched beyond sight. It was an army unlike any other that had walked the world. Nabila stepped away, trembling.

"What... what is that?"

"It is the darkness we have warned you of. It has come, and not just for us," said Imari.

"My Sulta, the forces of Khala and Kingshelm are moving toward the wall. Should I give the order to fire?" asked a captain who stood guarding the room.

Nabila did not break from her stupor.

"Sulta?" asked the guard.

"Even together we could not face such a host... who can stand against them?" she mumbled to herself.

"Nabila! You cannot face such a foe alone, let us help you!" Imari begged.

"Sulta, what is your order?"

The shouts of a charging army echoed below as they came rushing toward the wall. Nabila stood frozen, staring out at the blackened horizon. Finally she turned to the waiting captain.

"Open the gates."

"Sulta?" he asked in shock.

"I said open the gates."

With a rigid bow the captain moved to give the order.

"Nabila, thank you," Imari said with weary smile.

"I suppose we can all die together."

15: PART 2

LYDIA

S HE BRACED FOR the arrows that would soon come crashing down, but, to her surprise, no hail of darts arrived. Instead the large gate ahead slowly opened. A squadron of guards came sprawling out, waving a banner of peace. She lifted her sword, slowing the army at her back. With more than a little suspicion, she rode forward to meet the emissaries sent from Sahra.

"The Sulta Nabila bids you take up the defenses alongside us," said the captain.

"She wants us to join you?" Lydia asked, allowing her caution to tint her words.

The captain dressed in the crimson robes that distinguished his rank licked his lips. "Yes, our Sulta now sees the enemy we face and wishes to join forces."

Now that the threat is real you will show compassion, she thought disgustedly. She stared at each of the guards, making clear her disdain for their cowardice.

"We will accept your hospitality. I give you leave to dispense us where we are needed most along the defenses."

A surprised smile crossed the captain's face. "Most generous, Queen of Kingshelm."

"Just know if there is any hint of treachery it will be met with unimaginable force."

The captain gulped at the words but quickly stiffened his back. "Of course. You should expect the greatest of Sahra's hospitality."

"Good." Without waiting for a reply she turned her steed back to the waiting army. As she approached, Henry broke from the host along with Geralt, Lancelin, and Khaleena.

"What's the word?" asked Henry.

"It looks as if the Sulta has changed her mind after seeing what awaits them when they were finished with us." Her eyes lifted to the encroaching army.

"Word on Imari?" Khaleena asked.

Lydia shook her head. "I'm sure he is okay."

"We should hurry. We don't want anyone caught out in the open when the Felled Ones arrive," Lancelin advised.

"Wise words. Henry, go with the Sahra captains and make plans on where to station our men. Lancelin, give the order to allow the women and children to enter beyond the wall first." She paused as her eyes fell to Khaleena.

"Go and find your brother. I am sure it will lift the spirits of the Bomani."

Khaleena's face cracked with a smile. "Thank you, Lydia."

"You have your orders."

The others bowed and sped toward their duties. *When did they start looking to me for answers?* she wondered. She felt the loss of Titus at her side the most in moments like these. How she longed to stand together with him again. Her thoughts melted away at the sight of Aiden limping toward her.

"So the Sulta is feeling generous now?" he asked.

"It seems so."

"What would you have of me?"

"To fight like a Valkaran."

A wide grin stretched across his face. "That I can do."

It wasn't long before the last of their forces found their way behind the protection of the Grand Wall, and just in time. Like a deadly storm rolling in from sea, the army of the Felled Ones would soon break against all the Grand Wall had to offer. Lydia found herself near the center of the action. The Sahra commanders had come to the decision to spread their forces across the vast ramparts. Not an inch stood uncovered by a defender or a weapon of war. Soon they would need every one of them. As the Felled Ones approached she could see legions of men leading them.

"Ulric and his outsiders," she scowled.

The ominous clouds now covered the sky overhead, washing the desert stone in colorless tones. Thousands upon thousands of silver eyes stared out from the ghouls beneath them. No army like it had ever been assembled. Every manner of beast they had faced and more now stood ready on The Wastes. Corrupted men and monster alike stood ready to throw the full force of their hatred at them.

Good, she thought. *They will need all they can muster.*

A crack of lightning crossed the rainless sky, and so the assault began. In eerie silence the host before them moved toward the wall. A cry rang out amidst the breezeless air. "Fire!"

The thrumming of bolts and the satisfying thump of stone followed. In a devastating impact the projectiles landed among the enemy taking out hundreds with the first wave of fire. Still they moved without any hesitation, and, to the great dismay of the Sahra warriors, only Ulric's men remained slain.

"They are not made of the right material…" she found herself muttering.

"What was that?" asked the captain beside her.

"Eloy gave us special weapons known as Light Bringers. Only they can slay Maluuk's army."

The captain's eyes grew wide. "You mean to tell me our defenses are useless?"

"Not entirely. You need to focus on the enemy that still look like men." She pointed to the banner of the crescent moon leading The Outsiders.

The captain nodded and barked out the new order, "Focus all fire at that banner!"

The command reverberated down the wall. The next wave sent a hail of death streaming at Ulric and his men. Cries of agony reached their ears as more Outsiders were slain. Again the waves of rock and steel were sent out. Again they found their mark leaving a trail of bodies behind the marching legions.

A dark and ominous object came into her view. Out from the cover of the mesas dozens of towers streamed forth. Their height doubled any siege weapon she had seen. Her attention was pulled back as the first wave of foes drew near. From their midst arose ladders of lofty height. Their hooks came driving over the wall's parapet locking them into place. The Outsiders were first to attempt the deadly climb.

Crossbow fire rained up at the defenders to cover their climb. Lydia picked up a bow along with all the others to return fire. Reloading, she turned to the captain.

"Whatever we do, we can't let the Felled Ones on the wall, otherwise we are doomed!"

"How can we stand against them without the proper weapons?" he asked.

She looked around at the few men of her own who had been struck down by crossbow fire. "Pick up their swords."

The captain gave her a shrewd look and turned to his officers. "Share the order. Pick up the white bladed swords from the dead!"

The officers around them nodded as they notched another arrow to their bow. A wave of darts dotted the sky as they rained onto the attackers. She watched as a man was struck in the neck, leaving him in a free fall to the desert floor below. A short distance away, the first of the enemy leaped onto the ramparts. The Sahra and Kingshelm defenders quickly surged to the spot. The clang of steel now flooded the air. All of it was a distraction to turn their eyes and weapons away from the coming towers.

"Whatever it takes bring those towers down!" she cried.

The swift response of the ballistic's engineers resulted in several darts crashing into the towers nearest the wall. They creaked from the inflicted wound, but kept trodding forward in a steady pace.

"We need fire!" she barked at those who managed the weaponry.

Archers and engineers alike lit their projectiles and sent them flying. Several hit their target, starting a small flicker along the tops of a nearby tower. Soon the spark burst into a blaze that sent a deadly fire roaring across the siege engine. Felled Ones and men alike heaved themselves from the tower, illuminating the night as living torches.

The growing sound of conflict drew her attention back to the scene on the wall. She could see the flash of Geralt's sword as he entered the fray. He had insisted that he be assigned to a place close to her own. The opposing forces clashed with reckless abandon as they met with his men. This would be a battle written in history, she knew, and each man fought as though he knew it too. She only hoped it would be history worth remembering. Her eyes were glued to the conflict as Geralt strained to keep the invaders at bay.

One tower remained steadily trodding to their section of the defenses. Its looming presence cast a deep shadow over them all. Inside awaited the first of the Felled Ones, ready to devour flesh.

The archers focused all their attention to bring it down. Yet no flame would catch. A few flickering darts protruded from its side to no avail. Suddenly a ladder hooked in front of her. A man fastened with black armor and adorned with a blood red moon leaped from its rungs and over the parapet. His face was covered by a mask, its features the face of a demon. With ease he cut down two defenders with a thin curved blade.

More warriors rushed to meet him and more fell by his sword. She knew she must act before more would meet such a fate. Unsheathing Dawnbreaker, she moved to meet him. The warrior perked up as he saw her draw near. Bringing his sword before him, he eagerly awaited the worthy opponent. She leaped into the air bringing with her a downward slash. The Osaka warrior raised his own in defense but found it melted away as the two blades collided. Dawnbreaker tore with ease through the plates of armor, sinking deep into flesh. With a cry of both terror and agony the man fell to his knees, blood flowing from the cracked chest plate. He removed his mask with all his remaining strength. Caramel eyes stared into her own.

The seasoned warrior's face was decorated with wrinkled lines across its features. Each a tale of countless battles he had endured over the years. With labored breath he ushered out his final words, "You... will not... win."

She could see behind his faded caramel eyes a sense of dread and warning in the words. As if the fact was both a curse to his ears and the reality he had come to believe. She realized these men were an enemy that both resented their freedom and admired their stand. With one last breath the man from Osaka collapsed, leaving Lydia with a sense of hollow victory.

GERALT:

The battle was growing fierce as more invaders poured over the wall. He could see in the distance that the dreaded siege tower still had not fallen. His mind was forced back to his surroundings as a flash of steel filled his peripherals. He raised his sword with no time to spare. The ringing of steel pierced his ears and, with a reflex that could only be achieved from years of training, he slipped his sword under the man's guard sending it into his abdomen.

A sickening gurgle burst from the man's throat as he fell to the ground. He surveyed the battle once more and found that the tower was now only a few yards away.

"Men! Move to the tower! We cannot let the Sahra forces face the Felled One," he barked.

How could they have been so foolish to forget Sahra's weapons would be useless in this fight? he thought to himself. He rushed past the Sahra soldiers as they looked to fill the void he and his men had made. With a loud thud the door of the tower dropped onto the ramparts. A flood of menacing creatures came bursting forth to meet them. Like a tide they washed over the defenders who stood to face them. Even those equipped with Light Bringers were repelled by the onslaught.

Knowing he must stem the tide, he took Light Bringer in hand and jumped into the fray. He cut down a spider like creature, its legs buckling as he tore them free of its master. With another swing of his sword, he sent a deadly blow against the head of one of the large mouthed monstrosities. More and more came to face him and all fell by his sword. He noticed the attention of their forces begin to solely manifest on him. That's when the chant rose above the noise of battle. A foul sounding name was repeated.

"Draugr."

"Draugr."

"Draugr."

It echoed out until all grew silent as a manlike beast came storming from the siege engine. Its hair was long and matted. Lifeless eyes held the silver sheen of all Felled Ones, but his features remained human. His size was enormous and he wore no armor. Raw muscle was covered with dark and ruinous markings. Each testifying of the deeds he had done in the service of Maluuk. In his hand was an axe made of an ebony colored substance.

With a thundering roar the beast rushed to him. Spittle and foam flew from its mouth. With a great leap he swept downward with his axe cracking the ground where Geralt once stood. Geralt could feel the presence of both forces backing away to let the two of them fight.

"Thanks for the help," he muttered to those behind him. In return, all he received were terrified stares.

Draugr came charging once more. This time with a side swipe of its axe. It took all of Geralt's strength to repel the blow, and even still it sent him crashing into the parapet. With a quick roll he dodged the next swing that sent chunks of wall shattering into the air. It was in this moment the face of Draugr caught his attention. Behind all the markings and silver eyes he recognized this thing that was once a man.

"Fairand?" he said peering at the brute's face.

All he received in response was a gargled war cry, but he knew this thing had once been the esteemed commander of the Hillmen who had fought at his side on the Terras Plains. Where he once held only distain for this creature, compassion and pity took its place. He had traded service to Maluuk for his life, and it had cost him his soul. How many more Hillmen filled the ranks of that army beyond the wall? How many of them suffered horrid sacrifice rather than be turned into a slave?

In his distraction the next swing came from Draugr. It caught his sword, wrenching it from his hand. He now stood unarmed before his deformed kinsman. The beast formerly known as Fairand lifted the axe to deliver the finishing blow. That's when an autumn blur pounced over him. The flash of golden light streaked across the mountainous fiend. Before him stood Lydia, Dawnbreaker in hand and at her feet the head of Draugr.

The Felled Ones who had gathered around to witness the fight backed away at the sight of her weapon. With a fearless cry that would make her father Doran proud she ushered their men to press the attack. Filled with a newfound courage, they championed her battle cry and charged. She turned to him extending a hand.

"Now, now does the mighty Geralt need a shield-maiden to save him?"

He rolled his eyes but accepted the help, "Save it."

She smirked before rushing off, sending a teasing command as she went, "Ya best find your sword, yer going to need it."

He couldn't help but grin. A soldier came rushing to his side offering him back his blade.

"Come on, we don't want them to have all the fun," he said as he took it in hand.

LANCELIN:

Off in the distance he could see a tower had reached the center of the wall. They had their own problems to deal with. As Ulric's men approached, the main host of his forces had broken off and headed toward their section, likely thinking it would be less guarded than where the royal standards flew. They would be right to think it. If The Outsiders reached the top of the wall, they would soon be overrun. He glanced over at Izel who was ordering a battalion of archers to rain down fire at the climbing attackers.

For now it worked to keep Ulric's men at bay, but eventually some would be able to reach them. As he peered over the wall to see what progress the enemy had made, he could see shields covered by arrows slowly plodding up the dizzying heights. They had a tower of their own to worry about as well. It would soon draw within arrow fire taking away the precious bolts used to hold those on the ladders at bay. It was only a matter of time.

"Fire!" came the order from a nearby Sahra captain. The first wave of blazing darts crashed into the nearing siege tower. The hopeful flames quickly turning to embers. Another wave filled the sky bathing the hosts below in flickering light. Lancelin turned to the captain giving the orders.

"When that tower reaches the wall…"

"If it reaches the wall," interrupted the captain.

"If," Lancelin repeated, annoyed. "You must have your men dip their swords in oil and light them. It is the only thing that will affect these monsters.

The captain gave him a sideways look.

"Trust me," Lancelin said.

"Fine, but not until they reach the wall."

With the confirmation he moved with haste to Izel.

"We are running out of arrows," she said as he approached.

"I know. Soon we will have no choice but to confront them on the ramparts." He gave her a nervous look.

"I'll be fine. I may be at my best with a bow, but you did show Zuma and me how to use a sword, don't forget."

"When the fighting starts just stay by my side okay?"

Moving close she gently kissed his cheek. "Of course."

He couldn't help but feel the red creeping up his neck. "I don't need any distractions."

She smirked but her smile quickly faded as her gaze fixed behind him. He turned to see the first of Ulric's men climbing over the walls. Withdrawing his sword he didn't hesitate to fend them off. Dawn's Deliverer made quick work of them. Even as those on the ladders fell to his blade, he could see the dreaded tower was almost at the wall. He watched as an arrow from Izel whizzed by, hitting its mark. A small fire had caught just below the door giving them a faint ray of hope.

"Concentrate fire on the tower!" he shouted above the noise of battle. With swift obedience a wave of arrows fueled the growing flames. The flickering fire whipped into a growing frenzy. The siege weapon's door was now ablaze just as it reached the wall. It crashed into the defenses, sending shards of wood and metal flying into the air. A host of defenders were thrown back into the perilous drop below. Ulric's men who had been waiting to assault the walls leaped from the crumbling structure. They were met with the end of swords and spears alike. A small group of them were able to land safely along the allure, and that's when Lancelin saw him.

Ulric along with several others were slicing their way through the wall's defenders. He felt his blood boil at the sight of the man. With animal fury he rushed to meet them. Dawn Blade in hand, he cast aside Ulric's entourage with ease. Their weapons turned to ash at the touch of his own.

"Ulric!" he cried pointing the tip of his blade at the lonely foe.

A cocky grin stretched across the man's face. "Should have killed you myself. But now it looks like I've been given a second chance for my mistakes."

"Why? Why would you serve such a monster? Do you not see that all he does is bring destruction and death?"

Ulric's face shifted as he looked around them. Beneath a coat of floating embers the dead and dying littered the wall. Wails of those being cut down filled their ears. Death was the filter all around them.

"You think I have a choice?" he asked.

"We always have a choice."

"Naive," Ulric sneered. "The story I told you and your friends, it wasn't a lie. Maluuk does rule the world and he takes and he takes." There was a bitter hatred in his words. "But he also gives to those who will bow the knee. This fate would have been avoided had you only listened the first time. In fact, it was you who failed. You see, my father wanted to live by the old way of things, too. But it would have destroyed our people. Maluuk came to me with an offer to save my home if only we would serve him. So... I did what needed to be done, unlike you."

In that moment it dawned on Lancelin. Staring at Ulric now was like looking into a mirror. He was not unlike himself. Ulric was royalty, had charisma, and a passion for his people. He even believed Maluuk could offer him the power to save those he loved. At one time he had thought all these things could be true as well. Until... until Eloy had returned.

"What's that look?" Urlic said, annoyed. "Don't pity me! It should be me who pities you. You are the one who is about to die here. It's your home that is destroyed. Not mine! I saved my people! I have given everything for them!"

It was pity he felt for this ruined man. He had believed the lie that what he truly wanted was the good of others, while the allure of power ate away at his core. He had become a hollow shell in the hands of his master. He could no longer see that it was by his own hands that all this pain, all this death, was due to his master. He had become his tool through which he could pour out his wrath.

Ulric rushed at him with primal rage, forgetting the weapon that lay in Lancelin's hands. With one quick motion of Dawn's Deliverer Ulric was stopped in his tracks. In his careless anger he committed to the blow and found it a fatal mistake. The sound of his sword hitting the cold stone rang across the wall. Lancelin looked down at the feeble man clutching a stump for an arm. A stream of blood poured from the wound and gathered in a pool beneath him. All his majestic garments now ruined by the crimson liquid. Everything he had come to prize and cherish made meaningless by the fate that awaited him.

"Mer... Mercy," Ulric begged as he raised a feeble hand.

Lancelin stood over him with sword to his chest. "You don't deserve it. How many have you showed mercy to servant of Maluuk? But so that you may know what kind of master I serve, you shall be given your mercy."

"Thank you..." That's when a glint passed over Ulric's now silver eyes.

A sharp pain spiked up Lancelin's leg, dropping him to his knees. Ulric rose to a knee with a sinister grin. "You Islandians are so stupid to fall for the same trick twice." The small dagger in Ulric's hand came darting toward his chest. Just as the blow would be delivered, he felt the whiz of an arrow pass his cheek. The bolt found its mark in Ulric's throat. His eyes grew wide as he choked on his own blood. With a final gasp he slumped back. The dagger that had caused so much pain fell from his grasp down into the depths below.

With a grunt of pain Lancelin looked to see Izel with bow in hand.

"That's for Zuma," she said with tears streaming down her cheek. Dropping the bow she dropped beside him to examine his leg.

"Are you alright?" she asked, wiping away stray tears.

"Nothing I can't recover from," he said with a wince. "We need to reach the others before more Felled…"

He was interrupted by an ear-splitting boom. They turned to see the far side of the wall erupt, sending the once proud structure into a cascade of shattering stone. Dust and debris permeated the air creating a thick red haze where the wall once stood.

"What could cause such a thing?" Izel said stunned.

"Whatever it is, it has doomed us," he said with a sinking heart.

IMARI:

The full force of the Felled Ones was on them now. The Bomani alongside Nabila and her fiercest warriors stood at the center of the attack. Several siege towers had found their landing now. With the might of Ulric and the Felled Ones combined, they would soon be overwhelmed. Imari found his spear Daybreaker made quick work of his foes, but the Sahra defenders were not so fortunate. It went without words that Nabila and her men were unprepared for this foe. Only the Sulta herself had the power to keep this enemy at bay. Dawn's Light, the scimitar now returned, was the only beacon of hope.

The rest of her men began to retreat like a receding tide as they continued to see one comrade after another fall prey to their sinister enemy. Imari could see the tide of battle shifting, and with a cry he called his Bomani to take their place beside the waning forces of Sahra. Together they tirelessly fought to repel the endless hordes. With all his remaining strength he pressed forward, not giving an inch of ground to the menacing ghouls. The phalanx of the Bomani, bolstered by the two Dawn blades, fought until the remaining Felled Ones retreated in fear. In the short break from battle Imari could see Henry approaching with heavy breath.

"We have slain more than I can count, yet…" his gaze fell to the horizon where the sprawling number of foes still stretched beyond sight.

Imari shared his dread. Even with such a weapon as Daybreaker in hand, it wouldn't be enough. The strength of his arm would give before he would see the end of such a force.

"Is there a way to light them on fire?" Impatu asked as he approached.

"There is not enough pitch and tar in the world to light them all ablaze," Nabila replied disheartened.

Khaleena drew near with Amira at her side. "We have given the order for more of the dead's Light Bringers to be gathered. Still… the men grow weary."

"Maluuk hopes to outlast us," Imari said.

"And he will, sooner than later," Henry replied somberly.

Imari turned to Nabila who stood staring out at the enemy. He placed a gentle hand on her shoulder. "Thank you for doing what was right."

She turned to him with tear filled eyes. "I have failed my people, Imari. In arrogance and pride I have left them to slaughter at the hands of these monsters. All because I would not heed your words."

"The battle is not over yet," he said with a faint smile.

"Please, Imari, I am not a child. I can see what fate awaits us."

"There may be hope still."

"What hope is that?" she asked. But his response was cut short by Khaleena's voice behind them.

"I see movement!" she said pointing down at the forces below.

"Another wave of attackers?" Impatu asked.

"No, this is something different," Amira commented as she peered over the edge.

Beneath them dozens of large carts pulled by armored beasts of burden streamed toward the base of the wall. A mix of outsiders along with Felled Ones stood with shields raised to fend off any stray arrows. Fluttered dusty cloths covered the contents. Just beneath a thick black powdery substance could be seen.

"What could it be?" Henry asked.

Behind them a captain barked out an order to the nearby archers, "Archers! Focus fire on those carts. Whatever it is, don't let it near the wall!"

"No wait!" Amira screamed. "I've heard rumors of this strange powder. " But it was too late. A stream of arrows whirled toward their targets. Several found their mark striking several of the beasts of burden. One arrow in particular caught the side of a cart, starting a small fire in its side. Imari watched as those around it scrambled to put out the flame. But it continued to grow and those who saw it began to flee.

"Why would they?" That was all he could mutter before all around him erupted into a blur of flame and dust. He watched as the stone evaporated beneath his feet. It was all a violent fury. Indiscernible images flashed before his eyes and then… darkness. Nothing but cold, bleak, nothingness. His whole body was wracked with pain. He felt trapped in a nightmare of paralysis. Unable to move, unable to speak, unable to see, he was afloat in an ocean of meaninglessness. His throat was bone dry, and each swallow was a labored effort. Suddenly he felt a tug, as if something was pulling him up from the depths. A jolt of ringing stimulated his ears.

His eyes blinked open to an array of dust filtered stars in the sky. Time had passed with calloused precision leaving him with an even greater sense of disorientation. As he went to move, a crippling pain roared across his body forcing him to collapse with a tired whimper.

Shakily he lowered a hand to where he felt the pain radiate. He touched the source, feeling the pulse of streaming blood flow from his body onto the the thirsty desert floor. Raising his hand to his face he could see the crimson soaked fingers illuminated by the moonlight.

Slowly, he turned his head to see a landscape covered in rumble and ash. All around him chunks of debris and dead men littered the ground. With shaky breath he tried once more to lift himself up to no avail. Forcing himself to look he could see his legs crushed beneath the rubble. Panic began to rise at the sight, but he forced it back with several deep breaths. All sense of feeling below his waist had evaporated. Hot tears streamed down his cheeks as he let out an agonizing cry.

"Imari?" came a husky voice.

A shadow moved across the crumbled stone in his direction.

"Yes," he said feebly.

"Imari, it's me, Khaleena."

He swallowed, but the pain radiating from his wound robbed him of speech.

"Imari are you..." her voice faded as she broke into a sob. The dark shadow of his sister loomed over him now, blocking out the night sky.

"Shuka, Imari, you're... no, no." She began hastily throwing aside the rubble that covered him. "No, Imari, no," she repeated over and over as she dug.

After some time she was able to dig his legs free, but all it had done was reveal the true damage. His torso had been pierced by a shard of debris. The gaping wound leaking into a pool of blood beneath him.

"Imari... Imari... Imari," was all she could utter between gasping breathes.

He lifted a tired arm to her cheek. "It will be okay, sister."

"No! No, it will not! I can't lose you. Who else will I have?" She bent over washing him with her tears.

"You must keep fighting, Khaleena." His fingers fumbled for a small shaft of wood nearby. With his last bit of strength he grasped it and held it out to her. In his hand was the broken spear of Daybreaker. Reverently, she took it in hand, unable to speak. Slowly his eyes closed as the picture of Khaleena with spear in hand faded away.

LYDIA

Gloom was all that remained. The small beleaguered force postured themselves before the gaping hole that was once the Grand Wall. Amidst the rubble a small clearing had appeared where the forces of Maluuk could be funneled. With Geralt, Lancelin, Izel, and Aiden at her side they would make their final stand here. The grizzled veteran warrior showed no signs of giving up, but she knew beneath the tough exterior he must be wearing thin. Lancelin and Izel looked unscathed by the blow, a blessing only one section of the wall's defenders had received. The jade scales of his armor still shone with polish, and the woodland woman only carried a few cuts and bruises. Her brother Aiden had avoided the worst of it, but his forehead had a trickle of blood running from his fiery locks and his face was covered in dust. She could only imagine how she must have looked. Much like she felt, she was sure. Before pity could pull at her, something caught her eye. In the faint flickering of torchlight she could see a form sobbing among the ruins.

"Survivors!" she cried. A few soldiers rushed to the source and shortly returned with the weeping Khaleena.

"Imari?" asked Geralt.

A new wave of sorrow washed over her as she affirmed their greatest fear. Behind them a sudden shift in the rubble revealed a bruised and beaten Nabila. A few Sahra warriors that remained moved to help her free. She brushed them aside, eager to rise to her feet. Covered in soot and bleeding, she moved to join them.

"Imari is…" she said in a faint quiver.

Khaleena gave her a feeble nod.

"Show him to me."

Khaleena brought them to the still frame of the Khosi a few yards away. Nabila bent down in a pool of tears at his side. The others looked somberly at the corpse. Lydia felt the firm hand Geralt placed on her shoulder. "Come, lass, give her a moment."

She nodded in agreement and returned to those who remained. To their great surprise, Henry and the Bomani commander Impatu now stood among the other soldiers. Henry, not missing a beat, stood issuing orders for the needed formations for a final stand.

"Give yourself a rest for a moment," Geralt said taking note of his injured arm.

Henry gave a wincing shrug. "All soldiers get injured at some point. You fight through it."

"You Kingshelm men are tougher than you look," Aiden said, admiring Henry's resolve.

"You Valkarans think you own warrior-hood, don't you?" he said with a chuckle. His expression suddenly turning serious. "I heard about Imari."

Impatu's face turned cold at the words. "Where is he?"

"Back there," Lydia said pointing. Without another word the Khalan moved to pay his respects.

"Any other survivors found?" Lydia asked.

Henry shook his head. "No, they found Imamu, the captain of the Khalan guard, dead amongst the rubble along with many others. Besides that we don't know who is alive or dead."

A sudden sinister horn bellowed out from the shadows beyond the wall. A shiver ran down her spine at the thought of what was to come.

"Will we ever catch a break," she sighed.

"Not until the end," Aiden said gripping his axe.

Screeching out from the dark came a tide of vile creatures catching the remnant of their forces by surprise. Men fought with waning strength but were quickly dispatched. She could just make out the glow of Lancelin's sword among the dust that filtered her view. Its vibrant light thrashed at the incoming fiends.

"Go!" she could hear him bark. Out of the dark haze came Izel letting loose two arrows as she went.

"We need to retreat!" she warned.

"Where to?" Henry asked.

"To Sahra," came the voice of Nabila behind them with Dawn's Light in hand. At her side stood Khaleena and Impatu.

"You will not find refuge there," came a voice that chilled them all to the bone. It was a deep and menacing sound that carried the power to project itself all around them. From out of the impenetrable haze came Lancelin crashing to the ground with Dawn's Deliverer clattering by his side. Suddenly, among the debris that encircled them, thousands of silver eyes appeared. Outlines of haunting forms entrenched themselves on the rubble, cutting off their escape.

Appearing from where Lancelin had been thrown was a man of majestic stature. He wore black armor of heavy plating and at its core was stamped a blood red moon. His face was cut with regal form and his manner was that of a High King. Lydia watched as his piercing silver eyes examined them with disdain. In his hand was a sword of awesome terror. Its blade was as dark as the night sky above. The hilt was a dark gold decorated with lions whose eyes glowed a faint green light. It was the Dawn Blade of the High King now held in the hands of their greatest enemy.

"Do you see what it means to oppose me?" Maluuk asked, motioning to the devastation surrounding them. "You have brought this on yourself," he hissed with malice.

She could see in the eyes of her friends that terror had gripped them in the presence of this vile king. With weary strength and shaky hands she stepped forward.

"You may rule by the edge of a sword. You may destroy any who oppose your reign. You may terrorize our lands and destroy our homes, but you will never be a king worth serving," she said raising her sword.

"Foolish child," he said with surprising restraint. "I can see the defeat in your eyes."

He looked at those who remained.

"You," he said pointing to Lancelin who lay wearily on the ground. "You know the gift I offer, and now I will prove what kind of king I am. Even now if you will but bow to me I will spare your life."

Slowly Lancelin rose to his feet, causing a grin to cross Maluuk's face. All eyes fixed on the young prince.

"You once had a gift to offer me, this is true. But I have seen the name written in that cave. It is an ancient tongue, older than even you, but I have seen that name before in ancient scrolls. Dawn Bringer."

"And who holds Dawn Bringer, boy," taunted Maluuk.

"There is another way to read that word you know," Lancelin said with a grin as he raised his sword. "The name Eloy."

"You blaspheme me with that name!" Maluuk roared, his face flashing his true nature. A vile and sinister creature full of malice and hatred, sharp fangs hungry and ready to devour its prey.

"We will not bow to you. You can offer us no gift that we will accept. The true king opposed you unto death, and so we will fight you to the bitter end."

Lydia watched as his words reignited the fire in each of them. Geralt gripped his sword with an iron fist. Khaleena now focused her sorrow upon the evil before her. Nabila, whose once doubtful eyes found new resolution and hope, stood strong. Impatu blazed with the fire of a Bomani warrior. Aiden nodded to her with cool confidence. Henry gave an affirming smirk.

Maluuk's eyes flickered to and fro among them. A look of disgust filled his face. "Fine, perish along with this pathetic land. There will not be one stone left for history to remember this sad little kingdom."

He raised his sword and the host of creatures descended on them. With renewed strength they charged at their foes. A swipe from Dawnbreaker brushed away a wolfish beast as Lydia pressed toward Maluuk. She could hear the faithful steps of Geralt and Aiden just behind her. The Dawn Blade flashed in her hand as she thrust it at Maluuk. His eyes glimmered with confidence as he brought Dawn Bringer forward to deflect the blow. The collision sent her arm reeling with a jolt of pain.

Dawnbreaker was sent flying from her grip. In one quick motion Maluuk whirled his sword to cut her down, but Geralt leaped to deflect the blow. The impact shattered his sword and cleaved his hand at the wrist but it bought Aiden enough time to send his weapon sweeping underneath Maluuk's guard and into his side. The Felled King let out a roar of pain. With unbelievable strength, he sent Geralt flying back with a kick and dealt Aiden a devastating slash. Dawn Bringer ripped across his chest leaving her brother in a heap on the ground.

"No!" she screamed at the sight. Maluuk with a delighted grin turned his focus back on her. His attention was quickly stolen as an arrow slammed into his armor. Lydia turned to see Izel letting loose another bolt as Lancelin charged forward. He burst into the air swiping away Maluuk's sword and leaving a deep gash in the ebony plating across his arm. The wound did not restrain his malice. With a heavy blow Maluuk drove Lancelin back. Lancelin feigned a counter but was caught by a felled creature who had crept behind him. The beast ripped the sword free from his hand and forced him to the ground.

Izel let out a cry as she rushed to his rescue but was overcome by the sheer number that stood in her path. The last effort to stand against Maluuk came when Impatu, Khaleena and Nabila moved to face him. With both Dawn Blades in hand, they moved in a uniform strike while Impatu circled to flank him. Dawn Bringer danced with deadly precision in Maluuk's hand as he quickly repelled both attacks and turned with enough time to dodge Impatu's strike. Swiftly he countered, shattering the spear in Impatu's hand, leaving him defenseless to the host of specters that moved against him.

Next he moved upon Khaleena. With what remained of Daybreaker she deflected the incoming strikes, but they soon overwhelmed her as the shaft of the spear was thrown from her grasp. Out of the chaos of battle a lumbering figure rushed to save her. Lombaku, her faithful guardian took the killing blow on himself. His lifeless body falling to a heap beside her.

Seeing all hope was lost, in a final effort Nabila threw herself at the Felled King, leaving herself open for a deathblow in order to land her own deadly slash. Maluuk turned to shrug her aside, sending Nabila onto her back. His towering form loomed over her as he raised Dawn Bringer to finish the deed. A flash of white burst from the darkness beside them.

A small dagger slipped between armored plating landing its cold steel into Maluuk's ribs. He whirled sending an armored gauntlet into the face of Amira who had emerged from the shadows. Her thin frame crumbled to the ground as blood flowed from her marred face. Maluuk gloated over his defeated foes. Each of them overthrown by his overwhelming might.

Lydia looked up at the monster who returned his eyes to her. With a deep breath she accepted her fate. If this was to be the end, so be it. That's when she saw a faint light in the gap in the wall. A luminescence touched the horizon. It grew abruptly until she could see the outline of a mighty host marching toward them. The light now pierced through the darkness covering each of their faces. Maluuk turned in rage at the interruption of his victory.

Upon discovering the dawn, his expression turned to horror. Leading the mighty host, one that overwhelmed even the forces of darkness, was a man. The armor he wore was stainless and white and his face was set like flint. In his dark eyes burned a fury and passion that no creature could dare to face. This was the High King, the king over all others that led this army. Eloy had returned.

Maluuk, with a cry of overwhelming distain, roared for his army to turn and face their new foe. No longer could he hide his true nature as the growing light exposed him for what he truly was, a thin and ugly creature with gangly arms and elongated legs. He gnashed his fangs as he spurred his forces onward.

But he was stopped in his tracks as the vast host on the horizon declared in one voice, "Behold the true High King. He has given us the gift. It is in his authority and in his name we declare his lordship over all these lands."

That's when she could see who it was that marched with the High King. The faces of countless men and women who had lived and reigned over the years. Generations long past and those who still lived. The host grew silent as Eloy stepped forward.

"Maluuk, your 'gift' has been stripped from you, and now it has been restored to its proper master."

The Felled King could do nothing but shudder at the words.

With a command Eloy cried out in the ancient tongue, "Laqar Aintahat!"

As the words burst forth, the rising sun broke over the horizon. The dry and desolate ground of the Endless Wastes burst with life as the words rushed out like a wave. The declaration streamed forward melting Maluuk's army like wax. With that command Maluuk turned to ash, never to haunt the world again.

Tranquility filled Lydia as Eloy and the host at his back approached. The strange wake from Eloy's command washed over her. In it she found new life had sprung within. She watched with anticipation as Eloy stepped through the rubble to meet them. Slowly, she rose to her feet in reverence of the true High King.

"Imbaku? Father? Mother?" said a voice behind her. Khaleena rushed forward to a cluster of Khalans at Eloy's side. A grin stretched across the High King's face as the four of them embraced. Lydia broke into a tearful smile at what she witnessed next. Khaleena and the others turned in amazement upon hearing a familiar voice call to them. From the rubble a renewed Imari rose. His face full of the joy they shared. A new scene gripped her attention.

Lancelin scampered across the ruins as he spotted King Leon and his Queen Mother at his side. He paused, looking back to Izel whose head craned in search of her brother. Izel's face burst into a radiant smile as Zuma broke from the crowd, taking his place beside Lancelin's family. Giddy, Lancelin raced back to Izel. He took her hand in his as they ran to be united with those they loved.

Nabila looked downcast as though she doubted any in her family would be present, but Amira shoved her in excitement. Lydia's eyes were drawn to an olive skinned woman dressed in a red sari much like the one Nabila favored.

"Mother!" the two women cried as they sank into the woman's arms.

Now it was her turn to search for those she loved. A firm hand rested on her shoulder. She turned to see Geralt pointing with a grin. She followed his finger until a burly red haired king and a fair skinned queen came into view. Her mother's auburn curls fell loosely upon her shoulders. Her face radiated pure bliss.

"Mother?" Aiden said rising by her side. Tears streaked down his dirty cheeks. It was not just their parents, but at her side stood Brayan and Nara as well. Lydia suddenly found herself wrapped in their embrace. Laughter and exuberance poured out between them. But something still nagged at her. That's when she saw him. His wavy brown hair. His soft green eyes squinted with laughter. He stood patiently waiting for her to see him. With a nod of encouragement from her family she rushed to meet him, collapsing around his neck.

"I thought our road had ended," she said in broken sobs. Titus gently stroked her hair as he held her tight.

"Our road hasn't ended, love. It's only just begun."

A voice that sounded strangely familiar called all to attention. As she turned to face the booming voice, she was greeted by the face of

Cebrail. The man now returned to Eloy's side. His chiseled features and thick muscles only somewhat softened by the dawn's light.

"Behold, the High King has won the victory," he declared.

All around, the endless host kneeled before High King Eloy. She drank in the power of the scene. All they had suffered, all they had fought for had been made right in a way she could hardly explain or expect. Those who had looked for the New Dawn had found their long awaited hope fulfilled. It was strange. Her memories of all that had happened still remained. All the evil and vile things done to her and so many others she loved. Yet, bathed in the light of a new day, mysteriously appeared a greater purpose, as if all they had endured helped bring about this long awaited victory. Death had its reign, and by its own power had now come to an end. The victory that once looked like a defeat now secured forever.

Taking in the faces around her she was overwhelmed by all that she saw. From Yeshu, the first of the ancient kings to the nameless faces of history. An uncountable multitude had found their place in this new kingdom.

"Friends, I know you have suffered much, but the age of darkness has ended. Now is the time of the New Dawn, and you will be the writers of its history," Eloy said looking all around.

The vast host bowed in reverence once more. "And you are the High King we serve."

"Rise, kings and queens of the New Dawn, for our new task begins."

With that command Eloy faded from the center, but his presence was never far from each of them. Lydia observed his gleeful smile as he watched all those who were being reunited at last. She could see Geralt now stood among a remnant of his fellow clansmen from the Hills. His long desire for home finally fulfilled in the burst of laughter he rarely let loose. Impatu and the other Khalans gathered with Imari and his family, breaking out into a celebratory dance. Khaleena, however had broken from the rest to reunite with the Masisi gathered in the crowd.

"James!" Henry called to a man amongst all the faces, but the rest of his words were drowned out by the symphony of joy all around. She wasn't worried. There would be many years ahead to hear of all the tales that could be told. Elorah, the man who had saved both Titus and her life at one point, and time passed by with the captain named Dios at his side. They brought with them more tears of joyous reunion. As they departed, she could see her family conversing in the distance and she considered joining them. Turning once more to Titus she leaned her head against his chest. A flourishing of life spread out before her. Not just men and women reborn, but from the cracked and bone dry ground all manner of flora took root. In the barren valley a garden was born.

"The New Dawn is real," she said in a contented whisper.

"It is, and it is far greater than we could have ever known."

EPILOGUE

TITUS

FTER SOME TIME the celebration had moved within the city of Sahra. Instead of joining the others, he found himself standing alone amidst a blossoming field. The red rock and soil beneath had not been forgotten nor its beauty shunned. The life that grew miraculously from the once barren ground only enhanced the red stone's beauty. Before him rested the five Dawn Blades. Their silver edged blades protruding from the ground. Vines wove around the shining steel until a small bud of flowers rested around the hilts.

A faint grin crossed his face as he reflected on the mass reunion that had taken place. To see Imari restored with his family, and the two kingdoms of Khala and Sahra brought together at last. Geralt and his dancing had taken Lydia and him by surprise. Neither of them knew such a version of the man existed, but what other response was there when you have finally found a place to call home?

He was amazed to see his own father and King Doran meet not as enemies but dear friends. Ages of animosity washed away and in its place an old friendship was now rekindled. Lancelin was his typical swaggering self as he and Izel joined in the dancing festivities that had erupted. Music, laughter, and peace ruled the day after what felt like a lifetime of turmoil. Stirring him from these reflections was the soft treading of footsteps. Without looking, he knew who it was.

"Beautiful isn't it?" Eloy asked.

Titus turned to face his High King. "It is," he said looking at the flourishing valley surrounding them. "Yet, such a price was paid for it."

Eloy stopped beside him. "A terrible cost, indeed."

Titus looked to see a sober smile on Eloy's face. "A price we should not easily forget. The price of dealing with evil."

How true, Titus thought as he touched his side. His mind went back to the price he had paid to stand against evil. He knew better than to ask why it had all happened the way it did. Eloy would not shy away from the truth, but Titus knew that there were some things that only the High King would fully understand. What mattered now was evil had been defeated. Maluuk was gone and the true High King could now reign in full. With reverence he stretched out a hand and touched Dawn Bringer's hilt. The golden lions still roared with pride.

"Should we not hold on to these?" Titus asked.

A look of contentment crossed over Eloy's face. "The age where the need of such tools has passed. The time of the Dawn Blades has come to an end. Now comes the age of the New Dawn."

"What awaits us, my King?" Titus asked.

"An adventure beyond compare."

Their gaze drifted to the vast ocean stretching across the western horizon. The waves along the Vestlig Coast lapped against the shore in rhythmic harmony. All around him the world seemed to be singing a new song, one no longer restrained by a fractured chorus.

An adventure? he thought. Excitement deep within him came bubbling to the surface. A sense that many new songs, tales, and memories were just around the corner. He turned once more to face the High King.

"Where do we begin?"

Months later all of Islandia heeded the call of the High King. Among the white walls of Kingshelm, countless men and women gathered. Small signs of the siege remained but the scars drew little attention away from this day. Titus couldn't help but smile at the date chosen. The Day of Remembrance. The day all this had started for him.

The Grand Throne room was filled with royal figures of ages past. Titus stood in awe. Whether it was the first High King Yeshu or High King Bailian, the man who first stood against the Felled Ones, all of their regal splendor dimmed by the one who now sat on the throne. Tapestries and banners of the many kingdoms of the world were displayed among the marble columns. Illuminated by the sun's rays, all stood eager for the High King to speak.

Eloy stood and with a booming voice declared, "I have gathered you all for a Day of Remembrance." A kind look stretched across his face.

"Not for my long departure from this land, but to remember you. The faithful servants who were entrusted with it. And the remembrance of this city. One that has seen its fair share of sorrow. But no more! For she is reborn this day with a new name. The name of New Edonia."

A crescendo of voices filled the room at the surprising announcement.

"Quiet, the High King wishes to speak!" ordered Cebrail who stood at the base of the throne. The ebony lions at his back resonating his fierce tone. With a murmured hush the voices died down.

"Thank you, Cebrail. While there are countless men and women who deserve to be honored, and their day will come, I cannot help but bring forth those who have stood the greatest trial of our age and found themselves victorious."

Again a chorus of murmurs filled the room at whose names might receive such an honor.

"Khosi Imari, please step forward," Eloy said extending a hand.

With a humble bow Imari placed himself before the throne. His family stood off to the side, beaming with pride.

"Of all in the kingdom it is you who has desired to serve your people above all else. Even at the expense of honor, fame, and glory you laid your wants aside so Khala might honor her oaths."

"It is no burden, my King, to serve at your side," Imari said bowing.

"Because of your faithfulness, Khosi, I give you the title of High Khosi. There has never been nor will there be another like you in all Islandia."

Imari gulped as he fought back tears. "I am unworthy of this honor."

With a motion of his hand Eloy urged Cebrail to present a gift. As the King's guardian stepped forward, in his hands rested a pristine white cloak of a snow leopard. Along its edges rested the finest of gold.

"It is a cloak worthy of a High Khosi such as yourself," Eloy said smiling.

Without a word Imari dismissed himself, but Titus could see the shared awe as he presented the cloak to the rest of his clan.

"Lancelin, please come forth."

The Leviatanas prince broke from the crowd. His sandy blonde hair was swept back, and he wore a jade tunic embroidered with silver.

"My High King," he said taking a knee.

"Many in this court may question why you should be beckoned forth."

Titus could see a tinge of fear cross the young prince's face.

"But I have called you my dear friend because your name should be honored through the ages."

Lancelin lifted his face in shock. "My King... I."

"Dear Lancelin, you among men have tasted what the enemy had to offer. You who thought yourself doomed to darkness has seen the light. Even as the enemy tempted you, you proved yourself a conqueror over failure and temptation."

"Eloy it...it was and is my greatest honor to serve you."

"Indeed, and you have proven to be one of my most faithful companions. So the gift I give to you is this. Before all, I declare you, Lancelin, the title of faithful and true. Let no man speak ill of your name again."

Hot tears streamed down Lancelin's cheeks at the High King's words. With a gentle hand Cebrail helped the prince to his feet. They exchanged a look as if a mutual understanding resonated between them. In Cebrail's hand was a shield and on it the symbol of a bluejay.

"Your kingdom shall no longer be known by the serpent Leviathan. I give you a new crest. The bluejay shall forever mark your name as a faithful friend. Let all who look on it remember that fact."

Lancelin proudly took the crested shield and returned to those he loved. Quietly, he, Izel, and the rest of their family admired the new sign of their kingdom.

"Amira," called the High King.

Shock pierced the young Sahra princess as she stepped forward.

"You come from the proud lands of my family's founder." Eloy's eyes locked with the ancient King Yeshu who stood near the throne. Slowly he returned his eyes to her.

"You alone stood firm when all others failed. Without you many who represent Sahra today would have fallen into shadow. Your path may not reflect others, but do not think it worthy of less honor."

"I don't know what to say, my lord."

"Your actions have spoken for themselves and because you stood by Imari and Islandia, I honor you with this. Bring forth the crown."

Cebrail stepped forward presenting a silver circuit. The diamonds embedded sparkled with dazzling light.

"My King!" she exclaimed.

Eloy raised a hand. "I have spoken with your sister. She has wished this for you. She will retire to a life with her Khosi. A life she has chosen. Know this, Amira, no longer are you the unwanted child of a Sulta. You are now chosen as royalty."

In stunned awe she bowed before the High King. Silently, she moved away from the throne clutching the small crown in her hands. Nabila and many others from Sahra welcomed her with a bow reserved for royalty.

A grin crossed Eloy's face as he called the next name, "Geralt, please."

The grizzled vet stepped forward. A slight muttering permeated the crowd.

"Eloy, you don't need to..." Geralt was cut off as the High King motioned for the crowd to silence.

"Every man, no matter his kingdom, who has been a faithful servant deserves honor," Eloy said chastising the crowd.

With compassion he looked down at Geralt. "Without you, Geralt of the Hills, Islandia would lay in ruins. For all you have endured, my friend,, let it be known you deserve honor among all men."

"It is the second greatest honor of my life, my King," Geralt said bowing.

"Second?" Eloy said with raised eyebrow.

"Yes, my lord. I have no greater honor than to see the children I protected all those years stand with us now." His eyes caught Lydia's who stood at Titus' side. He could see the faint blush fill her cheeks at Geralt's words.

"Indeed," Eloy said smiling. "You have been a faithful servant to many, but I must ask Geralt, do you have a place to call home?"

The grizzled man looked up at the king. "I am home, my lord."

"Yes, yes you are my friend, and this is my gift to you. I declare Geralt of the Hills as my kin. Wherever you go you will bear my name, my clan, and my sigil as your own."

Those in attendance burst into a roar of shock. Even as Cebrail motioned for all to calm, Titus could just make out the shared look between Eloy and Geralt. Finally, the man who had given so much had found where he belongs. The grizzled warrior shot Lydia a glance. The once weary eyes now full of new life.

"For my final honors on this day, I call forth the two of you. Titus, Lydia."

He turned to his bride. Her red curls were braided and adorned with wild flowers for the occasion. His lips parted in a grin as he took her hand in his.

"Shall we?" he said.

"We shall."

They stepped out onto the red carpet that splayed across the floor. He could feel the host of eyes fall on them as they walked in unison toward the throne. Towering above, Eloy's eyes fixed on them.

"What can I say of such a couple?" Eloy mused. "Titus, you were faithful unto death. Lydia, even as all crumbled around you, you stood firm in the midst of the storm. Yes, you both have been faithful to the end and now..."

Eloy slowly descended the stairs as all eyes stayed glued on him. Without command, Cebrail moved to present the High King with the gifts that had been prepared. Resting in his hands were two marvelous crowns.

"For you, my lady," Eloy said extending a golden tiara with a diamond that shown like the sun.

"You who desired to see the Morning Star look no further, for it has come," Eloy said as he delicately placed it on her head.

He turned to Titus. "And you, faithful Steward. I present to you the Kingdom of Islandia."

"High King!? This is your realm. I could never," Titus stammered.

"Ah it is one of them, yes, but every king needs those who can steward his lands. Who greater among men than you?"

He felt the weight of glory at that moment. An undeserved honor, but how could he refuse?

"If it is your will," he said bowing to receive the crown.

"It is," Eloy said as he placed the seven pointed diadem on his head.

With that, Eloy turned to all present."Behold! I present to you High King and High Queen of Islandia." All that gathered erupted in a joyous cry. Titus could see the beaming faces of his father and mother as they looked on from the crowd. The faces of his friends grinned from ear to ear as they welcomed their High King and Queen.

Titus turned and whispered to Eloy, "What about you, my King."

Eloy nodded and addressed the crowd once more, "The reign of Maluuk has fallen from this world. Yet many have not heard the news of our victory. I must go for a time to proclaim that the New Dawn has broken through."

Those in the hall grew silent at his words.

"Do not worry. I will not abandon you. No, many of you will join me in this great endeavor. As for the others. It is time we begin to build a new kind of kingdom."

He placed a hand on Titus' shoulder. "Together."

A sound like no other echoed out from those gathered in the throne room. As Titus stared in amazement at the scene, he felt the grip of Lydia's hand at his side.

Before he realized it, he found himself crying out, "May your reign never end!"

All rallied with him, as they showered praise onto Eloy. As each moved to bow to the one who had brought about such a day, Titus couldn't help but think this truly was a day to remember. Surrounding him was the glory of a new kingdom and its king. He found himself unable to do anything but bask in the wondrous moment. Deep within him he felt a stirring, a tug of the heart, a call to worship. As he surveyed the towering halls and vast decor that adorned it, he found them frivolous objects. The jewels and gold that gleamed on every person were nothing but shining stone now. Even the hearts and minds of history's greatest heroes that encircled him seemed but equals now. His eyes drew downward until they locked with the only one worthy of such praise. Amidst the cheering crowd Titus could see Eloy's face crease into a faint smile. It was sent in his direction as if to acknowledge the thoughts floating in his mind.

It was this man, this High King, not any other object in all the world that deserved his praise. History and all its glory and death, its failings and triumphs, joys and sorrows, they all rushed like a stream to one place. It was in that merging that every memory of his life now rested. The wild banks of time came to their end, and in that place an ocean of tranquil new life had greeted them. Here where the High King reigns forevermore.

Among the ancient ruins a new day has passed.
Amidst the haunt of jackals life has sprung once more.
A peoples, a kingdom left in desolation reborn.
From the ashes of destruction they sing.
Bursting from their mouths a new song rings,
Rejoice! Rejoice!
A New Dawn is here.
The one who holds the Morning Star has drawn near.
By his voice he shatters the strong.
His commands make us break out in endless song.
O Kingshelm a city of ruin no more.

Rejoice! Rejoice!
The people shall have no reason to weep.
For Maluuk the defiler has been brought down in a heap.
The vile enemy has tasted the grave.
The New Dawn has sprung into glorious day.
Rejoice! Rejoice!
All who are near.
The day has arrived when all is made right.
Every generation comes to witness his glorious might.
In him the nations will cease their wars.
For the old way is dead and shall be no more.
Rejoice! Rejoice!
With one final cry.
The High King shall reign and never die.
We who serve will live evermore.
For the gift of Eloy has been restored.

THE END

EAST RASKU

WEST RASKU

DORMU

ESKALAN

MONTINBUS
ISLANDS

OSAKA

VALENAR

ISLANDIA

BARREN ISLE

Northland
Edonia
Vulca Islands
Kaskar
Scattered Isles
The Shields
Ishkar
Gurun

ILLUSTRATIONS
BY STEVEN BELL

DAWN BRINGER

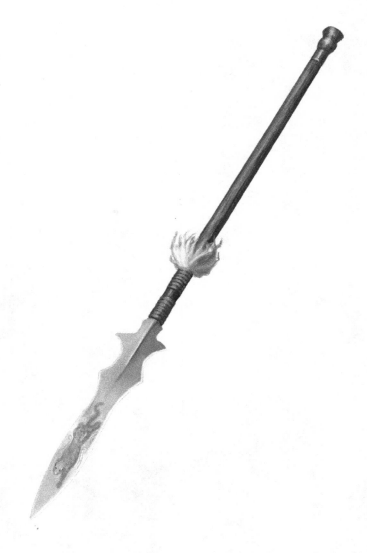

DAYBREAKER

DAWNBREAKER

Dawn's Light

DAWN'S DELIVERER

APPENDIX

KINGDOM OF KINGSHELM

People of Kingshelm:

High King Eloy: The true High King of Islandia. Descendant of Yeshu
and Saria
Cebrail: Royal bodyguard of High King Eloy, Commander of Eloy's
personal forces
Steward King Richard: Made Steward King after Eloy's mysterious
departure
Queen Eva: Wife of Steward King Richard, mother of Titus
Titus: Son of Steward King Richard. Later made Steward King after
his father's death
Elorah: Commander of Kingshelm's Army
Dios: Captain in Kingshelm's Army
Eli: Head Advisor to Steward King Richard
Henry: Kingshelm ambassador and spy, Sent to help Imari and
the Khalans
James: Guard of the Kingshelm ambassador, Sent to help Imari and
the Khalans

Places in Kingshelm:

Riverlands: The territory encompassing the Kingdom of Kingshelm
Kingshelm: Capitol city of all Islandia
Des Rivera: Large trading city between the Atlas and Fortis Rivers
Western Watch: Fortified city on the western edge of the Riverlands
Forest's Edge: Small village on the edge of the mountain chain known
as The Crowns

KINGDOM OF VALKARA

People of Valkara:

King Doran: Overseer of Valkara, Father of Aiden, Brayan, Lydia, and Nara
Aiden: Eldest son of King Doran
Brayan: Youngest son of King Doran
Lydia: Eldest daughter of King Doran
Nara: Youngest daughter of King Doran
Geralt: Captured Hillmen made guardian of the royal family and bodyguard to King Doran
Jorn: Royal ambassador of Valkara
Lokir: Royal ambassador of Valkara
Ferir: Commander of the Valkaran Army
Balzara: Mysterious advisor to King Doran

Places of Valkara:

Valkara: Capitol city of the Valkaran Kingdom
Thoras: A small port that sends trade to the southern kingdoms of Islandia
Rodenhill: A meager town on the way to the Lowland Hills and the Riverlands

KINGDOM OF LEVIATANAS

People of Leviatanas:

King Leon: Overseer of Leviatanas, Father of Lancelin
Queen Prisca: Wife of King Leon, Mother of Lancelin
Lancelin: Prince of Leviatanas and childhood friend of Titus

Places of Leviatanas:

Leviatanas: Capitol city of the Leviatanas Kingdom
Jezero: Port city for Leviatanas off the northern coast of Lake Leviathan
Founding Harbor: A harbor built in memory of the Founders' first arrival to Islandia
Levia Landing: Port city of the southern coast of Lake Leviathan, trade port with Kingshelm
Samadura Port: The largest port in Islandia, Known for its trade with other continents, Remains strongly independent from other cities in Islandia

KINGDOM OF KHALA

People of Khala:

Khosi Imbata: Overseer of Khala, Betrayed and murdered by Sulta
Fahim, Father of Imari, Khaleena, and Imbaku
Queen Mother Khali: Wife to Imbata, Mother of Imari, Khaleena, and
Imbaku, also killed by Fahim
Khosi Imari: Overseer of Khala, Became Khosi after the murder of his
parents, Married to Nabila daughter of Sulta Fahim
Imbaku: Brother of Imari, Son of Khosi Imbata
Khaleena: Sister of Imari, Daughter of Khosi Imbata, Leader of the
nomadic Masisi tribe
Impatu: Young Khalan warrior eager to prove himself, Friend of Imari
Imamu: Captain of the renowned Bomani royal guard
Imran: Captain of the Khalan city guard
Lombaku: Guardian of Khaleena, Masisi Warrior
Boani: Guardian of Khaleena, Masisi Warrior

Places of Khala:

Khala: Capitol City of the Khala Kingdom
Khala Desert: An endless stretch of dunes and sand swept landscapes
Cape of World's End: Most eastern tip of Islandia, A rarely visited port
along the eastern trade routes

KINGDOM OF SAHRA

People of Sahra:

Sulta Fahim: Overseer of Sahra, Father of Asad, Nabila, and Amira
Asad: Commander of the Sycar, Son of Sulta Fahim
Nabila: Daugther of Sulta Fahim, Wife of Khosi Imari
Amira: Daughter of Sulta Fahim, Trained Sycar warrior
Basir: Captain of the Sycar
Riah: Ally of Nabila, Conspirator in the plot to overthrow Fahim
Moheem: Ally of Nabila, Conspirator in the plot to overthrow Fahim

Places of Sahra:

Sahra: Capitol of the Sahra Kingdom
Wahah: A major southern port city, Hub of trade in Sahra
The Endless Wastes: An inhospitable land, Few who venture into the
waterless mesas are seen again
The Grand Wall: The shadow of the Grand Wall hangs over all of Sahra,
The inhospitable climate and sheer size of its fortifications have given it
the reputation of unconquerable.

NOTEWORTHY PEOPLE AND PLACES

People:

Hillmen: A people group who live among the Lowland Hills

Masisi: A nomadic tribe that wanders the Khala Desert

Founders: Established the kingdoms of Kingshelm and Leviatanas after fleeing from their homeland Edonia

The Felled Ones: A mysterious dark army named after their leader The Felled One, Waged war on the kingdoms of Islandia but were defeated at the Grand Wall under the rule of High King Bailian

Maluuk: Known by many names, He is the King of The Felled Ones

Izel: Native of the Dreadwood, Sister of Zuma

Zuma: Native of the Dreadwood, Brother of Izel

Valkin: Brother of Geralt and son of the dead chieftain

Thumdrin: Chieftain of the Hillmen tribes

Fairand: Commander of clan Harnfell's army

Gerandir: Elder of clan Harnfell

Ulric: Leader of the outsiders, disenfranchised prince of Northern Edonia

Cedric: Ulric's ambassador, Captain of the outsiders

Places:

Lowland Hills: Home of the Hillmen, A land ruled independently from the rest of Islandia, The Hillmen and Valkarans have often lived in conflict with one another

Dreadwood: A dark and dangerous woods, Home to an unknown people who seem to be ruled by a sinister master

Nawafir Mountains: Legendary home of the Dawn Blades, In the depths of the mountain a rare metal forged the mighty weapons used to repel the Felled Ones

Edonia: Home of the Founders, A place shrouded in mystery and ancient secrets

Desert Divide: A land of exotic wildlife that separates the north and south of Islandia

Terras Pains: A vast expanse of green pasture lands and prairie on the borders of the Riverlands

Lake Leviathan: A body of fresh water fed by The Crowns, Its size dominates the eastern portion of Islandia

The Crowns: The largest chain of mountains in Islandia. They span the entire breadth of northern Islandia

Check out the rest of the Kingdoms of Islandia Trilogy
and other cool merch at:

www.kingdomsofislandia.com

JACOB JOHNSON is the author of the Kingdoms of Islandia trilogy. He also is a Career Missionary with Assemblies of God World Missions. He along with his wife Vanessa and daughter Kynleigh serves in Botswana, Africa partnering with the national church to empower university students. Jacob has the heart to see students discipled with a deep understanding of God's love and purpose for their lives. He believes that it is only through living life together as a community can we truly be a light shining out into the world.